BOOK FIVE

FORGOTTEN RUIN

THE BOOK OF JOE

JASON ANSPACH
NICK COLE

WARGATE

An imprint of Galaxy's Edge Press
PO BOX 534
Puyallup, Washington 98371
Copyright © 2021 by Galaxy's Edge, LLC
All rights reserved.

Paperback ISBN: 978-1-949731-64-4

www.forgottenruin.com
www.jasonanspach.com
www.nickcolebooks.com
www.wargatebooks.com

TECHNICAL ADVISORS AND CREATIVE DESTRUCTION SPECIALISTS

Ranger Vic
Ranger David
Ranger Chris

Green Beret John "Doc" Spears

Rangers lead the way!

CHAPTER ONE

I don't think anything is broken. Having said that... everything sure *feels* broken. Real broken. Even writing hurts. Physically. Seriously. Like I just got used as a tackling dummy by every team in the NFL for about four hours straight. That is, if that National Football League that just molly-whomped me was an underground rushing river of dark nightmares in bones and rotting corpses and other... well let's just say *stranger wonders*. Oh yeah, and there were those long waterfalls and the forever drops that came with them. In the dark. Not being able to see the bottom you were inevitably headed toward, rocks or more rapids, as you went over the event horizon of the edge. Sometimes dark swirling whirlpools that tried to suck us down forever and hold us in grottos where I was pretty sure we'd meet some outer dark beast like the thing in the crack when Autumn and I ran from the centaurs and gotauri. We hurtled past these, struggling and using every Ranger trick of water survival to get spit into more rapids and avoid sharp rocks that might just hang you up and drown you right there in the constant flood. So yeah, writing this never-to-be-found *bonus content* for my Ruin journal with a Sharpie on what looks to be some old battered shield I found down here—and yeah, I'm hoping the ink takes down here in the wet and the dark—hurts.

Did I mention it hurts? A lot? So okay, unlike coffee, I ain't gonna mention it anymore. I've had my cry. *No one cares, Talker. No one.*

I'm cold, wet, and tired of getting beaten by physics and hydro-energy. Tired of listening to the constant watery disembodied roar as we were spat, shoved, sucked, and pushed deeper down into the darker parts of the earth for hours on end. I'm tired of the unending thirst for destruction that is the Mouth of Madness. A rift in the North Coast of Africa that sucks seawater into the crust of the earth.

For hours it has carried us farther and farther away from the Rangers at high speeds over dangerous rapids we barely survived.

Scratch that. I don't even know if Sergeant Joe is alive. The violence of the watery surge separated us, and I got thrown down a dark channel and ended up in a lonely pool of dark water, wet, shivering, and chattering uncontrollably as I crawled onto a gloomy underground beach.

After hours of not knowing where we were headed… off a waterfall into rocks this time, into a whirlpool no one could get off of the next time—and other, darker things— I'm smoked.

But I'm not bored, so there's that.

And I'm too tired to count all the ways we almost just got killed.

I'd have coffee if there was some. But I ain't even got a packet of instant from the MREs. And to think I was once the one-eyed man in the Kingdom of the Blind.

I had the caffeine market cornered, losers. Now all my vast addiction-wealth is gone. And I'll probably never ever see it again and Rangers who don't *love* it—you gotta *love* it—as much as I do, they'll just burn through it with a mouthful of dip ready to get their hate on because they just need the buzz. Pity the next chimera, werewolf, or whatever Kennedy's little game can cook up that comes at them next.

Savages.

Caffeine, hate, and high-ex is the Ranger's prayer. His blood. All that he asks for.

I get that more now than I did at first.

I'm writing by the light of a strange iridescent moss I'm burning down here. There are also sinister clusters of glowing sickly mushrooms in corners and near rocks. Sometimes growing out of the rotting damp skeletons of fallen warriors in ancient armor. Like they've erected small villages among the bones of giants.

Kurtz said we should always have three things: a Sharpie, a way to make fire, and a knife.

The Sharpie, because a good Ranger is always prepared to take notes. The way to make fire, because fire is used to make food (all meat is edible if it's cooked long enough), keep warm, and destroy the enemy. And the knife… well the knife is self-explanatory.

It was the only time I ever heard him mutter what so many of the other Rangers say when reciting such wisdoms. Kurtz never references Sergeant Joe. He has his own wisdom. Acquired across all the hard stretches of the marines, war in Iran, and a million other street fights and desperate battles that are his life.

But he respected Sergeant Joe. Everyone in the Rangers does. Might as well be part of the Ranger Creed. Hell… he is the creed.

Or was. I have no idea and cannot confirm his status as active or KIA.

One time, just the one I remember, Kurtz gave Joe's attributed wisdom to the weapons team like it was some gospel by which to navigate. Sacred text. A compass on the map of Rangering to the next fight you're headed into.

So I took it and made it mine. And it was this.

"Always have three things, Rangers," said Sergeant Kurtz after a good smoking about some task we were on top of. Some missed impossible standard. "A Sharpie, a way to make fire, and a knife. Book of Joe, weapons team. Book of Joe."

I need to write smaller. This shield ain't gonna hold all my verbosity, which every Ranger who reads this tolerates yet never fails to point out. But hey, no one else is keeping a journal of what the 75th Ranger Regiment did ten thousand years in a future gone all J. R. R. Tolkien. Not one that I know of at least. So this is my story. This is how I roll.

Then again, there is the other side of this battered old Spartan-looking shield. I'm glad it's a smooth shield. Just a few dents. It holds up. And the ink, if I give it a moment to dry, it stays on there.

Isn't that the only thing a writer wants? Asks for? That the words last, for at least a little bit, for someone to read? How else will anyone know I'm here? Writing it all down. Leaving markings on the cave wall, as it were. Telling the deeds that were done.

I'm pretty proud of that. Writing the deeds of others. I flat-out admire them. The Rangers showed up in a weird and unexpected situation and promptly proceeded to kick some serious... butt.

I'm probably gonna die.

Some Ranger will find this. Tanner will come looking. I'm glad I saw it. Saw the Rangers laying the hate on the strange weirdness that is this place. Asking for no quarter and giving absolute zero in return.

It was like watching *The Odyssey* play out IRL. In real life.

So I wrote it all down. They were here. So was I. For whatever that's worth.

It was pretty amazing, and I wish I'd live to see more of it. But… I'm pretty far down under the ground right now and I don't give myself high odds on getting out of here.

I do have those three things though. A Sharpie. A plasma lighter I picked up at the PX. 511 Tactical. And my knife. Which ain't much 'cause I ain't gotten so Ranger I've joined the knife cult yet. Just a basic knife to cut stuff. The tanto I got issued back at 51. My guess is, most Rangers have like five knives on their person at any given time. And even so, they really just use the one that's their favorite. Or it's lucky for some reason.

Usually a Benchmade. "But a Strider is what you want, Talker… that is if you're really in the cult," as Sergeant Chris likes to say.

This is just an observation from the detachment linguist who went along for the ride and got caught up. Became a true believer and even tried to Ranger as best he knew how.

So where am I? Where did Talker end up when he went into the surging waters at the entrance to the Mouth of Madness back at the battle between the Medusa of the Citadel's genie and the Rangers, to rescue Sergeant Joe? No clue. We went deep, really deep underground, the river sucking us into the farthest reachest of the Earth. And I have no idea how either of us survived a death waterslide of doom that would never have passed any kind of amusement park safety inspection for usage by ride goers. But they would've had fun.

Those that survived.

I never got knocked out the whole time going farther and farther down. Did not pass out. Didn't even close my eyes when I went over some of the drops. I kept my FAST helmet on when I shucked my other gear, just before I went in. That was a rare smart move on my part. And no that wasn't intended. I just forgot to take it off. But the bug turned out to be a feature because my FAST helmet saved me from serious lights-out hard knocks as we got tossed around in the embrace of the Mouth. Once Sergeant Joe went in and I'd shucked my gear, telling the other Ranger I was standing next to that I was going in after our NCO and then something stupid about Rangers never going alone, I hit the churning angry ocean surge flooding underneath the bridge and was sucked down into the rift itself. Beyond the bridge and along the cliffs that bracketed the citadel and made it nearly impossible to assault by land.

It was morning. The battle had started before dawn, but after house-to-house fighting to clear the eastern side of the citadel and then assaulting the bridge to link up with the sergeant major's galleys, the early morning sun had risen in golden dawn light as the both of us were pulled down into the Mouth of Madness. The shock of the cold water had my heart pounding as I tried to get to Sergeant Joe. It was then I noticed how *alien*—and yeah that's the word I want to use—the cliffs around the citadel were. I'm not saying I'm an expert on the geography of North Africa from the Before. Ten thousand years ago. But I'd been to Morocco once with Sidra Paredes. Of course it was with her. And yeah, crazy story short, it was real cray-cray. Forget that.

No room on the shield. But I'd never seen cliffs like these when I went there with her, ten thousand years ago.

Now as the undertow of the raging waters sucked us into the gaping black mouth in the cliff wall, the Mouth of Madness itself, I saw those strange alien cliffs revealed in golden morning light. Jagged cliffs rising high above us as we were drowned in the turbulence of the sea. On shore and along the bridge, the Rangers were slaughtering the last of the forces of the medusa. Gunfire echoed off the canyon walls as the genie hit the water and exploded. These cliffs were less Earth-like and more like high-res photos of Mars or other planets in our system. Like the rocks had boiled in some eons-ago comet strike and splashed up into cold space, freezing into sharp jagged tectonic formations like something out of the old science fiction magazines and TV series of long ago. Really un-Earth-like and very bizarre. Ravaged destruction frozen in the near-timelessness of granite as we were hauled by the rushing currents away from the battle.

Helpless to save ourselves. You don't realize how powerful water is until you're in it and it's having its way with you.

Going off the crumbling bridge and into the churn was like diving into a boiling pot of ice water. And no, I wasn't doing it to kill myself or make amends for what I'd written down in the journal about what happened in Portugon and the Purple Abyss.

And a waif who thought I was something I wasn't.

I went in because no Ranger goes alone. "I will never leave a fallen comrade" is a gospel in the Ranger Creed and in this case quite literally. Sergeant Joe was exactly that, and that scroll I wore would have been worthless had I not gone down the aquatic rabbit hole. That gets drilled into you in RASP and everything else.

Sergeant Joe fell as the bridge collapsed. The current was so strong, and the fight was on in all directions, so there was no way to organize and rescue him. I went in. I thought I could get to him, help him shuck his gear before it pulled him under, and the two of us could get to the side of the rocks before we went into the dark mouth in the cliff wall which I was pretty sure was bad.

Get back onto the rocks and into the battle.

That was my plan. And it didn't go that way of course. The skeleton lying next to the shield I found down here that you're reading in the dark is probably me and so *no... the plan didn't go as expected.*

Since arriving in the Ruin, I've gotten a lot of water survival training and what they call *drownproofing* on the humps between various ops we've pulled and killed weirdo monsters at. Also, I've been through Kurtz's unpassable Ranger School. Twice. Jealous? Anyway, Ranger School emphasizes riverine operations and water survival as a Ranger-critical task. Drownproofing and water survival training are key elements of RASP as well. The swim test bolos a lot of guys who've never gone in anything deeper than their bathtub. So those skills are hammered in the beginning.

Bolo means *no go.* It's not a good thing.

Swimming was one thing I was all good with at that level. Being here with the Rangers I got better. "Like ya do," as Tanner would say.

So I had skills when I went into the water, and the plan was to get the sergeant, who hadn't had time to shuck out of his gear before he drowned, time to do that, so we could get to the rocks and out of the water.

And back in the fight.

Getting out of the water was the plan and that is usually a good plan if you didn't intend to go in in the first place.

I knew what to do. Or at least that's what I told myself when I jumped off the collapsing bridge segment to rescue an NCO while a twisting tornado of a desert demon the Ruin called a genie tore everything to shreds and Ranger weapons cackled on full-auto murder as the detachment overran the indirect catapult positions surrounding the citadel.

I saw Sergeant Joe bobbing in the chaos of the churning water for just a moment and made my call right there. He'd gone in with his full kit, no time to shuck as noted. I popped out of mine and jumped, feet first, hitting the water and trying to spot the NCO who was probably getting dragged under by the weight of his own gear.

Once I was in, it was all chaos and I was struggling just not to drown. The water was excessively violent and there were subsurface undertows and rip-currents.

I saw him once and swam hard as he tried to keep his head above water.

Then the genie hit the water and exploded in every direction all at once. It felt like a bomb went off in there with us, shock waves passing right through your guts just as I got to Sergeant Joe. I have no doubt that is half the reason my insides feel like fresh-beaten ground hamburger. The other half is because of the hours-long, lawsuit-waiting-to-happen madcap amusement park ride of merciless darkness, rocks, and drowning. Let's give that part more than half credit. But my guts were certainly already shaken up when the medusa's genie hit the water and suddenly exploded.

I have no idea why that happened.

I had about a minute in the water before I realized what a colossal mistake I'd just made. It was never evident from the shore and the bridge we were fighting on, but the Atlantean Rift *is* the Mouth of Madness. That's where the comet fell and ruined the city of the Atlanteans, as the myths of Vandahar say. Or at least that's what I think now.

Maybe I'll find out more about that, and what really happened, and try to write it all down because I know the Rangers are going to come looking for my body. Right, guys?

Having said that, at this point...

Well, let's just say my confidence is not high right now about getting found alive. I just spent hours in a river of madness being dragged, pulled, and drowned, down and down, deeper than any cave I've ever been in. And now I've been lying here in the wet sand for about an hour, in this strange mushroom-filled cavern, listening to the smashing white noise of the distant Mouth in another cavern, and trying to figure how far I've gone from the main body of Task Force Pipe Hitter.

Eighty miles is my best guess. The river was moving fast, taking huge drops, and sucking me deeper and deeper into the darkness.

Us. Me and Joe. I'm gonna say we were in there for at least four hours. Maybe more though. Time gets weird when you're just trying to survive until the next moment.

I got to Joe just before we got sucked into the Mouth. I helped him get disentangled from his gear. It was his ruck that was dragging him down. We fought it and got it off, and he shouted at me to start turning it into a flotation device. We'd need to buddy-swim to carry it. But we didn't get much of a chance to do that. Mainly we both held on to it and tried to stay above water.

Then we got swallowed by an empty space in the universe, the gaping dark Mouth in the jagged cliff wall, and the battle and the dying genie weren't our problem anymore.

It might have been better had the darkness been total. It wasn't. I don't know where the light came from, and you'll forgive me that omission of detail seeing as I was too busy gasping and coughing up lungfuls of water and gathering bruises on every inch of my body to do a thorough exploratory assay. I mentioned the mushrooms though. That's probably it. And thanks to them, or whatever it was, I got glimpses I wish I hadn't. I saw things down here along the rocks in the dark that made me not want to get out of the ice-cold water that was carrying us away. Seriously. And then I got glimpses of tentacles and monstrous eyes under the surface that made me not want to stay in.

I have a Sharpie, a plasma lighter, and a knife. And now this shield.

I do not have a ruck filled with coffee and food on which to survive. Warm clothes, socks, survival gear. Or a plate carrier and a chest rig. Rifle. Ammunition. Sidearm.

I have none of those things and I'm eighty miles away from the detachment. At least. Underground with no clear idea how to get back to the surface.

I'm surprised we survived. That I survived. Sergeant Joe... I have no idea where he is at this moment. One of the waterfalls separated us. It was a big one, and again... not much hope that Sergeant Joe made it. But if anyone did, he would've. That guy's pure survival. We stayed together for as long as we could, pulling the ruck between us, and it took all our water survival skills to thread whirlpools, avoid rocks and other obstacles, and make the long falls into deep cold pools I felt like we weren't gonna get out of. Trying our best not to get smashed into the rocks as the Mouth carried us deeper and farther away into the earth under and beyond the strange cliffs we'd disappeared into. The best I could do at times in the rapids was to lie back, keep my feet pointed into the raging current dragging us down, and just keep my head above the angry dark waters.

Sergeant Joe shouted above the roar at me as we did so. Telling me he was there in those passages, which was most of them, that were so near pitch-black that we couldn't see a thing. Telling me what we needed to do as we approached each obstacle.

Laughing and swearing when we did… just barely.

The best I could manage was the occasional "Yes Sar'nt" through a mouth filled with seawater as we went down and down. Sometimes the best thing you can do is just try to keep it together for the other guy.

In the darkness with the rapids and the strangely iri-descent water, Joe's laughter and swearing were like navigational beacons on some dark night that was doing its best to drown you.

I'll adjust my eighty-mile figure. There were a few times when we got onto some rocks and managed to hold on for a little while until it felt like I was freezing to death just clinging there.

"Ain't no way outta this chamber, Talker," Sergeant Joe would shout above the roar of the water. "We gotta let go now. You with me, Ranger, you with me? C'mon bud, gotta swim. Dude, you still in the game? We havin' fun now, Ranger!"

Then I'd let go and off we went back into the rapids because there was no other path, no place there that seemed like civilization down in the darkness under the Atlantean Rift, a place the maps we'd carried just called the End of the World. No place to walk or travel in safety.

Just the ride in the rapids that was probably going to end badly underwater in some dark fall.

It was just a constant flume of white water and darkness for moments that seemed like forever.

And yeah, I even laughed when we made it through those moments. If just because I was losing my marbles and laughing at the whole thing was the only way to keep the madness of the situation at bay as we were carried deeper and deeper into the earth. Some demon whispering at the back of my mind that there was no going back the way we came. And that we certainly weren't going to like what was waiting ahead beyond the next waterfall.

My shocked and frozen mind was just carried along for the wild ride, trying to make some kind of plan to get out of this. Remembering Kurtz yelling at me when I was leading a patrol in Ranger School: "Make a plan, Ranger! Make one now or everyone dies!"

Now, sitting here on this wet sand beach deep under the earth, where the air feels ancient and heavy despite the rushing water, watching my strange little green fire that throws off a surprising amount of heat, I can say this: it's hard to make a plan inside a disaster. But you gotta anyways. So I did, and my plan was this.

Do exactly what Joe told me.

"Kick hard, Talker!" he shouted when we got into a current that looked like it was turning into a whirlpool.

"Grab rocks and pull yourself out! Hang on to the ruck! Don't let go!"

I didn't.

And: "Here we go, feet first, Private! PLF when you hit the water below! Feet and knees together!"

Then both of us shouting as we fell into darkness, hoping there was another pool down there to hit that we couldn't see. Hoping for *not* rocks.

Joe laughing in the dark cavern splashing madness as the current dragged us away again on the other side of the long fall into the pool and not-rocks. Coughing, sputtering, and laughing as you listened for the next set of approaching rapids in the darkness ahead and knew this ride wasn't over by half.

And that maybe… maybe it was never gonna end. Like it was hell or something. Like this was hell forever.

I'm only barely beginning to think now. I've been talking to myself down here in the dark as I scribble on the shield what feels like my last message. I'm serious… that was the most messed-up four hours of my life. Every freaky situation we've been through here pales in comparison to drowning in the dark for four straight hours. Now I'm only barely beginning to realize what I've gotten myself into down here. And whatever it is… it feels a lot like certain death. For a lot of reasons. Many of which I probably haven't fully comprehended yet.

Maybe I'm dead already? Maybe this is what death is?

Deep under the earth in some kind of netherworld of water and darkness. Cold, hungry, wet, battered beyond belief. Lost and not found. Alone. I think one of my fingers is broken, now that I've gotten feeling back into it. This little moss fire is throwing some heat inside this chamber I've found.

So maybe this is death. Maybe for all eternity I'll be down here, writing on this shield and burning lichen, moss for the illusion of heat.

No one cares, Talker.

Make a plan. Now.

That's what Kurtz would shout.

I just now took off all my clothes and I'm trying to dry them. I read what I've written and had a good long yell at myself as I got naked in the dark near the pool along the wet sand beach. Quit your whining, I told me.

I'm gonna get out of this.

It ain't death.

It's just... *lost.*

I have one other thing. The ring. The one that turns me invisible.

Oh, and I can do psionics. I've got that.

See, things are looking up already, Talker. With that and everything the Rangers taught me I just might get out of this, link back up with the main body. I'm writing really small now as I run out of room and I'm wasting room telling you that. But... I'm starting to think clearly again.

It's bad. Sure it is. No argument here. So what?

I've been in worse, I lie to myself.

Plus, there's everything I've learned from the Rangers.

Something Sergeant Joe said to me just before we went over the last waterfall and I lost him in the dark. "Odds ain't good, Talker. But at least we got 'em."

Then both of us went over the falls and it felt like the longest fall ever. A deep dark, colder than anything I've ever felt on the other side of that raging rapid we fell into. And

I couldn't find Joe, and I have no idea if he made it out of there. I let go of the ruck as we fell.

I let go.

Man, I'd kill for a cup of coffee right now. Seriously.

No one cares, Talker. No one.

Make a plan.

Now.

CHAPTER TWO

I'M on the other side of the shield I'm using as a writing tablet. Then that's it. Gotta find something else to write on. Hope the Sharpie holds.

I keep capitalizing the word Sharpie because I'm pretty sure it's a brand name. Like Kleenex or Band-Aid. A registered trademark. Wouldn't want the Sharpie Company or whoever they are to send a team of high-priced corporate lawyers in custom tailored suits down here into the bowels of hell to confiscate my shield under penalty of law. I don't figure trademark infringement is a priority here in the Ruin, but... lawyers, man, you never know. Tanner can tell you all about that.

Words. It's how I stay sane. Or try to. And I could really use a little sane right now. If you couldn't tell.

At least I'm starting to get dry-ish. It's cold and damp, but there's just not much you're gonna do about that down here in the Underworld of No Return.

It's not the underworld, I just shouted at me. But I'll be honest, it feels like it. A lot. It's weird, dark, cold, and lonely, and I can't see a way out of it if there even is one.

So... underworld, amirite?

I gotta do something about that. Stop talking to myself and get ahold of me.

Still, it's important to stay positive, Talker. Anything that doesn't kill you gives you a grim sense of humor, according to the Rangers. Right about now I'm wishing I'd learned more from everyone who ever taught me anything about how to survive just to make it through this. I've used everything I know, and it feels like I could use a lot more.

I'm starving and there's no way I'm eating one of these mushrooms and tripping out down here. There are fish but I have nothing to catch them with. And there were a lot of dead bodies in the water, in the Mouth of Madness. Fresh dead from the battle, and probably just Tuesdays around the Citadel of the Medusa. And from other... ancient times, or the sea, or so it looked. There were orcs. Goonies. Some *saw-haw-gin*. And the bones of humans. Old bones on every rock and in every pool.

In survival you got the Rule of Threes. That had been a big part of Kurtz's teachings in Ranger School. Three minutes without air. Three days without water. Three weeks without food.

Dead-body water was gonna be a problem, though there was a lot of it.

Food... well, I had time.

Coffee... don't get me started. Don't. Even.

Oh yeah, and there was even the wreck of an old pirate ship that had crashed down into the first pool after we'd entered the Mouth of Madness that looked like something out of an amusement park from ten thousand years ago. Dead skeletal pirates thrown in the ghostly rigging and draped from the shattered decks of splintered wood, their soulless black eyes glaring at us as we were sucked out of that pool and down the first set of rapids.

I don't know if it was the wind in the rigging but some of their heads turned. Some of their skeletal hands reached.

I'm trying not to think about that. And the implications implied regarding whether or not Sergeant Joe and I got sucked into some kind of Ruin Hell Netherworld.

Let's not get carried away, Talker.

And yet… the rapids told my mind to start thinking this was some kind of hell I'd ended up in. As though I'd drowned already, or was killed when the genie hit the water. The otherworldly sand and wind demon flying apart in some unnatural explosion of unearthly genie energy meeting the real-world elements of earth, wind, and fire.

Matter and anti-matter, kinda, I guess. But I don't know much about those things. Languages, yeah, let me lecture you on Japanese verb construction. But hard science… it's a method of investigation. That's all I know about all the disciplines.

The genie hitting the water was pretty bizarre to see. Like the water itself came apart at the molecular level while at the same time it turned into a living breathing thing that didn't want to be where it was in time and space. The air felt wildly dangerous in that moment but maybe that was because we were about to get sucked down into the darkness of the Mouth of Madness.

It doesn't feel like that now. Dangerous. Not down here now in this silent little carved rock chamber I've ended up in away from the water's edge of the raging Mouth. Now that I'm warm-ish and dry-ish. Kinda. But back in the water we saw strange arcane gates after the pirate ship remains. Gates beyond the rapids we were getting tossed along. Gates carved up there in the rock and the roof of the watery underground chamber. Looming in the mushroom-blue ghostly darkness. Two massive impossible bronze doors unlike anything I'd ever expect to see down here. Then… yeah, if I'm honest about it now, it felt like getting pulled down into a hell we were never going to get out of. *Then* it felt dangerous. Real dangerous. Like one guy carrying the C4, blasting caps, and det cord dangerous. Usually that's a three-man job.

It felt like that.

Not much room left now on the shield to write all this down, and I feel like I've wasted space just trying not to lose my mind and talk myself back to some kind of sense. How much of this was just me getting my head together? How much of this is just a message in a bottle to the Rangers to let them know what happened to us?

So, the gates. Gates of Doom or whatever you want to call 'em. That's what they felt like down there in the dark and water. As we got thrust down the underground river in the dark, they appeared out of the mist and gloom ahead. Fiery runes sprang to life, and I mean like two-forty forbidden-popsicle-barrel-red fiery. They burned through the dark, crawling like writhing snakes across the two massive bronze doors impossibly in the water we were being driven through.

And I'll add this here: these impossible and clearly magical doors were like five stories high. And on either side of the fantastic doors were two gray and silent sentry-like towers, barely visible as the mist of the mysterious chamber and the water's rush obscured everything else.

I thought, as the current swept us along, that we'd just smash into them and get hung up. Pinned by the flood and drowned by the wrath of the unrelenting water and the immobility of these fantastically impossible structures down here. Except, at the last moment, there was a crack in the doors, a bare parting between them, and in one sudden violent moment of watery vomit, we, Sergeant Joe and I, were inhaled and cast…

…*cast*…

Like the cockpit of the *Millennium Falcon* jumping into hyperspace.

That's the word I wrote. *Cast*. My hands have stopped shaking from the cold down here and the cold of the shield I'm writing on. Writing on it like I'm leaving some record for the Rangers to find.

Didn't I already do that in my journal? Confess all my sins? Will Tanner read that? Will he still be my friend knowing I almost walked away from the Rangers once?

I don't know.

I'm alone now. And when you're alone it's hard to know things.

But *cast*. That's the word I wrote and that's what it felt like. So that's what I'll use. *Cast*. That's what it felt like now that I think about it. The waters on the other side of the door cast us. Flung us. Flung us out into the darknesses of other rivers. Like some otherworldly C-130 drooling jumpers in the dangerous night. Falling toward the LZ and a desperate mission no one was coming back from.

Feels like the psionics is taking over now as I think about the *cast* and the long fall afterward. Explaining things. Showing me… things. The psionics that is.

If what I'm seeing is true… if what the psionics are showing me… then maybe I've gone a lot further than I think I have.

Maybe I'm more than lost.

Maybe there are other... QST... gates... than the one we came through to get here to the Ruin ten thousand years ago. Here ten thousand years in the future now.

I don't know. Down here in the dark, time passes, and I think I've kinda lost track. My Timex got lost in the river. I doubt it would have survived submerged that long.

How long?

The question echoes in my mind. Echoes down here in the darkness.

How long ya been down here, Talker?

Where am I really?

* * *

I took a break. You can tell from the last sentences, whoever you are, whoever finds this shield, maybe it's even you, buddy. Don't tell them I almost lost my marbles down here, Tanner. Don't tell 'em cool-as-ice Talker couldn't keep it together.

That ain't Ranger.

I worked hard to fit in, to seem like one, but I wasn't. Even if they said so. So don't let 'em know I cracked up if you find this shield, Tanner.

Tell 'em I was stone-cold to the end. That I didn't forget nothin' like it says in Rogers' Rules of Ranging.

I started walking after I lost it a few sentences ago. Needed to get away from the water. The Mouth and all its echoing roaring madness. I concentrated on what I knew. I was in the water, even after the gate. The water kept flowing. There was some hang time after the gate... the *casting*. But I was in...

I followed the beach. The wet sand littered with the crushed and cracked bones of the dead. All the dead of all the worlds who have been sucked down here to wait for whatever comes next.

All the worlds. Is that the psionics talking? Or just your friendly neighborhood Talker losing his marbles in the dark, alone?

Concentrate on the facts. On what you got. Reality. No one cares, Talker. No one.

I have a knife, a Sharpie, a… plasma torch. This shield. And the ring.

I'm alive.

Ain't dead yet.

Tanner. Tanner sees the dead. Can talk to them sometimes.

So maybe I got that to look forward to. It's actually a comforting thought.

I've managed to get away from the water, but I can still hear it through the thick stone, its never-satisfied rush and roaring. Up the beach were two obsidian pylons that marked the beginning of some cut trail leading away from the rapids and torrents and down along the rocks that have toppled over each other. The trail became wet stone steps, crudely carved into the granite of this place. I followed those for a while and when I got tired, I sat down and started writing again.

The writing helps me.

First, I collected some lichens and moss, a few mushrooms—

Oh, hey, that's another thing I have. My Oakley assault gloves stayed on the whole time I was in the water. And my FAST helmet. But the gloves are good because that way if there was any contact poison on the strange glowing mush-rooms, I have some protection.

I have the gloves, fire, something to write with, an old, dented shield as a writing tablet, and... my knife.

And the ring.

Away from the water I feel better.

It's right to call that massive titanic hungry rush the Mouth of Madness. It'll drive you nuts if you give it long enough. If you listen long enough... you can hear voices, and other worlds. Maybe. But that's what it sounds like. Makes you start thinking you died and went to hell.

Ha.

I'm listening now. And I hear...

Someone's coming.

CHAPTER THREE

OKAY... maybe it ain't hell, but I just killed a demon. So maybe it is. I've got about half of one side of a shield left to tell you all about how I almost just got my throat cut by what clearly looks to be a demon or a devil. I'm not sure what the difference is. But wait... there's more. The demon had a tube filled with parchments. So we got that going for us, Talker. I don't have to write so small now. We can leave more for the record for whoever comes looking on how not to survive. Young Rangers will learn by my misfortunes. And honestly, I ain't opposed to that.

I think I'll finish filling up the shield first though, before moving on to the parchments. Got the hang of it now.

After the demon who came out of the dark was dead, I unrolled those parchments in the tube I found on his body, doing some sensitive site collection as taught to me by John who wasn't really John in the Vegas that is no longer, and then by the Rangers as we rifled dead sorcerers and plundered dragon hoard at various times.

Looking back, we've had a pretty good time here in the Ruin. Alas, all good things must come to an end. And this looks like mine.

Back to the SSE. The parchments all appear to be blank, but the psionics are telling me something else. Telling me there's some kind of writing on them I can't see with the naked eye. Like Last of Autumn's Moon Runes. Whatever, I'm still gonna write all over that stuff and attach the parchment tube to the shield in case any Rangers ever find me. Because of course, my story is more important than what are most likely bad demon jokes. More probably horrible spells though really. Maybe I'm canceling them out with my blather. Who knows?

Palimpsest. That's the word. It's what they call a parchment where someone erased what was there in order to write something else on top. Or maybe the words were so faded they didn't even need to erase. Like when some medieval farmer finds a valuable ancient historical document and decides to use it to write up his grocery list or tally his grain stores.

To be fair, there are worse things a farmer could do with a piece of paper. Archeologists and historians should count their blessings.

Archeologists and historians. Is that who I'm writing this for? No. Tanner will come looking for me. He's my buddy. He'll find me. Even if I am dead by then. Still, I'll get found and that's important. And maybe Tanner and me will have a chat. Even though I'm dead.

You gotta count on something, and right now I'm counting on my friend to come and find my corpse.

Also, I would cut a dude for some coffee right now. So maybe I'm not dead and in hell after all. A cup of cold brew would be pretty great right about now. *Coffee!* Can I get an amen? The cavern and the surreal drip of water and the echoes of loneliness it creates here say no. And also no, the demon didn't have anything in his kit that even looked to be anything remotely like coffee, or even tea, that I might want to drink and savor.

Snake eyes.

I don't really know if it, he, whatever, was a demon. But he was evil. That's for sure. It was definitely male. An elf of some kind, I'm pretty sure. Was. Was an elf. Now he's dead. Like Last of Autumn is an elf of a kind, so is he. But whereas her people are vaguely Korean, skin tone a soft golden tan, this one was black. Not like Chief Rapp black. More like black almost blue. Like coal. Blue tongue and white teeth. Red burning eyes. Eyes wider than Autumn's... Last of Autumn. Like psychotically knowing wide. Unsettling serial-killer-rushing-on-their-run wide.

Just before we met, I was sitting and working on my little fire in the small chamber along the stairs, a round strange square cut into the stone, ignoring or at least trying to ignore the distant crash of the Mouth of Madness, when I heard him coming up the way I was going to head down next to see if I could find Sergeant Joe. The demon was humming to himself as he moved along the passage, tapping at the rock as he went.

I was almost in a trance writing, working on my fire, and ignoring the distant rush of water. But it was the tapping the demon was doing, occasionally, that caught my attention at just the last second. You know, 'cause I'm an elite predator killing machine like the Rangers instead of a linguist pretty much convinced he's down to his last few hours.

But I caught it. The tapping. Caught the tapping and my body tensed instantly despite the battering of the Mouth. Like I was coiled and ready to get it on kinetically even though I had no carbine or sidearm with which to get it on. Kinetically that is.

Still, Sergeant Kurtz, I was ready, Sar'nt. I was gonna go combatives and knife work. That I could do.

Then, in perfect Hindu, the demon who appeared in the chamber spoke. "Well hullo, what's this we have here, lovely?"

Hindu is rough for me. So maybe he didn't use *lovely*. I never count it as a mastered language. I know some—a lot even—but I ain't fluent and that's bothered me for a few years. Now it bothers me a lot more as I write this down. I'm probably gonna be encountering more Hindu in what remains of my life.

Like I said, I've been pretty much out of it since the pounding I took in the Mouth of Madness. I'm cold and tired and remember I'd just fought for close to twenty-four hours at the citadel, so… my survival skills weren't on high right at that moment. I just sat there and looked up to see this strange figure standing at the narrow entrance to this section of the chamber cut into the rock.

I knew I was gonna respond with violence if I needed to. It's just… I was slow.

A note on the chamber we both found ourselves in. The cuts in the passage, the doorways, they're all crook-ed and off in their angles and measurements. And that's disconcerting to the mind more than the eye. Like it ain't right and wasn't built, carved, hewn, or whatever you do to make underground dungeons, by rational minds. I remember that being a feature back in the Atlantean architecture surrounding the citadel.

It makes you feel unsettled when you stare at it long enough.

I looked up, slack-jawed, to see this pure bluish-black elf in a stone-gray cloak, carrying a small green candle in one gloved hand and a serpentine dagger in the other. The cloak of his hood was pulled back and I could see golden hair, pure gold, pulled up into a topknot.

A large brooch shaped like a black widow spider fastened his cloak. Or it looked like a black widow. I'm no spider expert. Arachnologist is probably the correct term. His boots barely made a sound and perhaps that was why I'd only heard his approach at just the last second when there was nothing I could do about it in a meaningfully defensive way.

Although I still had time to write, "Someone's coming." I did. I got that done.

Despite my lack of inspiration, since my body has been trained in Kurtz's constant Ring of Death and the relentless survival game we've been playing for months now here in the Ruin, I got ready instantly. *Coiled* is the word I felt in that sudden everyone-holding-their-breath moment. Like, if I needed to, despite the injuries from four hours in the rapids, I was ready to explode with violence if just to survive another moment.

My gloved hand reached for the knife.

Now that I write this down on the last of the shield and get ready to switch over to the parchment from the tube, I remember thinking… well, I could just slip on the ring and disappear.

That was the last thought I had before the blue-black demon with the vibrant blue tongue leapt at me. He had two fangs among his brilliant white teeth. They were bared. And the strange gold hair gleamed in the green light of his candle.

I threw up the shield, and the serpentine knife the demon was ready to plunge right into my heart connected with a sudden savage *CLANG*. I didn't even have the shield strapped. Its strap still worked. Which was amazing, considering I'd found it abandoned down here in the damp. All the shattered weapons and smashed gear I'd encountered so far had rotted and succumbed to the damp of the water and ruin of the Mouth. But this plain old shield seemed to have held up. Interesting.

I want to say, *The pen was mightier than the sword*. On account of how this shield is actually my writing tablet. But that's a stretch even for me. More accurately, *The Sharpie-inscribed shield proved sufficient to deflect the serpentine dagger*. Not as pithy. Shakespeare would shake his head and give me a *yeah, not so much* look. Though it is kind of cool, when you think about it, that I, the linguist, just defended myself with what is, effectively, a book. I know there's something clever there. I'll keep working on it.

"*Heeeyyaaah!*" screamed the psychotic nightmare elf as he swirled away from me and cut wide with the gleaming serpentine dagger whose surface seemed like it was made of shiny flint, but sturdier.

I dropped the shield because there was no time to strap it on, gained my feet, dancing back to avoid my small fire, and got my own knife out.

A moment later the chamber was filled with flying purple sand that extinguished my green glowing fire. In the last Kodak flash of light, I saw that the demon had flung something across the cold rock chamber. Yeah, as the sergeant major would say, "this was a real hippy walk."

Everything got trippy for a second. Green fire. Midnight-black elf. Purple sand. Obsidian dagger.

It was the sudden darkness that followed that felt like a smothering blanket thrown over me. The elf had flung the equivalent of fire-extinguishing pocket sand and blinded me was my only guess about what had happened.

I fumbled in my pocket for my plasma lighter, intending to use that as both light source and weapon with my off hand. Getting my feet under me as Kurtz had made us do in the endless beatings of combative practice, I crouched and waited to get the shape of my enemy within my grappling reach.

Instead of finding the lighter I found the ring.

Might as well, I thought, and slipped it on.

Two can play at hide and go seek, buddy.

Neither of us could see each other now. But I could hear the demon breathing in the darkness of the chamber. Heavy and ragged as though he were kind of asthmatic.

I quickly got control of my breathing, forcing myself to get oxygen through my nose. *Never let 'em see you breathing through your mouth*, Kurtz shouted at us in whichever Ring of Death he'd set up that day to abuse us with. *Breathing through your mouth means you're tired, Talker.* That was straight from the Terminator back at RASP. No breathing through your mouth during PT. So that had been at least one thing Kurtz couldn't gig me on.

Spoiler: he found a dozen others. In time I learned to stop resenting my lack of killing and survival knowledge and embrace the beatings—I mean *teachings*—of my combatives sensei and personal torturer, Sergeant Kurtz. I know, and am, nothing, Sensei. Ready… *fight*.

Try it sometime. It's real fun.

Now, in the dark and with just one chance to save my life, I realized all of it, every fight I'd been in, was vital to this one.

THE BOOK OF JOE

I felt the cold stone wall of the deeps of the earth at my back and I could hear the demon across the chamber, wheezing and laughing softly in the dark.

"Samir will find you, lovely," the thing whispered in Hindu. I think. Maybe. "Samir the Finder finds even the smallest things. Samir will find the Spider Queen."

Soft boots sliding across the floor. Finding his way to me. He was smelling the air, peering hard into the darkness to try and find invisible me. Waving the dagger and trying the occasional savage backswipe to prevent me from getting behind him. I could tell all this even though neither of us could see anything. I just felt it. Like the ten thousand beatings in Kurtz's fighting pit had given me the ability to *feel* the combat as much as see it. For a moment I thought I saw both burning red eyes in the dark chamber's confines, just for a second, so I lunged, exploded savagely forward, full predator mode now, slashing with the tanto in a reversed grip.

Looking to plant it and rip hard.

Instead, I cut air hard and found myself bouncing off the opposite wall of the chamber. In an instant, this demon was on my back and strangling me from behind.

Let's just stop there and have a cup of coffee. You'll love this part, Tanner, if you've found this account and are reading of my demise.

So there I am. My knife is out and away from the enemy. He's got a reverse chokehold on me, and I can feel the flinty knife against my cheek. It's pitch black and both of us are struggling, except I ain't got no incoming air to work with and what I got left ain't gonna last much longer. I'm stamping and trying to smash his feet or throw him off. I have no idea if I'm blacking out because it's pitch dark. But I feel like that's happening at that moment.

Yeah, since I arrived in the Ruin, I've had a few desperate fights for my life. This is the top one. Death felt close, had felt close in the Mouth of Madness for four hours and then the loneliness of the bone-littered beach where I lost it for a few minutes there.

"Like ya do, Talk," I could hear Tanner saying as I began to black out.

The ring's invisibility feature does nothing for me in the dark. It's just two blind warriors fighting blind. Even stevens.

I was in the dark fighting a demon who had me in a chokehold. Like ya do. Then I think about how nice it would be to see daylight just one last time and my mind lands on the plasma lighter I bought from the PX. The one still in my pocket.

The one there because of the passed-on wisdom of a sergeant who went simply by Joe.

I got it out, flicked it open, and jammed the plasma flame right against the demon's exposed arm. It was slender and smooth.

He wasn't strong. Fast and wiry, sure. Agile yes.

He screamed and flung himself away from the white-hot pain of the plasma connection. I stumbled forward, gasping, stepped on the shield, and smashed into the side of the chamber once again 'cause I'm pro like that.

A regular cat, one might say.

Stars were everywhere inside my skull and as I felt myself going out, I did my best impression of Sergeant Kurtz and motivated myself to hang on for just one minute more to see this thing to its conclusion.

I saw the red eyes in the dark, moving fast for me suddenly. I grabbed the shield off the ground and just flung it, heaved it really, like a frisbee, right at those incoming psychopath's red eyes.

I threw the book at him.

There it is. I knew I'd find something clever. *I threw the book at him.* Tanner will get a kick out of that one. I guess words are violence after all.

The shield went low and crushed the demon's throat. I figure that out later once I got another fire going. Until then, in the darkness, all I heard was him hit the floor and begin to gurgle, gagging and strangling as he tried to breathe and couldn't. And no, I didn't have a nasopharyngeal tube to clear his airway. Not that I would have.

He did try to kill me after all.

I'm not saying I'm all Kurtz. Hard and stone-cold killer. But I concentrated on just getting the fire going as the dying thing on the floor gurgled and died, crawling across the floor to get away for all the good that didn't do him.

By the light of the green fire, I stood and saw a dark and silent shape on the floor of the chamber.

A corpse. And that's when I took a breath and knew I'd won.

I'm not gonna write something prosaic like *for whatever that's worth.*

I know what it's worth. I live. I won. I get to go on living for the next few minutes. Add those up and maybe I get back.

If this is hell, the underworld, the nether realm, would he really be dead? Can you die in hell? That's a question you never really think to ask until you do, and then... you can't stop thinking about it. Even late in the night when you're awake and it isn't even the Hour of the Wolf yet.

I didn't think so. I didn't think you could die in hell.

So maybe I was still alive. Maybe the corpse is a clock judging by the lifeless shape at my feet. It just took some killing to prove life was still a thing. That was a Tannerism he'd said once on a battlefield we'd swept. "You know you're alive, Talk, when everyone else is good and dead."

My hands weren't shaking as I got the fire going again. That told me something. Something about me changing. Changing because I needed to. It was thrive or die, Private Talker. That's the way Tanner would put it.

"Sometimes you gotta adapt, Talk. It's that or just die badly. Ain't no two ways 'bout it and all."

There was a better way to say that, and I just didn't know it yet. But I knew I'd learn it. I'd have to now if I was gonna make it. Or I just wouldn't be anymore. No two ways about it, right buddy?

And I wasn't ready for that yet. Death.

I heard some… and this is stupid, but I'll put it down anyway and I don't want you to think worse of me. But I heard some trumpet that wasn't there… some call to arms. It wasn't there but it was like it was in my head. Maybe the Rangers still needed me.

Maybe I needed to put all these moments of survival together if just for that.

My hands weren't shaking, but I could have used a cup of coffee. Of course that. Junkie gonna junkie. Otherwise I wouldn't be me, now would I?

And the difference between me and the dead demon on the floor was that I was me. And that he was dead.

Sometimes it's that simple, Tanner.

Sometimes.

CHAPTER FOUR

I'M feeling more like me. Now. Or at least the me I've become living among the Rangers like some *Heart of Darkness* Jane Goodall. Knowing the whole time I was going upriver, whether I admitted it to myself or not. Not just looking for, but becoming the Brando character in *Apocalypse Now*. In the end… a true believer.

Chanting "one of us" in whatever chaos the Rangers are creating to kill more of their enemies and get the mission done.

I'm good with that now.

Ranger gonna Ranger, right?

I'd told myself, when I was enlisting, that I was just gonna get close to the river. I was just gonna look and see. I definitely wasn't going in. You know, the lie we all tell ourselves. That I wasn't worthy to Ranger, was the excuse. But being close to the world's most elite fighting force would find the edge I'd seemed to always need to find.

Now, with the dead guy at my boots, let's just be real honest about everything: This is where it was going all along, wasn't it, me? It just took going this far beyond the boundaries I'd established to realize I'd fallen in the river I'd only ever intended to get close to. Metaphorically speaking, referring to the Rangers. I had, in fact, actually *jumped* into the Mouth of Madness. But that other river, the River

Ranger, I'd merely stumbled into. Having meant only to tiptoe along the shore.

That was just the lie I told. But don't we all? We all just whisper in the dark that we're just going this once…

… and then we stay forever.

But I ramble now that I've got parchment. Like some drunken sailor in from the seas with pay to spend blocks from the port. Tomorrow will never come. The bill will never need to be paid.

Remember, no one called me *Talker* before they started calling me that in the Rangers. My last name is Walker. And no one in academia ever called me by that proper last name either. First names there because we were all elites. Ivory tower elites destined to govern the masses. At least that's what they thought without ever directly saying it out loud. It was just assumed. But I listened long enough to know that was deep inside them. And that I wanted no part of that. That way lies madness. Control. Ain't interested. Just here for the thrills, kids.

And I'm a talker. Hence the tag.

But now… I'm someone different now. Different than whoever I once was. I'm Talker, I thought to myself while looking at the body of the dead demon on the cold stone floor of the stone-cut deep cavern lost in the shadows and mist of the dark down here.

I'm Talker now. I accept that.

So then I rifled his body, ignoring the psychotic dead eyes of the elf-demon glaring upward as though seeking some kind of dark salvation above our heads, something unclean watching the both of us from the dark shadows there.

Sorry pal, this ain't charity. I beat you fair and square. I get your stuff. Dem's the rules, as Sergeant Chris likes to say.

The lost and the dead.

Like I said before, I'm keenly aware at this moment that if I'm going to survive, I need to concentrate hard on the task at hand and remember everything every Ranger ever taught me in the six months we've been here. I'll win this battle in the details. By the inches. Anything that comes my way is mine and it's going into play for the high score.

So I'll start here as I ignore the lonely drip of distant unseen water and the hysterical disembodied cackling I heard five minutes ago. It just came out of nowhere and seemed to echo over vast spaces and lonely forsaken halls down here that must be nearby and along the strange course of the rushing Mouth of Madness. The psychotic laugh had that bouncing, reverberating effect, and then it got lost in the distance as it faded.

I don't know which was creepier. The cackling, or the loneliness of it fading into the nothingness.

For a full two minutes I sat there listening to it wander and fade, wondering what kind of creature would make a mad sound like that down here. Insane. Mindless. Beyond a rational state of mind.

Lost.

I made up my mind I'd need to kill it if I ran into it down here. I'd need to have a plan for that. Ranger NCOs love to remind their lower-enlisted charges to *be polite, be nice, have a plan to kill everyone in the room*. It's an old quote and they don't quite have all of it down, as in embodying all three pillars. *Polite* and *kind* specifically. That's not their way. The killing part? *Definitely*. They've got that down in spades. But they aren't long on politeness or being nice. Rangers like being grim and fatalistic and often find, as I have noted, horrible things to be incredibly funny to them and their particularly gruesome senses of humor.

Now Chief Rapp, he's different, but then again, he is a Green Beret. He's got all three down pat: *polite, kind, professional killer.* Nicest guy you'd ever wanna meet. He can kill you dead in about six ways to Sunday and a dozen others I'm sure he has in his toolkit.

But yeah, back to the unseen laughter that was the sound of madness. It made my skin crawl and turn cold all at once in the same instant as I listened to the hysterical babble in the distance. I thought, in the unsettling silence that followed, that there was no way I was getting out of this. That this situation was gonna roll me no matter how hard I came at it. The despair came at me just like that— like some monster we'd just discovered. A sudden dark hopelessness that whispers how deep in over your head you might actually be on this one.

Just a… *You're gonna die down here, Talker.*

I laughed a little at that.

Then shook my head and decided I wasn't gonna.

I got down to the business of survival, which meant rifling the dead elf. I remembered something Captain Knife Hand once told us. After a pretty weird fight that almost went real bad for even Rangers.

And yeah. It's not a demon I'm searching the pockets of. It's some kind of elf for sure. Autumn told me there were many races of elves all across the Ruin. That's what she called them. *Races of elves.* She said most were difficult to get along with because of the long lives of elves and the sacred traditions they live by. One time she told me about a race of elves she hoped we'd never meet. Bad juju. Or big bigga juju as the assistant gunner for Kurtz's weapons team would say.

She called them *Lost Elves*.

Dark elves straight out of all the myths of legend even from our day. Elves who had gone deep into the earth, driven there by the other races of elves, collectively in great battles and campaigns, secret wars the Cities of Men never knew of. Almost every other race for that matter despised them. The Lost Elves were universally hated. Apparently for good reason.

"They…" She spoke in the halting English I was teaching her then. Why? Because there'd been a reason to. The Cities of Men. We were us then. And we had a dream of a boat. Just the two of us. Her no longer a queen and me… I don't know. I'm not that guy anymore.

The memory is like gossamer to me now. I tell myself it will fade one day, and I won't even remember it eventually. But I also know that whether it's some bad day going worse with the Rangers, Winchester on ammo with more enemies than allies inside the wire, or it's some day when I'm old and can no longer hang, or chew whale fat as it were, that in those last seconds I will think of her, and the memory of a dream that was once ours.

But like I said back in the journal before the attack against the citadel…

That was then, this is now, Talker.

"They… seek the destruction… of the Ruin," Last of Autumn had whispered to me regarding these Lost Elves. "They worship the creator of Ruin. Hunt… her… the Spider Queen… everywhere they… go. They seek her death. Seek… her powers."

I'd delved back then because sometimes in myth there is truth. And truth in intel. And intel is advantage. And the Rangers need every ounce of it here in the Ruin. So I contribute by getting it whenever and wherever I can. Vandahar had translated those pages we'd recovered and there had been some mention of someone called the Spider Queen among those yellowed and brittle fragments.

"It was the Spider Queen who... destroyed...?" I asked, struggling to frame what I was trying to ask. "The time I came from?"

She nodded.

We were eating summer apples. Thinking about it now, I can still taste the bite of them. Wish I had one now. But... I got nothing down here in the dark.

Now I'm thinking about coffee. But you knew that.

Back to what the captain told us one time after it got real hairy and kinetic all of a sudden. It was on the movement south from Tarragon after smoking the dragon. Our assault packs filled with treasure from the hoard. It was a night march and the captain had made the decision to move by cover of darkness because we were being stalked by what Kennedy told us were most likely goblin tribes.

Jabba confirmed this just by scenting the air like a dog. Lifting his cracked FAST helmet back and tasting the night.

"Smell lika Shivah Mountain Gobs comin' down dem passes. Bad juju. Big bunch. Bigga bigga bunch. Moon Gobs hates Shivah Mountains. Big wars for bigga times with Shivahs. Killee all, Shivahs. Killeee now!"

The Rangers weren't afraid to fight the goblin trackers that had been dogging us for three days after we'd cleared Tarragon. But the truth was, the fight with the dragon and clean-up operations afterward against the Saur expedition-

THE BOOK OF JOE

ary force had left us low on ammo. So for the moment we were just fading into the south and trying to make the walls of the FOB. Moving by night through as much of the swamp as we could as fast as possible. Going into all the tangles and bayous where it was real hard to be followed.

Vandahar was with the captain's element, which consisted of scouts and the weapons team. Last of Autumn had gone south with the new king of the Shadow Elves, and I had stayed behind because I was in no hurry to get back to the new normal of no longer being... us. The Cities of Men and the dream.

Vandahar had said, as we caught sight of the distant goblin trackers moving through the late afternoon shadows in the dark hills behind us, "Many evil races will now come for the dragon's hoard knowing Ssruth is truly dead. Those goblins can smell gold and it is why they are ever at the dwarves' throats for it."

Max the Hammer, champion of the Dwarven King, was with us and nodded gravely at this truth in the early evening shadows of the halt as we took a knee and waited for the scouts to find the way forward through the difficult swamp in the night. Humping hoard and as much ammo as we could do in case it got hairy.

"But there are other dangers here worse than goblins," murmured the old wizard who merely chewed on his unlit pipe now that we were moving by stealth. "'Tis best we be through this edge of the Charwood as fast as is reasonable," noted the old wizard.

Later, after the fight we got into, Kennedy would hypothesize that we ran into what his game might have called an *aboleth*. But at the time, creeping through the thick swamp, as the scouts opened up ahead, all we knew was we'd run smack dab into pure insanity all at once.

The scouts had come upon the remains of a sunken old city there in the swamp. None of the old maps mentioned it and they were threading the near sunken bridges to cross to the other side of a foul-smelling lake that seemed silent and evil in the hot and sullen end-of-summer night. All the water here smelled worse than foul. Taco Bell bag-of-diarrhea death ripe. It was undrinkable even with boiling and drinking straws, so we'd steered clear of it as a hydration source. Problem was, it was late summer by then and the hump was hard and sweaty through the sucking biting-insect-filled mud and stagnant pools of the snake-infested marshes. We were thirsty, and gold is heavy to hump.

Suddenly the scouts were engaged forward in the middle of the hot and humid night. Fire everywhere and Sergeant Hardt calling for support ASAP over comm.

"Let's go, weapons team!" ordered Kurtz without delay as he received the sitrep from the scout team leader.

The captain sent us off to the left to get eyes on the lake and see how we could support the engaged scouts with effective fire. Meanwhile, he took the remaining Rangers and went up along the swamp path to relieve the fighting forward scouts from the rear.

The ground was soft and spongy, every step sending up sour awful-smelling spores and biting gnats as we pushed through the dense murk and sucking muck to reach the overwatch position along the lake.

"Gobs gonna hear. Bigga bigga Shivah Gobs gonna come fast now!" shrieked Jabba as he followed the gun carried by Soprano as fast as the two-forty gunner could.

Kurtz broke through the undergrowth first and found a fallen log, rotting through, on a small slice of sandy beach overlooking the lake. Directions to emplace here were quickly given and the Rangers went to work on delivering high-cycle death within the next thirty seconds.

"He ain't wrong," muttered Brumm, bringing up the rear with the SAW. Across the middle of the lake, the scouts were strung out along an ancient barely-submerged-at-points crumbling stone bridge from another age. They were firing wildly at nothing we could see. Automatic gunfire in wild bursts, frenetically streaking off into the water and causing a series of small volcanic plumes in the stagnant moss laden murk. At the same time, their squad designated marksman was shooting into the cracked and fallen circular towers that guarded the path of the sunken bridge out into the gloomy mist-shrouded lake.

The whole scene was wild and beautiful all at the same time and made no sense to me. Tracers. Suppressed fire. Hulking stone sentinels in the cracked and broken towers strung across the dark lake in the moonlight.

But no enemies I could spot.

"Weapon up. Ready to engage, *Sergente*. But I can no see what they shooting at!" shouted a bewildered Soprano, eagerly looking for something to kill a lot.

"Something in the water…" mumbled an almost mesmerized Kurtz as he studied the situation. "You guys hear that…?" Then: "There!"

He directed Soprano with his targeting laser and the two-forty opened up with a quick eight-round burst as the gunner muttered, "Two-forty entering the chat." The high-powered seven-six-two smashing into the muck-and-moss-laden surface of the lake farther out where some dark and monstrous shape moved like oil and quicksilver in the moonlight just beneath the surface.

Whether the outgoing rounds hit or not, we had no idea. But what happened next felt like getting hit by a tidal wave of fear. The thing in the lake charged us as though it sensed the two-forty was now the real threat to its continued existence.

Later, the scouts swore they were fighting ogre archers that had come out of the water like giant hulking Navy SEALs all kitted with wicked curving swords, huge bows, and war paint, ready to get their kill on. Except there weren't any of those murder behemoths we could see out there and as we did the after-action report later, the scouts all agreed that of the enemies we'd faced here in the Ruin, the big ogres that had attacked us back at Ranger Alamo had been some of the most cunning and deadly they'd faced. Those ogres were eight feet tall, built like 'roided-out MMA fighters, and moved like Abrams tanks on the hunt. You had to shoot 'em a whole bunch just to put 'em down. Standard Ranger doctrine concerning them was a full mag of five-five-six was gonna do the trick. Make sure to shoot fast, and accurately, but fast for sure. Because those things would be all over you before you could spit. One of them had chopped a scout, Corporal Davidson, right in half with an axe.

So those things were, in the scout's mental hard drive, listed under nightmare fuel. Which meant, for Rangers, that they really wanted those things to appear so they could kill them a whole bunch and then kill them some more. And then probably piss on their corpses and draw obscene stuff with Sharpies on their ugly faces. Rangers didn't mind fear. They just dealt with it differently. *Homicidally* one might say.

"That's a lot," Tanner had remarked regarding the five-five-six requirements to kill the ogres. "Over in the sandbox, if hajis were wearing body armor, it took three to waste your average bad guy. Thirty is a real serious romance, if you get my meaning, Talk."

I did.

I'd seen a lot of those hulking murder ogres, dead and alive. You didn't have to convince me.

But that would all come later during the AAR as we tried to figure what trick the aboleth had played on the scouts when they'd tried to cross the lake by stealth. Spoiler... it turned out, the scouts collectively considered the close-combat ogre archers to be something they would rather not run into and get involved with. This aboleth dug around in their minds and then concocted something for them to be concerned about while it played its mind games.

"The abomination of the deeps can read the thoughts of its victims. It will take their terrors and make them even far greater," remarked Vandahar in the aftermath of the battle. Now with his fragrant pipe lit, him stirring it to life, and musing almost to himself about the events we'd been through. "To think the lesser cults of the Dragon Elves worshipped these evil beings is beyond comprehension. But so were the final days of every empire of the Ruin. Corruption and perversity. And..." he said, turning to me. "I suspect even the kingdoms of your time. Evil always seems to find a way to become an idol that the degenerate must worship."

So during the battle, the seduced scouts thinking they were getting overrun by ogre operators coming out of the swamp at them from all directions, were suddenly shooting back at phantasms. Mental illusions they had created with the help of the aboleth. Then with the gun team suddenly getting focused on by the charging bull in the water causing all this… it was instant chaos.

I started shooting.

Sua sponte. Of my own accord. Because whatever this thing was, I was immune to it. Probably because of the psionics, but I don't know. My Ruin-revealed ability was doing something for me, probably. I'd put it down as that later, though at the time I had no idea. I couldn't feel anything in particular. It was more… *Threat identified. Waste it. A lot, Talker.*

I heard Soprano swear the thing was screaming in his ear as he pulled the trigger on the two-forty mounted on the rotten log and burned a whole belt like we were going to Ammo Costco the next morning because there was a sale on 7.62. Jabba fed the belt, doing his Jabba yipping in the explosive excitement of the moment. Kurtz moved to his three-twenty grenade launcher as Brumm watched the rear and Tanner pulled perimeter security on the left flank.

I was on the right.

The nightmare fish thing was bigger than I'd at first guessed. The aboleth seemed to grow as it charged the beach, coming straight at us, swelling in the water like Monstro the whale from the *Pinocchio* cartoon. But creepier in an *Outer Dark* way. Then the first rounds from the two-forty ripped straight into it and the thing surfaced, its gaping mouth just a sucker-like circle filled with jagged needle-sharp teeth.

Nightmare stuff for sure.

It screamed like some alien mind not meant for human consumption. Pain and rage and destruction all at once.

I shot it as much as I could and then, as it took fire from the two-forty, it fishtailed along the narrow scum-laden shore and sped off fast like a thresher shark, throwing green moss and mud from the black bottom of the bayou all over us.

Then the tail, like a feathery whip, shot out of the water and hit Kurtz, knocking him senseless and down the beach. Like he was a small bothersome fly who'd just gotten swatted into next week.

Tanner was on Kurtz in a second, sensing the weapons team sergeant's intention to put fragmentary grenades into the lake and now unable to do so. Explosives in the water are the fastest way to end a threat within that terrain medium.

Tanner had the launcher up and was dropping rounds where he thought the submerged beast might be now. Kurtz was on one knee, coughing and still pointing where he wanted the two-forty to put fire.

There was a momentary pause as the next belt got loaded because Soprano had burned the last one too fast for Jabba and the little gob had missed the link-up.

Then Tanner stopped launching grenades from the three-twenty and just turned like he was in a trance toward the two-forty team. I watched as he raised the launcher and aimed it at them.

I ran straight at Tanner knowing he wasn't in his right mind, hit him full bore, and the both of us went into the midnight-dark scum-laden water of the smelly lake. Bad move, Talker. Both of us would reek for the entire trek back to the FOB and ultimately we'd burn our cryprecisions because the stink of the swamp never quite washed out.

Plus the memory was unsettling.

At least Tanner, who'd been *enslaved* as Kennedy would put it, by the aboleth, didn't blow up Soprano and Jabba.

Or the two-forty.

We struggled in the dark water, Tanner and I. We had both sparred in Kurtz's combatives, but this wasn't like the full at-combat-speed fighting Kurtz liked to see us go after one another with. Tanner was barely there, and I could tell that as I attacked him. I yanked the three-twenty away from him almost effortlessly like he was fighting to take control of himself on the inside, and I flung the launcher up onto the beach and out of reach.

Then I got my feet under me in the muddy water and pushed Tanner down into the muck and around so I could get him in a chokehold. I remember hoping he didn't drag a grenade off his belt and just do us both right there.

Later he'd tell me, after the AAR in which he'd just told the captain, "That thing got into my mind and told me to take out the two-forty," what really happened.

"It told me its name was *Summoth Gulak*, Talk, and that it was as old as the time of the Delta Kings. Told me in just half a second every lie I ever wanted to hear, Talk. Told me to *let it happen*. But I shrugged all that off even as I could feel its... tentacles... pushing around inside my mind trying to figure out what would work for it to get what it wanted done... done, you know, man? This was all while I was dropping rounds in the lake trying to get it to pop. But it was when it told me it knew where to find... the girl that killed me that I just said... okay. That jester. *Harlequin* I think they're called. Well, I wanted that. Want it, you know. Real bad. And then it took over just like that. After that, I had no idea till I came to on the lake with you trying to choke me out. And by the way, Talk... I'm dead. I don't think you can choke me out. But good try all the same, man. Sorry about my superpowers and all. But I'm hard to kill. Steven Seagal. Again. You know what I'm talking about?"

So that was my part in the battle against the aboleth, or whatever it was Kennedy said his game called it. Making sure our own guys didn't attack us. The fire from the scouts was so wild, that could have happened, too. Them hitting us out there with outgoing fire going every which way. But in the moment where I was trying to choke out a dead guy who didn't need oxygen, Soprano and Jabba burned another belt on the fishy horror, and the captain's element deployed the last Stinger on the thing in the lake. Because even though it had hypnotic powers and lived in a cold dark lake in the deepest part of the swamp, it still gave off a heat signature below the surface of the water.

And as Sergeant Chris likes to say, "Stinger's the greatest sniper rifle ever made."

Fighting there in the smelly and rank water, all we heard was a sudden streak of a whooshing roar as I wrestled with Tanner and then an explosion, and water rained down muck and aboleth guts all over us.

Then the thing was dead, and the hypnotic *enslavement* or whatever you want to call it, the power it had, faded. Oh, as did the fact that some of the Rangers in the captain's element were literally being attacked by the water itself. Yeah, weird, huh? The dark mucky water of the swamp, when the aboleth was fighting us, came to life and attacked them as they tried to fight forward, turning into watery tendrils and even sudden columns of water rising out of the muck. Grabbing the Rangers and flinging the ones it could get a hold of out into the stagnant lake.

In the aftermath, it was Brumm who came out of the dark clutch of the swamp to our rear to see Rangers in the lake, Kurtz gasping on the sand, and me trying uselessly to choke out Tanner.

Soprano was whooping that he got the fish-horror, but Jabba corrected him and said, "No... Stinga.... Stinga got big bigga monstah!"

Then Soprano slapped the goblin and said, "That ain't how it went, little monkey. Gun team got the kill. Got that, monkey man? Gun team for the win!"

Jabba immediately jumped up and down shouting that the "Gun team killa bigga big monstah!" as though this was the truth and so ever would it be.

Brumm put two and two together. He'd heard the Stinger go off and he could see the now-floating dark bulk of the dead aboleth out in there in the swampy lake.

"Carl G may not care. But that Stinger is a stone-cold killer, man."

So, now that I have enough parchment from the dead Lost Elf, if that's what it is, I tell you that whole story to tell you what the captain said later after we *didi mao'd* out of that section of the deep swamp, trying to lose the goblins by going farther into the areas they didn't want to go. Hoping not to run into anymore horrors from the outer dark in quiet little murder grottos.

This is what Rangers do when it's time to fade. Go where the enemy can't, or won't, or would be stupid to follow. And if they do... they'll pay. The Rangers will go there even if it's on the wrong side of hell. Which, as a survivor of that swamp, pretty much describes the geography for the rest of the march that night and the next few days.

Let's just say I'm glad Kurtz didn't take us back there for swamp phase of his Ranger School. He chose one closer to the FOB, and to be honest, that place was no picnic either. Unless you count tying yourself to mangrove trees to sleep in water up to your chin while poisonous snakes swim through your legs, a picnic of some kind.

Which you don't because only psychos—or Rangers— would think that.

I told you all that to tell you what the captain finished the AAR with that next morning after the strange battle with an aboleth and before we went to sleep for the day, cleaned weapons, stood guard, and got ready to make our way through the next section of the worst swamp ever that night. One star. Would not recommend. After Captain Knife Hand quietly and calmly listened to how all of us had operated under the strain of the battle with something that had new and strange supernatural powers. Powers that got into the dark parts of our minds and messed with our heads.

Unpleasant stuff.

Rangers AAR everything. Even nightmares from the outer dark that hack science fiction writers aren't clever enough to think up. If they could, Rangers would AAR the very enemy firing squads that lined them up and shot them, if such a thing were to occur. Recommending improvements and promising dip-fueled threats from beyond the grave.

The morning sun felt warm and clear in the small clearing the Rangers had secured for the patrol base as we finished up the AAR. The captain stood there in the middle of us, tired, that permanent look of indigestion on his face gone for the moment. If just for a little while, then. He looked more... patient now in the morning light after listening to all sides of the surreal battle. Then he spoke to us like he was explaining some truth he'd had to learn the hard way. Out there in the dark and weird parts of the world that had always been there long before the Ruin ever became a thing. As the sergeant major had once told me about our captain, "He's been up some real dark alleys, Private Talker, and sometimes the only one to walk out of those fights. He's tougher'n a two-dollar steak, and we drew the short straw, or maybe the universe likes us a whole bunch, to get him as the GFC on this never-ending hippy walk."

The captain spoke to us like he knew exactly what we were going through right now because he'd been there before, once and a long time ago. The weird blank spaces in the universe that are dark and unexplored for a reason. And many times since.

The truth was, and we all knew it, the rest of the night's hump after the aboleth fight had been pretty freaky. The images the dead thing in the water had left inside our heads were still messing with us. Every shadow, every tree, every dark and smelly pool, a place of danger and no return, even for Rangers.

You didn't know what was real, and what wasn't. What could be trusted, and what couldn't. Which is a lot of extra baggage through a dangerous swamp you could drown in with every step.

The Ruin is a beautiful place. A strange place to be sure. But... a deadly place in ways that just hadn't occurred to us yet. We'd smoked a dragon and felt pretty good about that. Then met something... *other*... something *weird*... on the way back. That bothered me. And I think it bothered everyone else too.

"We didn't lose anyone, Rangers," began the captain just after dawn. "We made it. We fought something outside our anticipated capabilities. Now… it's dead. That's the way Rangers do it."

He said that matter-of-factly. Like it was carved in stone somewhere and maybe we'd forgotten that, or just needed to be reminded of it in the warm light of a new day. And it was true. Now he knew we needed to accept that truth once again. That there were weird things out here that were going to try and kill us every day we were here. Attack us in strange new terrible ways and we'd just have to deal with that as it came, the best we could. Expend brass, use the whole kitchen sink, knife, and knuckles. That's survival.

"Being afraid of weird stuff is fine," continued the captain once he bluntly put the first part out there in the warm and humid morning air, and we'd accepted it. "It can make you paranoid," he said. "Paranoid enough to keep you out of some bad situations and stay alive. But fear… fear'll kill you, Rangers. Fear will vapor-lock your brain to the point that anything can, and will, walk up to you and just cut your throat while you're bug-eyed with panic and fear. That happens. And it happens to pros all the time. Trust me on that one."

He stared at all of us for a long moment as the swamp flies buzzed and strange birds hooted forlornly out there in the all the dark pools and lost mangroves we'd have to crawl through out there that night. Again and again, until we were out of it.

We'd go where the enemy wouldn't. It's that simple.

"But you met it and fought it, Rangers. And then you killed it. Just like the first time you got into a fight. A real incoming fight where you can hear the rounds moving past your helmet and you're doing what you gotta get done. Next morning nothing's different. Wasn't then. Isn't now. Breakfast still tastes the same. You've done it before. And you'll do it again, Rangers. And you'll survive and do anything to survive… because that's what Rangers do."

I had to write all that down just as I remember it now.

I need it now more than I ever thought I would.

I've got the dagger, the elf's lantern. The parchment too. My ring. My lighter. This shield. And a knife. If Sergeant Joe is dead… then that ruck is still out there somewhere. It's got stuff I'll need to service. And if he's alive… then I need to link up and maybe he needs help.

I'm going to survive.

That's what Rangers do. I've done it before, I'll do it again. It's that simple.

So… I'll do that.

I'll go find Sergeant Joe now.

CHAPTER FIVE

I heard the distant gunfire echoing and rolling off the rock walls and cut tunnels down here, sounding much like an M18 being worked both economically and aggressively. Before that, I'd walked for a long time, following twisting narrow caverns, wide carved halls, and other dank dark passages that generally followed alongside the constant rush of the Mouth's long and turbulent journey down through the depths of subterranean rock.

How far down had we been carried? How lost were we? Eventually I'd need to figure that out if I was gonna get back to the rest of the detachment.

I've seen, and run into, other strange, weird, and horrific things down here in the dark.

Go on, Talker. Tell the Rangers who'll find your rotting bones down here what exactly were your last adventures on this lost and unofficial recon of the End of the World, or so the maps call these grid squares beyond the edge of the markings.

Well…

For example, a cube of quivering translucent greenish jelly came down one of the larger and more finished passages, a wide stone-worked hall really. The carving in the stone walls became more and more finished the farther along the passage I was probing. I was definitely headed down. Deeper into the earth. Or at least it felt like that. So maybe usage of *definitely* is a little too *definite*. It's hard to say down here.

But let's just say I'm not headed back or toward the surface as far as I can tell, and I'm pretty sure that is the direction I want to be heading.

But back to the quivering jello cube I found blocking my path forward along that route. It was at least one story tall, so... big for a dessert, you might say. It was greenish, shimmering, and almost translucent... what I can only assume was some kind of living bio-material jelly. At first I thought, as I took the passage off the main one I'd been following, hoping to get closer back to the river and perhaps find Sergeant Joe, or his body, and in that case hopefully the ruck, I at first thought I might have run into some kind of magic shield. That's what the horror jello cube looked like initially. So I approached cautiously, thinking it was some kind of barrier I'd either need to negotiate or turn around because of.

I've found it's best to be apprehensive about magic of any kind here in the Ruin. Arcane sorcery, or what they call na-no, has a way of making people real dead in weird and truly horrible ways.

So measure once, cut twice, because your life probably depends on it. Your mileage may vary but not by much. Be careful.

Then I heard it singing... and yeah, this is the weird part. It was quivering and producing a barely audible sound that bothered my brain. Like some thin violin playing disharmonious notes across an alien landscape mankind was never meant to cross. That's what it felt like inside my brain. That's the only way I can describe it for you.

Enjoy.

The sound the thing made was as though it was mindless and possessed no actual language except the song of its own horrible gelatinous quivering. A song that seemed to convey lifeless alien destruction and a happy endless hunger for same. Definitely not Top 40, and no beat you could dance to if you were so inclined and didn't decide to just run screaming from it as soon as you ran into it which would have been the smart choice a pro would make.

So... I decided to investigate.

When I got close I saw the corpses inside. The translucent horror-jelly seemed almost to magnify them in the near darkness of the lonely hall. Someone once told me not to look too closely when you came upon car accidents. Might not like what you see and might not be something you want to live with. This felt like that. Other things were trapped there within its gooey embrace. Swords and shields, broken and shattered. Rings and coins glimmering like promises made. Fantastic gems that seemed huge and beyond anything I'd ever seen at a jewelry store in the mall.

Like *Aladdin and the Forty Thieves* big. Fantasy fantastic is the description I've been thinking a lot when we encounter things in the Ruin. In the dragon hoard the Rangers plundered, this really came into usage. Most gems in real life, or rather the life... or the world... no that's not right either. Most gems from the *time* we came from are small. Even some of the most fantastic and expensive in the world. Nothing like in cartoons and fairy tales or video games. But here in the Ruin, I've seen an emerald that would choke a horse. Things in the Ruin are... bigger. Fantasy fantastic. But of course, you've probably already figured that out by now. I'm just articulating it. But it's been that way all along.

Back to the deadly dessert cube.

I didn't know it yet, because its movement was so slow and ponderous, *lugubrious* one might say, but that giant cube of translucent green quiver-sad-singing jello was moving. Slowly. And that word, *lugubrious*, was spot on, Talker, I told myself as I watched its sluggishly melancholy process, mentally awarding myself linguist word nerd points for using it to describe the thing. *Mournful, dismal, or gloomy, especially to an exaggerated or ludicrous degree. Lugubrious.*

So slowly, yet steadily, down the passage toward me, the quivering thing undulated and slid its sucking *unguent-y* bulk, hey look at me inventing words, toward me. By that time I'd gotten close enough to stupidly approach it, surprised that my mouth wasn't half open like some slack-jawed yokel seeing strange lights on a lonely county road. I watched it, utterly fascinated. Staring at the treasures and corpses trapped within.

From this distance I could finally tell it was a cube indeed, by the light of the torch I'd made to see my way along without NODs or blue-glow mushrooms. The entire passage beyond its bulky shape changed with refraction, and I could see that this wall of quivering jelly was truly a compact cube. A slow-moving cube, quivering and filled with rotting corpses.

Mostly.

I was just a few feet away from it, sure I could outrun it if I needed to, and definitely aware that this strange and alien thing held a kind of grim allure for me, when I saw the freshest corpse within its jellied embrace... twitch.

Another Lost Elf. A warrior of some type. Trapped within the gelled volume of the cube. Flesh being eaten away. Dissolved. I'd assumed it was just another corpse sucked up by this bizarre jelly vacuum down here. Until it moved.

And then I saw the psychotic eyes of the Lost Elf trapped within the green translucent gel go suddenly wide as he noticed me through the hell of that prison he was trapped in.

His mad eyes immediately implored me to do something. Anything. To reach in and help him.

And to be honest… I had every intention of doing just that before I could even think about it. On some level, the back of my mind had been contemplating just something along those lines. Now that I was in survival mode. Now that I'd suddenly become a gear hound, knowing that as much as I could collect down here could add seconds and even minutes to my survival and perhaps I could turn those small slices of gained time into something like days. Given enough of them, I might make it back to the Rangers. Alive even. The stupid plan my mind was playing with as I approached the jello horror was to find a way to get that gear out of there and use it for my continued survival.

Swords and axes as weapons. Maybe they were magic even. Coins and jewels as currency for trade, should I happen to eventually run into someone who could sell me food or water. Or even point me the way back to the Lost Coast and across the Atlantean Mountains.

The Rangers, once the medusa was smoked, would continue on to objective Mummy in the Valley of the Kings somewhere in the Land of Sleep. South of Sûstagul, in what we once called Egypt.

I could find my way there. I just needed stuff to make that happen effectively.

The dead guy inside the jello cube of slow death moved and wordlessly screamed in horror at me, begging for help. So of course, Ninja Ranger that I am, I backed up quickly—hey, I didn't run away—and tripped as I tried to back up to what I considered a safe distance from a possibly very dangerous dessert.

It was at that moment I realized the jelly monster was capable of a sudden burst of speed. As I landed on my butt, the entire cube suddenly quivered violently, ecstatically one might say, and that was pretty horrible to hear and see up close and looming, and then the entire deadly mass of gelatin surged forward at me. I am assuming it intent was to run me over, suck me in, then digest me for… *let's hope not a thousand years.*

At that point I got a good look at the psycho Lost Elf trapped inside the gel. His half-dissolved face in pantomime that I should help him out was replaced by a new horror. He wasn't asking, begging, or silently pleading for help now. His former pleas and unending torment had now turned into insane laughter as performed by some terrible street mime you can't avoid. Wordless and silent, which honestly made it all that much weirder and creepier, as I watched from the floor while the looming cube heaved its bulk to run me over and suck me up.

Quivering excitedly as it did so. Like some mindlessly fat gourmand racing for the latest buffet to open aboard a cruise ship of the damned. The two a.m. Captain's Snack featuring stupid linguist sashimi.

The elf was laughing hysterically in slow motion, trapped within, and knowing that soon I'd be foolishly trapped in there along with him. Suffering in torment for who knows how long.

Company in hell and all. Something about misery.

It's at that moment as you're about to get rolled by a one-story murder dessert, you remember the exact quote from the *Star Wars* movie about being trapped inside an all-powerful sarlacc. You swear you can hear the golden robot's voice right in your ear, delivering the gloomy promise on behalf of the space-gangster giant slug about your suffering.

So I crabbed backward, got my legs and soggy boots underneath me, and then ran for all I was worth, hoping the horrible green jelly cube was actually mindless and that it didn't control some function like opening a pit ahead of me for me to fall into or closing off the passage with some secret wall and completing the trap. Because then... well then I would be joining the psychotic elf for what remained of my horrible existence inside that thing.

Breathing heavily, I made the main passage and found other carved halls and distant stairs to follow the course of the vast underground river farther and farther away from the green quivering monster.

In time I heard the gunfire. Lower down. Single-shot and sounding like an unsuppressed MK18 carbine. A minute later I felt a sudden hot blast of desert wind coming at me from a new angle in the darkness I was making my way through. I could smell dry sage and heavy dust in the draft coming from off to my left, out over a vast open space in the dark down here I'd been crossing through, when all this new input suddenly overwhelmed my tension-filled senses.

The torch guttered and wavered in the blast of warm desert air as it crossed the great cave I'd discovered.

How did I know it was desert air? I've smelled enough of that in the southwest on visits to my dad and the ranches he was working on, training horses. It smelled of sage and desert and after all the gloom, dark, and rot down here, it was like suddenly seeing a lighthouse cutting the night in a rough storm at sea. When you know there are rocks all around and no way to see them. Then suddenly someone throws you a line and shows you a passage to safe harbor. A way out of this place. It was like that.

Then the hopeful draft was gone just as suddenly as it had come.

More gunfire farther below rang out in the darkness, distant and sudden, and I had no idea how to reach it. Shots came in quick succession, three usually, then it would be quiet for a short interval, then another rapid succession of shots as someone else got smoked.

Sergeant Joe, I had to assume, double-tapping? That was my hope. That meant he was still alive.

I followed the direction of the breeze when it came once again from the same quarter. A few more sudden gusts, then nothing at all. It took me a few minutes, but eventually I found the far wall of the great dark cavern down there I'd been crossing through. There were hairy webs the farther I went toward the wall. Hot and itchy as they touched my exposed arms and face. My torch struggled against the thick gloom here, and the weird warm drafts continued from some unseen desert, fanning the torch to sudden and erratic life.

I had my knife out and I was slashing my way through the strands and columns of old and new web to get to the source of the gusts. I could see the breeze making the ancient sticky strands ripple.

And then my torch caught some of the nearby webbing. Greedy flames grabbed the spider-silk and ate hungrily, crawling upward quickly and illuminating a vast cavern far above my head.

By the light of the flames, I saw six of the worst spiders I've ever seen in my life. Including cartoons.

And by *worst*, I mean huge, spindly, and an almost translucent red that screamed, *Hey, I'm super poisonous.*

Up there in the heights of the cavern, the flames made them seem like hiding, crouching, demonic monsters as they scurried away from the climbing fire, chittering screams. One of them got caught by the flames and suddenly fell, smashing into the floor nearby, the flames consuming it at once.

I've seen a lot of horrible things in the Ruin. Spiders are at the top of some list I've been making all along. These spiders were twice my size, and it was clear, even as they ran from the flames across their ghostly cathedral of webs, that they were still intently focused on me and considered me of primary concern.

Like shoppers eyeing the chickens in the meat case for a sumptuous Sunday dinner.

And yeah, there were corpses bundled within the webbing up there. Of course there were. Corpses the shape and size of the two Lost Elves I'd met. And other, bulkier captives. Some of the webby bundles twitched as the flames got close, but maybe that was just the heat drafts off the developing inferno and not an indication that some of those prisoners were probably still alive and filled full of sickly poisons inside those webbed coffins, waiting to be devoured and wide awake for the whole horrible show. Feebly struggling to get free with what little energy they had left before the flames reached them.

A moment later, huge sections of flaming web collapsed across the cavern floor in the direction I'd come from, cutting off any retreat I might have wanted to make. Other spiders, on fire, smaller than the six hulking reds up there, ran away in every direction as smoke began to fill the cavern.

I had no time for this and followed my original course through the swiftly developing smoke. I found a crack, a fissure really, in the cavern wall, and now I could smell the desert and feel the hot dry wind and air close at hand. I pushed into the crevice, regardless of other unfound spiders that might be waiting in the dark in there because burning alive here was becoming a real possibility real quick.

The smoke followed me and filled the tight fissure as I squeezed through, stepping on broken bones I couldn't see, hearing their brittle snap, curving around warm rock, and finding handholds to pull me farther past areas that were so tight I had weird moments of panic where I thought I might be stuck for good. Wedged in the dark and choked by smoke. Bitten by angry spiders who considered their hunger more important than their vengeance that I had torched their empire.

"Ain't got time for that," I grunted at myself in the dark smoke-filled well of the fissure as I forced myself onward, embraced by crushing rock and not knowing if the passage would even continue to be passable in this direction, if just barely at that. More gunfire sounded from ahead in the direction I was going, clearer now, ringing out over the desert light I could see beyond the darkness.

And then I was out of the claustrophobic crack, my lungs able to expand fully once more, and I had to shield my eyes against a vast desert plain unlike any I'd ever seen before. White sand dunes, dazzling and bright, stretched away as far as the eye could see. Out there, in the distance, I could see buried palaces, ruins, rising obsidian obelisks, all of it sinking into an endless sea of sand that seemed to go on forever. And the bones of ancient leviathans, too, larger than any we'd ever seen save Cloodmoor the Giant, lay out there bleaching in the sun, half-swallowed by the burning sands.

Out here was no evidence of the Mouth of Madness and its violent course, and I could hear nothing of its ever-present subterranean roar as I scanned the vast and endless waste before me. Within the space of a few moments, a few steps across through an impossibly tight crack in the wall, it was as though I'd been born anew into a whole new world unlike anything I had ever imagined or anything I'd left behind.

Again, I wondered how far we'd gone. And a strange vertigo, unlike normal vertigo, hit me. It felt like... like growing old and thinking you're still young in the same instant. The feeling that time had passed and you hadn't paid attention to its grind. That the future was unexpected and real and faster than you could believe possible.

I gazed upon this desert of strange and distant monuments being swallowed by an endless arid region that stunned the mind to consider in its immensity, and I was sure that if I went into it I would die there because it was so devoid of any kind of life. My bones would eventually join the waste and bleach out there among those strange skeletons in the infinite sand, their white vertebrae reaching up out of the dust as if to signal that they were once as alive as I was and am and will soon be no more forever.

That way, out there, was death. To go into it was madness.

Then I heard more gunfire and looked down. I was on a ledge. A carved ledge in the face of a looming cliff. The crack was the result of some long-ago earthquake, or Ruinquake, that had marred the facade of a city along the walls carved all around me. That's what it looked like to me, that dwellings had been carved into the face of the mountain cliff that rose sharply above my head. Like old cities from our time, ruins of the southwestern Anasazi, carved into the walls of wind-blasted cliffs. Barren and alone for hundreds of years.

But this, the carvings all around me, were more ornate and looked to be the work of thousands of years. Towers and minarets, stairs, and strange temples, some collapsed and crumbling, others silent and brooding, had been carved all across the face of the rocky cliff I'd emerged onto. And the ledge I was standing on was a part of it all. Demons and strange animals were cut expertly into the rock all around me, rendered in the minutest of detail, so lifelike that for a moment I had to make sure I wasn't about to get done by more weird and alien monsters coming out of the rock.

Gibbering hyenas with tongues that lolled as they walked upright carrying swords like paddles and circular shields adorned with the madness glyphs I'd seen before. Animal eyes alight with hunger and something more.

Hulking humanoid crocodiles with whips, casting spells symbolized by carved stars, standing within magic circles while human slaves were sacrificed en masse. Crocodile snouts open and devouring slaves like unlimited candies tossed to circus animals. Scenes of horrible carnage and sacrifice.

Terrible demons like something left from the Toltecs or the Aztec ruins of our time. Boxy and wide-eyed, carrying axes over cities that burned with smoke and corpses. Forked tongues drooling flames as they went.

All of it was dark and unsettling. Horrible to consider as I searched for a way to find the source of the gunfire I was hearing, and hopefully Sergeant Joe.

Off to my left lay a vast entrance back into the cliffs, a pyramid-shaped gash cut into the rock of the mountain. The gunfire was coming from there, echoing out across the apocalyptic desert from below.

I had to lower myself off the ledge and then work my way across the carved demons, down serpentine steps that were dangerously steep, past demonically horned altars stained rust-red with ancient blood. I made it to the edge of the cut into the rock and saw him below.

Sergeant Joe.

He was three stories down inside what looked like a vast entrance to the cavern complex, working his way down a series of stairs cut into the rock, past a massive statue of a carved and grinning demon holding an immense brass bowl between its crossed legs. Gleaming rubies the size of steamer trunks stared out from the demon's malevolent face, gazing maliciously at the unending desert beyond.

The maps had called this region... The End of the World.

Below, harrying the Ranger NCO, were Lost Elves armed to the teeth and working in small clusters. Warriors with scimitars and other archer types with curved bows pursued and closed in on the Ranger from all directions. Arrows hissed and whistled across the cavern in the intervals when there wasn't ringing gunfire. Joe was moving from cover to cover despite the closing noose, firing if they rushed him, knocking down charging psychotic Lost Elf warriors dressed in dark chainmail and purple cloth. They wore capped helms and dark purple masks over their mouths. Swirling cloaks of midnight purple seemed immune to the desert light sifting into the cavern as the lithe yet heedless warriors rushed to gain some kind of advantage over the deadly Ranger in their midst.

Despite all that, Joe drilled them economically with the carbine, backed them off, and dashed for the next cover position before their archers could draw and fire at him.

Missed shots bounced off stone idols and shattered on blocky altars that seemed eons old.

In my mind, I could put it all together using what I knew of the geography of our time, the maps of the Ruin I had seen, and the desert vista that stretched off to the south, east, and west.

The Mouth had taken us from the top of North Africa, or what the Ruin called the Atlantean Rift, where some comet had hit in the ten thousand years since we'd been gone, and shot us out on the southern side of the Atlantean Mountain range, looking at what had once been the Sahara Desert. But now it was filled with the sporadic ruins of some long-ago lost demonic civilization. East and west ran the crooked line of the mountains that guarded the rift and the coast from the End of the World. Each peak rising up like a jagged canine tooth thrown impossibly skyward by the tectonic destruction of that ancient comet. The range to the north seeming impassable from here at the edge of the burning sands, and all other directions, everything to the south, east, and west, was swallowed by an endless desert that seemed like a place no one could ever stay long and survive, or even find their way out of.

To the north I couldn't see. That was over the jagged mountains, back the way we had come through the earth along the underground river I could imagine no way of navigating back. Through the dark. Up the Mouth and past things probably far worse and much more horrible than the quivering cube that took its time eating your flesh and equipment. All that you ever were.

But directions, geography... that was for later. Now I had to effect linkup with Sergeant Joe and get out of Lost Elf Central.

So... what then? Do I shout at him?

He was heading down the stairs, trying to reach the sandy floor of the cavern, dodging arrow fire and suicide charges by fanatical Lost Elven warriors, purple tongues lolling like those demons carved on the walls all around, blue skin demonic if there ever was such a color, eyes wild with fear, hate, and murder. To me, they, the new hated elves, were worse, in different ways, than the ogres the scouts didn't like too much. There was something wild and dangerous about these elves that was darker and far more sinister than the raging ogres.

And now I understood, at least a little, why Autumn had said they were almost universally despised by the denizens of the Ruin.

Clusters of them massed ahead of Joe, and behind him...

Behind him huge black spiders the size of bulls crawled out from deeper within the cavern where I could not get a visual from my location along the cut in the rock. And atop these gargantuan arachnids—a kind of black widow if the red hourglass on their backs was any indication—rode the knights of the Dark Elves. Imperious and haughty. Heavily armored in dark plate and carrying wicked barbed lances. They were coming out to do battle against the so-far-unkillable Ranger sergeant.

The trap was closing about the Ranger NCO.

And there was more.

Dark-robed figures, their wraps purple and close about their gaunt bodies as though they were corpses prepared for burial but taking one last walk around, the cloth adorned with sliver stars and moons and other unholy symbols that bothered that psionics part of my mind, were gathering in the clusters behind the front line of savage warriors. Hand gestures shot forth spells of dark bluish illumination, like Lost Elven star shells and pop flares for their archers to target the difficult Ranger working his murderous way through their lines.

I ran down the suicidally steep stairs, still three stories above the main floor. There was a balcony below my current position where I could signal him from. Another one lay on the opposite side of the cut-into-the-rock entrance to the cavern. Probably once some ceremonial guard post to watch over all the pomp and circumstance of ghoulish sacrifice that I had no doubt had once occurred here and probably still did.

I reached the stone-cut balcony, panting and surprised I hadn't broken my neck, leaned over the stone lip, and tagged my sergeant's progress. He was now on the sandy floor where the dunes had invited themselves into the ruins throughout the long years. Joe was moving among purple tents and ghostly blue witchfire lanterns.

The scene looked to me like some version of a Lost Elf FOB. Elves from within the tents, these wearing more ornate breastplates and robes, came out against Joe and were violently double-tapped, sometimes getting a quick stab to the neck or face if they were clueless enough to have wandered out into the chaos thinking the danger was farther away than it actually was.

The sergeant was the living embodiment of the concept of Violence of Action. A textbook example of professional murder and mayhem for others to understand why some animals are more dangerous than others. Sergeant Joe moved like a compact whiskey keg of unending violence and economy of savage gunfire without mercy in the slightest.

"Rangers lead the way!"

It was the only thing I could think of. I shouted it to get his attention.

Joe shot his head up, caught sight of me waving at him.

"Talker!" he shouted back, his voice booming out in the cavern below. Then he domed a Lost Elf who came out of a tent carrying a spear just steps away from him.

Domed is Ranger for blowing off the top of a bad guy's skull. It's considered pro shooting and something to be attained, remembered, and shared with others in the group. Rangers will recount domed shots like family members remind you about best-ever Christmases past.

"Man... I domed this haji coming out of his ambush position one time and it was the closest I ever felt to being a rock star. You shoulda seen the look on his face. Talk about surprised," is not an uncommon thing to hear from Rangers.

For the record, anyone I've ever domed was purely by accident and probably due to the fact that they moved just enough to make it happen right as I fired.

But I do aspire.

"Sar'nt, you got two fast movers coming up on your six," I called out. "Big spiders!"

I should have added *Really big ones*. But I didn't. Things were weird enough and hectic already.

He wouldn't have seen those from what I could tell. The huge spiders with their mounted Lost Elf knights moved fast and silent on delicately long legs, picking their way over and through the rich fabric of the purple tents that marked the forward operating base of the Dark Elves.

The Ranger sergeant pivoted, dropped to one knee, and shot the riders off their mounts as the hulking arachnids approached. The first knight took rounds and toppled off into the darkness. The second was quickly missing a head and just flopped over in the dark saddle to dangle, along for the spidery scrabbling ride while both grinning beasts bore down on the NCO.

They didn't need masters to know it was feeding time.

I'd already figured out what I could do to help, but I wasn't super-excited about doing it.

It hurts a lot when I do.

But I had no choice in the moment. Those spiders were gonna tear Joe limb from limb if they got on top of him, carbine or not.

I summoned that mental cone of destruction I'd used to knock off the headless riders back while holding the gun position when we were going up against the Army of the Dead, and I turned it loose on the two spiders.

Like that X-Men guy with the eye beams… but with thoughts.

Cyclops is the guy's name, Tanner told me when I described what it felt like.

The blast hit both of the huge spiders and my mind touched theirs as the lines of contact opened up. And by *touched*, I mean I mentally punched them in their tiny brains like Mike Tyson wrecked faces.

I smashed through their surface mindless hunger, their desire for fleshy treats at the hands of their elven masters, and ripped into their survival brains.

I'll use a metaphor because that's the best way for me to explain what it was like. Their spider minds were like old rotting Victorian mansions where spinster aunts lived among dry dark lace doilies and gossamer curtains made of the memories of ghosts. Everything delicate, sinister, and steeped in decades-old brittle corruption and parched evil. Even the details of their minds were unspeakably macabre as I rushed in.

I'm getting better at this. Still hurts though.

I ran in there, threw open the curtains, and the brutal Arizona summer sun suddenly decided that every dark thing in that decrepit mansion that was their mind needed SPF 3000 to survive, or as Kennedy and many of the younger Rangers who have joined his little gaming cult like to say…

Save versus Worst Day Ever.

I have no idea what that means. But the spiders failed to save.

In my head it was like watching old newspaper burn, fanned by a sudden whirlwind providing all the oxygen the flammables needed to combust quickly. That was what it was like inside their malevolent spider minds. I roasted them all at once with one massive mental blast and barely missed Sergeant Joe as he made it through the ornate and dark purple tents while more spiders, Dark Elf infantry, and hissing archers closed the knot on the sandy floor of the cavern and barely missed pinching the Ranger in their hasty trap.

"Run, Talker!" shouted Joe as he made the desert floor, cleared the tents, and ran for it.

He was sprinting for open desert now, MK18 held high, ruck strapped tight. I had a blinding headache. Thank you, psionics.

But I needed to move because it was time to get out of Dodgistan. So I ran.

I had no idea what would happen next. All we'd done was stop a few attacks on our rear and get out of the trap for the moment. But it was that kind of situation. Play for inches. Not yards. There were easily over a hundred of them if not more, boiling toward the entrance of the cavern. All we'd done was gain the desert floor and maybe fifty yards.

They'd mass and overrun us in the open shortly, screamed my sudden and tremendous headache.

"Run for that dune, Talker!" shouted the NCO who, despite being small and built like a whiskey barrel keg, and humping a massively overloaded ruck, was easily doing his best to make the six-minute mile. "We'll make our stand there."

I hit the desert floor without breaking my neck and ran for all I was worth through the thick sand. Black-shafted arrows landed all around me. The shots were wild, but something fired inside my swollen psionics-overdosed brain and caught sight of one shot coming in straight and true. It was gonna skewer me for sure.

I suddenly threw up the shield without thinking as I ran, tripping in the sand, and the shield caught the incoming arrow strike solid center mass. Coming in *just*—and I emphasis *just*—between me and death.

The missile shattered harmlessly and caused no recoil in impact.

I mean, it ain't *doming* someone. But it's pretty cool all in all.

I made the dune right behind Joe and we gained the lip, threw ourselves down in the sand, and made ready to give a good account of ourselves in what was probably going to be a last stand as the sun began to fade toward the horizon in the west.

Joe skinned his secondary and handed his M18 sidearm to me. I took the pistol and press-checked to make sure I had a round ready. He was handing me his magazines next, four total, while breathlessly telling me the plan to defend ourselves.

"We fight from here, Ranger. You're on perimeter and rear security. I'll work the carbine and handle the front to take out as many as we can. Each round is a kill. That's the game for today, bro. Make 'em all count 'cause that's all there is, kids. Once we're out of kill sticks, we do pickups and fight back-to-back for as long as we can. I got a few grenades and one stick of high-ex left. So the only way we lose this fight is if they cheat better than us."

CHAPTER SIX

THE attack we were expecting didn't come immediately. Lost Elf arrow fire, badly aimed, catching the hot bursts of desert wind and of course sand coming off the dunes, went wide or planted itself in the dune we were ready to make them pay for. The dark cavern they were clearly massing in remained a blank space in the mountain range we'd come through. It felt like, as we waited under the last of the hot sun of the day, like we were watching a boil getting ready to burst.

I would've cut off my left pinky finger for a Carl G in order to burst that boil from our position. Alas, no Carl, no joy.

A dark-shafted arrow slammed into the dusty white sands right in front of the small position Sergeant Joe was quickly improving to give him a better field of fire and less exposure to enemy attack. I checked the flanks. One dune to our left we could pop them on as they came over, that's called a reverse slope defense, but the right was nothing more, defensively speaking, than a wide-open alley bracketed by other dunes, and if they came at us from that direction, attempting to flank us, we were gonna get overrun real quick. To our rear and due south was another dune. Tall. A real monster to get up was my guess.

I had the secondary magazines secured and the sidearm ready to go when I circled back to Joe and lay down in the sand next to him. I carried the dented yet reliable shield strapped to my other arm, gripping a small metal grab that allowed me to control it better.

The wind was picking up as the day faded, and I guessed we had about two more hours of daylight left. As I had that thought something tickled my brain. Something about the enemy we were facing and what their capabilities and requirements were. Assessment and intel.

More fast-moving arrows came out to try and find us in random spurts that seemed of no value or direction. Some soared overhead as though they'd been lobbed. Others didn't even reach the dune as they fired forth from the gaping black maw of the crack in the mountains. Still others caught desert wind and sailed wide.

"They're using skirmishing bows," Sergeant Joe noted. "No range. Plus, no massed fire. While I was in there and among them, I realized their tactics consist of little more than suicide charges. They're more like wild animals than trained warriors. But I wouldn't rule out that they don't got no training. The gear and organization indicates they got some kinda game. If they were smart, they'd try to mass fire and take us out with a charge while pinning us. So what I'm wondering right about now is why don't they just move on us and get it on."

He had an OD-green tactical monocular out, scanning the deepening shadows within the great cut into the mountain. I have good eyes but I could see very little in there with any definite resolution. As though the darkness was more magical than a condition of the fading light in the area within and under the rock of the iron-gray granite mountains covered in desert dust.

"They're gonna wait until dark, Sar'nt. They're underground dwellers. Sun probably makes it hard on them to get out in the daylight. That's my guess, Sar'nt."

Joe grunted and swore softly. "Yeah. That's what I was thinking. Okay. Let's roll. Time to beat feet then."

Without thinking, I grabbed the nearby ruck he'd been carrying and shouldered it on.

He shot me a look that basically equated to *What the hell.*

"Figured you been carrying it for a long time. I can hump it now, Sar'nt."

He nodded but told me to take it off for a second. And my boots too. One eye on the cavern, as though the both of us were waiting for the Lost Elves to suddenly get motivated and come screaming out of the darkness there at us, waving scimitars and riding giant black widows. Just go for broke now that we were pulling a fade.

Joe muttered in his ruck about them doing that. "Try it, sewer-weenies. Because I would absolutely love that right now." He tore open the ruck and dug out a spare pair of boots. Then pulled a Ziploc filled with rolled socks.

"Shuck your boots, Ranger. I ain't got a spare pair for you, but I got socks. Change 'em now. We don't got time for my lecture on trench foot but you'll get it, trust me. It's dry feet or dead meat."

He changed his socks and swapped into his spare boots.

My boots were still wet enough. Not waterlogged, but soaked. We'd been in that rushing river for a long time. And even after all the time spent tracking through the underground halls and warrens, they were still wet through and through. And now I had desert sand in there too and the feeling was exactly as pleasant as you'd think it would be.

Which is *Not*.

"Your feet are gear and they're more important than whatever you got to stack skulls with, Ranger," said Joe as he angrily jerked the laces on his fresh boots tight and double-knotted them. We had little time to burn, and I could tell his intention was to make tracks fast. "Take care of your gear so it can take care of you. Socks'll keep the rot off and make the long walk back we got ahead of us a lot easier."

At least my boots weren't waterlogged, just soaked. So when the new socks went on my feet, they mitigated some of the damp.

New boots and socks on, Sergeant Joe handed me a piece of beef jerky, every movement fast and quick, and I tore into it as we began to move on the bastard dune just to our rear.

"Walk fast, choke it down, Private," he ordered. "Wife's secret recipe. Once you got it down, we gotta haul fast and faster."

He had his piece swallowed by the time we reached the dune's base and went up the steep incline like some kind of hill-climbing monkey that didn't mind squat day, every day, all day in the least.

I wrapped my mind around the standard being set and followed. The enthusiasm wasn't genuine, but I did my best imitation. Plus, there was the promise of getting overrun by psycho elves, so that, I had to confess, was a motivating factor. Getting stabbed to death out in the sand without a last coffee haunted my thoughts and so I dug in hard and climbed, humping a ruck heavier than any assault pack I'd ever carried on my back.

I wanted to ask him what he had in this thing, but I didn't have the spare oxygen.

"I heard him ahead and above me, grunting and intermittently chanting as he pulled through the thick sand. "Every day that ends in 'y' is leg day in the Rangers, Private."

My legs were burning halfway up, but I followed flying sand and we made the lip, cast one fast glance back over our shoulders, and saw that the arrow fire had stopped from the not-distant-enough entrance into the mountains. The mouth of the cavern was a black and ominous darkness at this range.

All around us, atop the dune before heading down just as fast as we'd come up, for a moment that seemed to be every moment in an endless desert that never changed and changed all the time… the desert was silent save the slowly building howl of the wind out there.

"Storm's coming," said Joe as we practically ran down the other side of the steep dune. "They'll chase. We'll lose 'em in it."

In the distance, strange towers and temples rose up from out there in that sea of unending dust. But with the purple haze of afternoon being swallowed by the distant sandstorm roiling up out of the south, was it a mirage? Was anything out there real? This was the Ruin. Illusions were real. And I wondered if we were heading into a dream that might just be another nightmare.

Things you think about when you're running for your life.

"Storm ain't a problem," shouted Joe ahead in the thick silence as we moved as fast as we could, knowing it wasn't fast enough if those murder elves caught up with us out here in the open. "It's a cleverly disguised opportunity for greatness, brother."

CHAPTER SEVEN

WE had an hour and change until dark. We moved as fast as possible through the thick, almost chalky sand, crossing quickly, breathing heavily as we jogged through the gritty trough between the dunes, then hauling up as fast as we could.

Sergeant Joe worked the plan for our survival. Talking over his shoulder as I followed, humping the ruck and shield.

"Mission is we gotta E and E, Talker. Escape and evasion. Situation is… we're in it, bro. Execution. We're gonna put as much distance as we can between us and them, until dark. Then pick up a new course track, hope the desert covers us and our tracks. Maybe we lose 'em, maybe we don't. If they make the mistake of winning *hide and go seek* then we kill 'em and keep moving. Maybe we booby-trap the corpses if they manage to sound the alarm for help before we waste 'em. That way their buddies find out Mr. Grenade is not their friend."

This was said as we climbed a near-vertical dune. My cardio was great, but… c'mon. Even Joe was breathing heavy, but he continued to walk us through how we'd execute the plan for our survival while climbing like a madman.

Then he gave me Rule Number One.

"Don't get caught, Ranger. We may be running, but we're stalking too. Stalking's about discovering what your prey finds essential, then killing them when they show up to get it. That goes for anything."

I gasped, indicating I understood this rule, as we crested the steep dune and stared out at an unending scene of more of what just ate my lunch, figuratively speaking. Literally. If I'd just had lunch I would have hurled everywhere. I was tasting ammonia, that's how brutal the cardio was. My calves and legs finally gave up and just said... *Whatever, Talker. We'll make you pay later.* I heard myself suck hot end-of-day dry desert air. I sounded weak like I was done already and there was no end in sight that I could see. So... I knife-handed my own brain. I told me to start breathing through my nose and stop showing weakness. If this Ranger Sergeant could fight for two days back at the citadel after coming ashore on a hot LZ, attack and det the bridge, then go for a slip-and-slide fatal funnel down an underground river of death for the better part of a day in which we almost got killed more times than I have fingers and toes, and *then* fight his way out of an ambush while escaping psycho elves with scimitars and supporting archers who might not have great skills at extreme ranges but managed to compensate for that by firing fast and frequently with what I had a very bad feeling were poisoned arrows... then I could climb some dunes with his impossibly overloaded ruck on my screaming back and not act like it was my first PT run.

Sure, I thought I was gonna die. But that's just Tuesday in the Rangers. I'd learned to ignore that a long time ago. I'd seen enough real dead people, and even made a few, to know the difference.

Then Joe continued a conversation we'd been having as we worked our way through sands and up higher dunes, trying to put as much distance between them and us. "You remember the number one rule?"

"Don't get caught, Sar'nt," I answered.

"Number two?"

We were headed down a slope so steep that its thick sand was swallowing our boots whole, with maybe forty-five more minutes of light left. I had no idea what Rule Number Two was for escape and evade getting killed by Pyscho Elves, but I was keen to hear it if just not to think about dry-heaving and of course... coffee. Because... me and all.

"Negative, Sar'nt," I gasped as calmly as I could, breathing through my nose and trying not to go face-first to the bottom of the dune.

Joe told me. "If you get caught, kill everything in sight until you're not caught anymore. Got that?"

"Copy, Sar'nt."

"Number three?" asked Joe as he led the way, scanning, head on a swivel and watching for other predators in the sandy valleys that got deadly quiet as we descended between the high quad-killing dunes.

I made an attempt at number three not because I knew it, but because I didn't want him to know how badly I needed air at that moment. So, breathing through my nose, I took a stab at rule number three.

"Don't stop for nothin', Sar'nt. Keep moving to get out of the net they're trying to throw over you." That was intel training from John-who-wasn't-John in the two-week quick intel course on the wrong side of Vegas that was a long time ago and now is not.

"That's a good one, Talker. Do that too. But no, number two don't always work on big groups, so number three is, convince them you're real dead so that you're not caught anymore. Then show up two years later and knife them in the kidneys when they're waiting in line for burritos. You got that one?"

"Make 'em think I got killed. Find 'em later and stick 'em when they're waiting for tacos, Sar'nt. Copy."

"It's burritos, Talker."

"Burritos, Sar'nt. Can do. Will stab."

He laughed, impossibly, as we dashed across the next bottom of a sand dune valley and hit the next incline up another massive dune a lot faster than my quads would have liked.

My mind showed me all the dunes out there and told me this would never end. Never. Ever. I told me to shut up and followed, matching the Ranger sergeant's pace step for step. I did have one advantage. I was taller. He was built like a small whiskey barrel.

Still, he seemed to move a lot faster than me.

We made the top a few minutes later and Sergeant Joe called a halt. He rifled the ruck on my back and came out with an old-school square collapsible canteen.

It wasn't coffee but it was everything I needed at the moment. Warm, chlorinated water. I hadn't ingested fresh water since the day before, moments before we crossed the phase line to hit the bridge in the attack on the citadel.

While I relished tasting water and not having dust in my mouth and throat for a moment, he got some five-fifty cord out of his ruck and popped a flick knife. He fished around in one of the cargo pockets of his Crye Precision pants and pulled out an army compass.

Inwardly I fell off a cliff at the sight of the cursed thing. You know that feeling when your heart stops? That's the one. Me and compasses... *shudder.*

Land nav had been one of my weaknesses in Kurtz's Ranger School for people who will never actually get their tab. It's tough. I stuck some of the patrols and got a go. But on one I spectacularly failed and got everyone "killed" while we were lost in the middle of the night. Eaten by a Draw Monster somewhere in the Charwood's least hospitable regions.

Kurtz scouted high and low to find the worst possible places to run his school. He's a giver like that.

Sergeant Joe handed me the carbine as we knelt on the far side of the lip of the high desert dune. Then he checked the sky, and we could both see that the front of the dust storm was sweeping up out of the south fast. It would be all over us sometime after nightfall. And it looked like a real doozy.

But as Sergeant Joe said... *opportunity for greatness.*

There were millions of stars out, twinkling in the purple nepenthe of night as evening came on. It was beautiful and I'll tell you, at that moment with death out there and looking to come get us, way down range and beyond the perimeter, I'll say this... it was simply beautiful, and I was glad to be there if just for that quiet moment in the middle of a sea of sand dunes. This never would have happened to me had I not joined the Rangers, and in some weird way, it was worth it. Even if we were gonna die. Out there across the sea of dunes lay the mysterious sinking ruins and the whole thing was a picture of ageless calm, a quiet that few men would ever know.

Tanner told me one time that Rangers do things other men never will. I understood that now more than I ever thought I would.

We heard the horns out there in the coming desert night. To our north. Not the *Uroo Uroo* blasts of the orc hordes. Or the unsettling bone drums of the Army of the Dead. These were disconcerting and chaotic. Almost ululating out in the night like cries of sudden pain. Not triumphant... but shrieking and mad with fever.

Then there were quick, fast drums with a Middle Eastern tempo dancing beneath the bleat of the distant ululating horns. And as the wind came and went there on the dune, rising and moaning now, blowing sheafs of sand off the tops of the dunes all around us, you could, if you listened closely enough, hear small bells. Like the bells a dancer might wear around her ankles or something as she twirls madly and stamps her feet.

"They're hunting us now," said Joe as he worked at cutting lengths of the OD-green five-fifty cord. "They're all riled up now and on our track. We're gonna give them a reality check on who they're dealing with. In my experience, that'll either slow them down some, or it'll speed them up recklessly. I'm good with either."

Then he muttered some oath to himself and told them, "If that's the way you freaks want it, then... come get some, losers. I got somethin' for ya you ain't gonna like too much."

Again, I marveled that as much as both of us had been through in the last seventy-two hours, this guy wasn't tired, or at least didn't show it, and if anything, he was promising them a good old-fashioned bar fight with a follow-up street brawl, broken bottles and all, if that's what they wanted.

He was happy to provide the service.

"All right, Private. You're gonna get us out of this. And by *get out* I mean you're gonna take point, lead, and land nav like a stud."

While he said this, he was busy dummy-cording the army compass to me. Tying it off on my belt.

Then he pulled out another compass and dummy-corded that one to his own gear, saying, "If you got two you got one. You got one you got none. Read me?"

I read.

"All right… this storm's gonna be all over us in an hour. We can't see pursuit, but this is their playground, and we have to assume that even though they're night creatures, or I don't know what you wanna call 'em…"

"Underground dwellers," I suggested again.

"Yeah. That seems about right. So yeah, they're all over the *down there* and all. But we gotta assume they come out at night and hunt, and that they know this desert. But we're lucky, and we're Rangers. We're gonna use what looks to me to be the worst-ever haboob developing out there to the south and lose 'em in it."

He stood, keeping below the lip of the dune as he did so. The distant horns were growing. Shrieking out from all directions to our rear as night came on. They had an excited, party-like quality to them. Even from here I could tell they were breaking off into hunting parties. Spreading out to throw a net over us.

Joe confirmed so and said that was good. "They come at us in smaller groups, and we got a good chance they'll come in smaller numbers. They'll try to pin us down and isolate us. We'll kill 'em and keep moving."

He scanned the endless horizon of dunes and ruins. The sky a thin red strip to the west. The purple night coming down like a blanket. The wind peeling away white sand from the dunes that were like a sea in which nothing lived.

"Okay, Private… pick a structure out there in the desert between ninety degrees and one six zero. East and left of south. We're gonna break off from our due-south track and try to make one of those. See that tower-looking thing?"

I spotted the obelisk he was indicating, a tapered tower with what looked like a small pyramid at the top. It leaned awkwardly in the sand. The light fading now to early night.

"Shoot it, brother."

I shot the azimuth through the army compass. I'd used this many times. A little in Basic. Some in RASP. A lot in Kurtz's school for wayward Rangers.

"I read one three four, Sar'nt."

Joe muttered to himself.

"I count about seven large dunes between us and it. All of them at least one hundred and ten steps high. Was that your count going up this last one?"

I hadn't counted.

"Didn't count, Sar'nt."

Unlike a lot of Ranger NCOs, and especially Kurtz, there was no sudden scowl and verbal beatdown about meeting Ranger standard.

Sergeant Joe was a very easygoing Ranger in a lot of ways. You were afraid of him only because of his competent reputation and the legendary status with which he occupied his place in the regiment. But he was uncharacteristically easygoing. That was the thing I didn't expect now that it was just him and me out here. I'd been wired tight and doing my best to meet standards as though he were Kurtz and Hardt who never seemed to not have the time to light you up and improve you to their ideal and impossible standards regarding the killing machine called Ranger.

And if they didn't have time... they were gonna make time. That was how they NCO'd. If I sound bitter about that... the truth was, they were right. They achieved results. Their teams Rangered.

Instead of the Kurtz scowl or even the "Sergeant Hard" beatdown, Joe stayed on the problem. I knew what he was doing. He was establishing a pace count for each of the seven dunes between us and the objective. Pace count upwards to indicate *mean* height of all seven dunes. The objective was that leaning pylon of obelisk out there in the desert being swallowed by the night and the sandstorm.

The only unconfirmed hope we had. The lighthouse to our lost ship of two.

If the pace count matched one hundred ten, then we could count that as a dune we had crossed to reach the objective. One of the seven. If the dune didn't match the pace count, then it was smaller and something we hadn't been able to see due to our elevation and the other dunes in between us and the location we were attempting to land nav our way to. At night, in the desert, and in a sandstorm, I'll add.

This would not be easy by anyone's standards. And apparently I was gonna lead the patrol.

I'd night land nav'd once. Got eaten by what the Ranger NCOs called a *Draw Monster* and gotten a *no go* out of that one. Chief Rapp had been out that night doing medical evaluation on the candidates, and he'd laughed about the Draw Monster.

"Boy," he told me as he checked my feet the next morning and shot a blister up full of cortisone. I didn't scream, but I grunted and bit my tongue for the brief second of living lava fury that the blister became. Then the pain was gone just as quickly. "Boy, don't worry about that Draw Monster. Draw Monsters eat up Green Berets going through selection back in North Carolina like they wasn't even breakfast. Ain't no shame in that. Avoid 'em when you can and better to go around 'em was always my rule. Box that noise, son."

A draw is basically a terrain feature formed by two ridges with low elevation between them. The lower area is the draw. They're like small valleys and it's easy to get physically stuck in them due to the slope or vegetation, or both in the case of my epic night land nav failure in which everyone I was leading got killed very easily by OPFOR. Opposing Force. They're also great ways to just break a leg. Which happened on another patrol. I was the gunner on that one and all I had to do was hump the two-forty and keep following the guy in front of me. That guy broke his leg, missing a step on a slope just shy of vertical.

Recycle. He'd get to do it all again someday.

So, one hundred and ten paces would mark a dune we topped and one of the seven we needed to reach to arrive at our objective along the one-thirty-four radial as indicated by the compass.

I set the bezel showing the course mark I needed to keep the needle on as we got ready to move once again.

This was going to be an exercise in pure "dead reckoning." There was no route to get to our point out there besides a straight line. If I just kept my head down and made sure this needle stayed lined up with that bezel mark, then in theory we'd bump right into that obelisk out there. Even if the visibility became nothing due to the pending sandstorm. Just dead reckon that needle and count the dunes we crest.

Simple, right?

"Got it locked in?" asked Joe as he measured out a length of dummy cord between us and tied it off. "Good. I'll take rear security and keep them off of us. I'll also clean up our trail even though I think the wind is about to do that work for us if it really gets blowing. Even if you lose me, in fact don't even look back, just stay on course and keep moving. We're tied off with this cord. You gotta keep two pace counts. The dunes and the distance to the objective so you can recognize that we're there. Out here that ain't gonna be easy.

"So, every one hundred meters is seventy-two steps. We gotta go about three thousand meters is my guess to reach the pylon." He stepped close. "I'll keep playing out line if I need to drop back once the storm hits. But no matter what… you keep moving on the oh-bee-jay. I know this is a lot—night, sandstorm, creepy-crawlies looking to do us in and all, and hey… it's land nav, it's one of the hardest things you do in the army. But you're not lost, you're just getting acquainted with the neighborhood.

"Last thing, Talker… we get lost out there or we don't make our objective, which I'm hoping is some kinda choke-point we can kill them good and plenty at, our chances are gonna shrink real fast, know what I mean? Plus, we need water and I'm hoping there's some there. So I'm gonna give you another one from the Book of Joe and I know you're gettin' the master class out here and all, but everyone says you're real smart even though you talk too much. Here it is.

"*Bros don't let bros stay wrong.* You're running this, Ranger. You discover you're not on the right bearing, the rest of your crew, me pretty much, depends on you owning your mistake and fixing it real quick like so we're all not lost out here with stabby elves. We all make mistakes. No sin there. The sin is continuing to live in that mistake outta fear of being told you're dead wrong. Book of Joe, brother. Let's move."

CHAPTER EIGHT

IT was when the sand began to scour our faces and the wind rose from a keening moan into an ominous otherworldly howl that Joe gave me the last advice for the night's move to the objective at the end of our compass track. Right before he fell back to deal with the shadows in the dark haunting our tracks in the sand. Shadows of Lost Elves ranging out into the sands for prey. For us. Working the back trail and looking for prey they must've felt was close.

I was working the count on the steps and following the compass needle, keeping it center line within the bezel mark I'd set for one-three-four.

"Don't know if these guys are true believers, bro," began the NCO. "But let's act as though they are, and that we are in fact in their kitchen."

We'd just surmounted the first dune, and the other six ahead were now obscured by the front of the haboob and the night falling on us in full. There should have been a moon up but there wasn't one we could see through the storm. Stars were gone too, obscured by the massive front of the sandstorm, and light was dropping to nothing by the second.

Joe had NVGs. I had nothing but the tritium glow-in-the-dark needle on the compass and numbers by which to navigate our way out of this. Still there must've been a moon somewhere and good desert starlight, because descending into the trough of the next dune the skies were more dark chocolate than straight-up blackout.

The sandstorm was pushing us backward as I let the climbing step-count go, now that we were headed down, and continued with the seventy-two steps to mark our true line-of-sight distance to the objective.

"You know what a true believer is, Talker?" bellowed Joe over the storm. "You got 'em all over the sandbox, throughout Southeast Asia, hell, you'll find those bastards everywhere."

He was preaching above the screaming winds, behind me and scanning our back trail, sweeping the tracks so they disappeared faster if the pursuit was that close. Head on a swivel and pointing the carbine at any sudden collection of sand rising and skirling in the wind that looked just like the shape and mass of our pursuers.

But they were just sand devils, and we trudged on through the storm, humping our gear and ignoring the muscles screaming for relief and hydration. Joe's wife's magic jerky had satisfied hunger and protein requirements for the moment.

But the sound of their music, the Lost Elves out there in the storm, rising and disappearing on the wind, was coming from almost all points of the compass to our rear now. The shrieking and ululating you'd catch on the moaning wind made your blood run cold. Joe was right, without a chokepoint to kill them in, we were very exposed and outnumbered out here in the sands. If we got caught... it wouldn't be good.

Bad position to hold, but so far, we hadn't been dealt a good one. Still, the Ranger way was to make it happen.

Even if you needed to hump several dunes at a high rate of speed for the hope of a killing field. We were gonna fade until it was time to hit. And then we'd hit hard.

"You don't ever get to choose the battle, bro. Best you can do is pick the spot for the graves," thundered Joe over the blast of the wind.

Ours or theirs, Sergeant? I didn't say.

I ignored the sand in my eyes and mouth, the howl in my ears, and concentrated on that kill zone we were gonna find. At that moment... and hold on to your butts here... it was more important to me than coffee.

I have sinned.

Joe was close now as we pushed forward through the deep sand. His bombastic voice no match for the banshee scream of the wind as it rose in pitch to an almost ear-splitting decibel. He had a shemagh up over his mouth. He shoved another at me and held the compass while I tied it off, maintaining the azimuth. Finishing his sermon on The Nature of the True Believer while I got sorted.

"The true believer, Talk, he's training every day and every night with little food, sometimes no water in conditions we would consider extremely harsh. The only thing he cares about is his weapon. It's the only thing he keeps clean. It's the only thing he loves. It's the only thing that's ever loved him back. He doesn't work out. His ruck weighs a ton and he's used to it because it goes everywhere he goes and does everything he does. He never stops because he *believes*, so fatigue and sleep mean nothing to him. He don't care how hard it is and he knows either he dies... or you do. We are in his kitchen on this one, bro. He only knows what he considers the truth and he's willing to die for it.

This ain't Kurtz's Ranger School. This is for all the marbles. How's that count, Ranger?"

I told him where we were at.

"Good to go. Back azimuth lines up. Stay on course and watch that point, I'm gonna drop back and jack up a few I can smell on the wind good and proper. Stay on course and never mind the line. If it goes slack, I'm dead and I cut it. Cut yours and get lost. Then get me some revenge when they go for burritos. Copy?"

I copied. "Burritos, Sar'nt."

Then I was alone in the wind and the sand. Following the compass up the next dune. Counting the steps as I trudged through the relentless sucking sand, leaning forward, legs burning, mouth dry and hot, the breath inside my shemagh ripe and rancid, my heart beating harder than I'd ever felt it.

Coffee tried to come and get me to think about it, but I absolutely could not go there right now. Two counts and a course track, checking in every twenty-five steps with the needle, which is excessive on normal land nav, but hey this is a sandstorm and everything is freaky dark and if we miss the objective we're probably gonna die and Kurtz will laugh at my bad death.

It's probably the closest thing to joy he'll ever experience.

I heard what I thought were suppressed gunshots to my rear. Felt the line of five-fifty cord shift and pull as the sand swept my back trail, covering our tracks. He was still there. Hit the count for the top of the next dune and was still climbing hard, as this dune was steeper and taller than the others. An extra twenty steps and I crested breathing hard.

I thought for just a moment I should scan the horizon and try and see what I could see from here, ahead and behind us. I took one glance up from the compass repeating the numbers of the count in my head like they were the sacred chantings of navigational holy text and must be committed to memory for all time.

Even up there on the crest I saw nothing but maybe five feet of visibility in all directions around me. The night was black and filled with ghostly sand coming off the other dunes. It felt like my exposed skin was being flayed alive. The white noise in my ears was so loud I thought I would be deaf forever, which is really cool for practicing linguists. Not. Maybe Sergeant Kang could teach me demo. His tinnitus is so bad, the only joke the stoic master breacher ever makes is for someone to "answer the telephone."

Up here, the sand had wind-sculpted the surface of the peak to zen perfection. And even so, it was dragging sheets of itself across my boots as I took a moment to catch my breath, knowing we had none to spare. Yeah, there are limits. But those died hours ago. Now we were on let's-see-how-close-to-death-you-can-perform-your-tasks-and-stay-upright.

We were operating on Roman Legion rules now. It was march or die. Or, if the psycho elves caught us... march *and* die.

In RASP, the Terminator talked about none of the tasks in Ranger School being really all that hard. But then he said, "It's just we gonna add no sleep, hunger, and some high-ex, little Rangers, then see how ya do when yer on the high wire up there and trying to meet task, condition, and standards."

The storm-filled sky was angry all around me. Best case scenario was that the storm was making things as miserable on our pursuit as it was on us. The weather was pure maelstrom, and in that moment my heart stopped as I feared I'd suddenly become disoriented and lost my bearings to the objective as I stared around and nothing made sense.

I got back on my compass, holding it flat in the shield arm as I carried it forward and watched the needle. The dented shield-slash-journal strapped about my forearm protected it from the wind as best it could. Joe's sidearm was in my right assault-gloved hand. Sand whipped my eyes making them water, which was surprising because I was so dehydrated. My flesh, inside and out, felt parched and papery like the moisture was being sucked out of it with each new buffeting blow of the storm. My feet were already half buried as I shrugged and tried to adjust the massive ruck on my back. I could almost hear the old Tanner howl and yell, "We Rangerin' now, son!" Always delivered when some limit of endurance had been reached and there was still a lot more to go.

You figuring out *limits* were just a thing in your head. A thing that meant nothing if you decided it was gonna be that way.

I decided it was going to be that way.

And every step for a few, I was having to recommit to my new faith. Just like every new believer in something.

The drag line behind me was already covered by the sand once it fell down into the endless shift of that ever-moving silt. If I fell down here and stopped, it would bury me within half an hour.

I didn't want that.

But my legs didn't want to move either and they only did because they had to and I told them they had no other choice. I was Compass Man. This was my patrol. No-go was not an option. Everything was locking up, everything was past the point of endurance. I could have used a good drop-your-ruck, watch-your-sector-and-hydrate-while-the-team-leaders-and-the-squad-leader-disseminate-info halt.

Tanner calls that the "rucksack flop."

Others call it the Long Halt.

But it was just me out here in front on point and so there was none of that. I started down the backside of the steep dune, shuffling through the chalky sand that whipped me relentlessly. Stumbling toward the edge as things began to work again.

I wanted to go through the litany of how little rest I had, or coffee, or love... but who cares, Talker. Amirite? Without even telling my mind to shut up, my legs just carried me off the peaked plateau of the dune and down the sandy incline of the next as I balanced the huge ruck, and the shield, and watched the compass every twenty-five steps while chanting the numbers of the count over and over, whispering under the wind. I stumbled once and tried to remember if that was the second or first dune I'd gone up. I recited the numbers of the count and reminded my-self it had been two dunes with five more to go and then I should start looking for the objective.

Recognizing that you've arrived at the point you've been navigating toward is a critical element to successful land nav. There are many ways to do this. One is to plot a backstop, so you know when you've gone too far because you've hit your backstop. But there had been no backstop observed from our start point, so if I was a few degrees off and we passed it... well, we'd just keep walking out into the abyss.

For this movement I had worked out a rough error box instead. This meant that in my head I had our objective in mind with a roughly five-hundred-meter box around it. Once I hit my final pace count we would stop. If we weren't already right at the base of the thing, then we would assume we were somewhere inside that box. Short of our target, past it, to its right, or to its left. From that point it becomes a simple matter of doing a starburst recon in straight lines out and back until you find it. Again, a simple matter.

And flat-out crucial when stabby elves, as Sergeant Joe called them, are stalking you in a sandstorm straight from the gates of hell.

More suppressed gunfire dancing around on the wind, and I wasn't really sure where it came from other than off to the left, but maybe it could have come from behind.

Did I add that you had to fight a creeping sense of vertigo in the storm and sand? Also, I was afraid that if I fell down, it was gonna be a real fight to get back on my boots. So... best not to go there.

I stayed focused and made the top of dune number three. Four more to go. The wind cleared in spurts and sudden breaks up there, and as I started down the backside and quickly neared the bottom of the dune, I saw within the sandy trough down there a small group of ruins.

It wasn't the obelisk that marked our navigational endpoint, and for a brief moment I freaked out and worried we were way, *way* off course.

Fat, scalloped columns rose out of the sands. Below those, the remains of sand-covered stones, like some broken structure or platform, lay half-buried in the desert wastes. My course track led just to the right of this structure, but there was something unsettling about this strange place suddenly appearing out of the maelstrom of hurling sand and howling wind raging all about me. Above, the sky got suddenly dirtier and darker as I approached the odd collection of sand-sunken ruins. The air felt hotter and denser, alive with some current of electricity I could barely feel.

I checked the drag line connecting me to Sergeant Joe, saw it was taut and even playing out some without me moving, shifting off to the right and rear. Then I memorized my count, feeling things were getting confusing and that I might have to concentrate on the new LDA of the ruins I'd just discovered because psionics, or Spidey sense, your call, told me something in there was dangerous.

ODA is Ranger for *Open Danger Area*. It describes areas of threat or caution you encounter on your patrol. Heads-up-ball areas where you are most likely to be attacked or detected.

Hey, I learned something in Ranger School. Take that, Kurtz! Or, as I mumbled in the howl of the storm, half joking to myself because of the fatigue starting to mess with my mental clarity, "After-action report. You identified the ODA, Talker, but you still got turned into a purple undead skeleton bat by the bad guy. No go."

I almost lost the count making my pathetic joke.

Then I remembered my Sharpie, got it out of my Crye Precisions, and wrote on my exposed arm the current count. I stowed the marker and continued forward, following the compass needle with the G19 ready to engage anything that might turn me into a purple undead bat. Or any other color of undead bat.

Thoughts about flying sand and grit and long submersion in the underground body-choked-at-points river water made me question the weapon's ability to function reliably and long-distance punch holes in things that needed to have holes punched in them. But what else did I have? Joe would have no doubt cleaned it once he was out of the water, I reasoned, because Rangers, and armorers but that is another story for another time, believe your weapon can never be clean enough. One comforting thing I'd learned about Glocks, the M18 is the military version, is they always go bang when you need them to.

"Even if they rattle like a blue-haired maven ready to hit the slots in Vegas," as Tanner likes to point out at every possible opportunity.

Five double-stacked mags, and I had a lot of rounds to punch holes into anything that wanted to turn me into something other than me. Then I remembered Joe telling me every shot was a kill out here. That was tonight's game we were playing. We had a long way to go and a short amount of ammo to get it done in.

So "Shoot to kill and get it done in one," as Chief Rapp liked to chant while walking the firing line.

I followed the one-three-four azimuth right up to a raised corner of the platform sticking out of the far dune I'd need to head up next. The sand-sunken platform was like the bow of some lost shipwreck drowning in a sea of sand.

I could see five columns on top of the platform of raised stones, just barely. Blocks of heavy carved limestone like those used in the pyramids of our time formed the base and construction of the platform. I cast a quick glance at the nearest column, rising above me among the wraith-like blasts of sand coming at me from across the desert. The keening howl screaming here like a wounded animal. I saw that hieroglyphs were imprinted on these fat and ancient stone columns, stamped into their wide graceful curves. The markings uniquely disturbing.

A lone inky figure was carved in the stone, line by line and row after row, repeated over and over to the exclusion of any other identifying marker.

There was something... compulsive about that, and it bothered me just to look at it. A legion of that one figure made many times over. The only other feature stamped into the fat columns was a black line that wrapped around the circumference in the center of the column and seemed immune to the harsh blast of the desert. It was so clear and dark, it seemed the most illuminated thing out here in an upside down and ironic way. I could make out its definite stamp feature in the swirling chocolate of the sands and the lack of light that tried to strangle the air and any moon or starlight. As though the darkness in that dark circular band was... something else other than just black. Like it was a blank space in the universe one didn't mess with lightly.

Remember, Talker. Curiosity did indeed kill the cat. And it almost killed you with the Death Jello.

Unsettling had been my first instinct, and now I had upgraded that to *thoroughly creeped out* as I passed by the lost place. It was like walking into some old collapsing house you find in the country and seeing not the graffiti of the local kids and smashed beer bottles on the rotting walls and missing boards, but instead a thousand small chalky handprints covering every wall. Every surface. Obsessive and evil.

Then I had the feeling this place had just surfaced in the storm... *for me*. Calling the winds to come and remove just enough of the sand for me to want to come close and take a look, son. And that when the storm was over it would be gone, buried by the desert in the harsh, relentless morning sun if it ever rose again.

And if I was dumb enough... me buried with it.

Down there forever.

My course continued past the emerging ruins the sand was uncovering before my eyes. I continued on, though the salt mummies had already formed on the platform, swirling to dusty life out of the passing sand... and they began to shamble toward me, their horrible mouths working silently in the howling wind and blasting sand.

They moved faster, not seeming like mindless undead in the least. The first one rush-shambled toward me as two more circled behind and the last two moved ahead, five in all, watching me warily as they shuffled down rotting limestone steps, covered in sand, along the far side of the half-sunken platform.

I raised the G19 and superimposed the front sight post on the head of the first mummy, took a short breath, and pressed the trigger. Bang as advertised! The elements be damned. The first round went right through the weaving, herky-jerky head of the mummy. Chief Rapp drills us constantly on shooting with sidearms. And yeah, I've been getting better due to practice and occasional real-world application.

Remember when it took me three rounds to retire Deep State with him sitting not two feet away and not even paying attention as I pointed the smaj's weapon at his skull?

I'd get that done in one now.

It's important to track your progress in life. Know how far you've come. And occasionally have a sense of humor about the gruesome stuff you had to do to get the job done and keep everyone safe.

Still, despite the conditions… I was impressed with my own first shot given the circumstances.

How did I know they were made of salt? The mummies. Well, despite raising one crusty hand, its arms covered in dried bandages that were flapping and falling apart in the wind, making it look like a nightmare thing that wasn't even in this timeframe and reality, it slammed a fist into my shield. That's the arm holding the compass. Salt exploded everywhere. I could smell it as it blossomed out and away, and oh help me, taste it on the wind that suddenly carried it away.

Yes, I ate mummy dust, probably. In my defense, I tried to spit it out the entire time the rest of them were trying to kill me.

But the first hot round of nine-millimeter spat forth from the G19 and nailed the thing right in the face as it got close. Sand, dark like volcanic ash, spat out the back of its skull and to the side, then immediately got carried away by the wind. But if it had brains, the salt mummy that is, my first shot didn't do much toward killing it as I had intended. Its rotting toothless mouth opened and it raised its other hand to its head to feel the wound, as though it was suddenly experiencing the worst headache ever.

It moaned, emitting a raspy papery moan-roar I barely heard over the wail of the wind.

I couldn't move because I had to hold my position in order to hold the azimuth I was leading us to the objective with. I had five seconds in which to assess my situation and see what had just happened without actually really knowing what had happened.

The round had done something to it. I could tell that. If it was the salt I could taste in my mouth—*yikes I got mummy sand in my mouth*—now I needed the darkest, most bitter, high-nitro cold brew known to man to chase the taste away forever.

Spoiler: Talker got none.

The round had given it, the mummy, a severe headache. It hadn't killed it dead. The fast-moving projectile had gone straight through, ventilating black sand from its necrotic bandage-wrapped skull.

Black magic, I thought, and had no idea what I was talking about. Psionics or instincts, again I had no idea.

So. I could keep firing, hoping I got better with each shot instead of what usually happened, which was that I got worse with each shot as muscles got tired and my grip started to slip thanks to firing something that explodes in your hand every time you pull the trigger. At Chief Rapp's School for Legendary Gunfighters, I noticed my first magazine usually landed great on the target. In my opinion. Chief Rapp would adjust my grip, stance, something, and then the next rounds grouped even tighter. After that, my marksmanship began to degrade. Or as Chief Rapp put it, my mental focus degraded. "You overthinkin' it, Talker."

Surprise, surprise—I overthink things. Have we discussed coffee in the last fifteen seconds?

It's not like I was thinking all this in the middle of a fight. I just knew that two mags was the best I was gonna do in one gunfight. After that, things might get a little desperate and chaotic with salt mummies danger-close and my aim degrading.

Sand, my inability to shift from my position, and five tangos to kill my way out of this, said things could go from bad to worse real fast.

But...

The salt mummy that had attacked, smashing its dried, bandaged hand flapping madly in the bursts of wind rocketing across the trough and through the strange dark columns, was now missing that corroded arm.

The arm had exploded on contact with the shield. Now the malevolent thing was just standing there, using its one good arm to rub its scabby bandaged head like it had the worst headache ever. Or was it just stunned to be missing an arm?

I had no idea. I just knew I needed to kill it. Right now.

Like I said, these weren't mindless undead. These, in their first movements, had shown some kind of intelligence. Breaking off into groups to close me in like hunting predators. Even their empty black eye sockets and groaning cavernous mouths conveyed anger and a desire to destroy life.

Rage, but the quiet kind. Endless fury. That's what I got from them.

I brought the shield up with the leading edge and slammed it right into the mummy standing in front of me, hitting it in the neck. I think I was hoping just to knock it back and get some fighting room, but the way I jerked the shield up, in the wind, fighting the drafts, and put all my core into an off-hand strike, wasn't aimed. I was just getting myself some room to think.

Instead the shield cut the head clean off the mummy like it was the flying hat of death from some old kung fu movie. The bandages of the decrepit old thing caught fire in the wind as the dented found shield connected and went straight through its papery husk. In a moment, the raging windstorm extinguished the flaming black scraps as the empty shell of the headless mummy carcass just felt over in the sand, turned to salt, and blew away like something that was never really there.

I holstered the M18, switched the compass to that hand, and planted my feet as the next two mummies came at me from behind.

They were closer than the two in front, and I had to deal with them fast.

I shoved the shield up to block at the last second and the first of the two caught it right in the chest. His ancient bandages ignited, and he fell to his knees in the shifting sand, turning to dust and salt and blowing away an instant later, the fragments of burning bandages dancing away in the blast of the storm like fireflies in hell.

Mummy number two dodged to my right and reached out its scabby claws for me, one hand grabbing my arm through my Crye Precision combat shirt, and I felt a cold deeper than anything I'd experienced in the underworld river. I watched as the fabric of the shirt began to turn black and disintegrate before my eyes like some fast-moving CGI movie plague taking effect all at once. At the same time, the mummy made what I can only call a Karate Man Open Palm, raised it back over its shriveled head, and clearly telegraphed it was about to slam the open palm right into the side of my head.

I fell to avoid the mummy judo, going down to one knee just to get the shield up in time to intercept and absorb the blow.

Then a booming thunderclap went off and destroyed the mummy, exploding the moment the punch connected with the dented shield. Either the shield did this, or the mummy's attack was so powerful that the magical effect came with the punch and reflected off the shield, destroying Salt Tutankhamun.

The Ruin is a strange place, and I don't underestimate anything. Mummies doing mummy-fu with Bonus Thunderstrike, call it what you want… sure. All I know is the shield rebounded the thunderclap, which I heard almost distantly from behind its dented circumference. As though the echo of thunder was somewhere else far away. As though the shield was more than just a barrier in the present, but in time and space also.

The mummy in front of the dented shield was instantly destroyed. Sand exploded away as though a very large brick of C4 had just been used to effect. The storm winds carried off the flying sand, but it was clear the thunderous impact of the blow against the shield had just cratered the mummy.

I stood, amazed I have to confess, then remembered I had two bad guys coming at me from the other direction.

I turned, unsure if I had shifted off my radial and relieved Sergeant Joe had dummy-corded the compass to me. The explosion and my reaction to intercept the strike had caused me to drop the compass in the sand. It was already buried but I saw the cord sinking down into the depths beneath my boots.

I had no time to get it because both mummies had flanked away from each other and were trying to come at me in a pincer attack, shambling forward at the same time to arrive at the destruction of me in the same moment.

I crouched low, getting the shield up in front of me, gauging their incoming shambling undead progress. They were going to hit me at the same time, and I could see that these two had the same kind of thunder-fist fist the previous mummy I'd smoked had tried to punch me. Both of these had theirs held back this time as whisps of necrotic black smoke erupted from each fist. The area around the fists was shaking, as though space-time energy was vibrating from the energy contained within those bandage-wrapped fists.

So, it wasn't the shield that had created the shock wave... it was their fists.

Still, they were both gonna try to hit me at the same time and there was every chance one of them was gonna get past the shield and land a thunder blow right on my head. With bonus black stuff eating my shirt as I watched.

I skinned the Glock at the last second and shot the one to my right in the face. That stopped it as it stumbled and stepped back, disrupting the timed attack as it reached to its dirty bandaged head in disbelief trying to understand why, or how, fast-moving nine-mil had just cauterized sand within whatever passed for its black magic thinking brain of malevolent evil.

Whatevs, I whatevered. Some day I'd be a Specialist and my Sham would be on point if Tanner were my Sensei and taught me everything about the Sham Shield of the E-4 Mafia.

The other one got a full shield swipe right across the mummy-rags-abdomen. It split nearly in two and black scorpions ran from out of its ripped-bandage belly as the rags caught fire and turned to black wisps of glowing scraps on the sand. The mummy threw back its soundlessly laughing skull as though laughing at the ironic horror of it all, and more scorpions ran out of its cavernous mouth, a visualization of its death scream.

Thankfully the scorpions ran off into the storm and the sands of the desert. Instead of stinging me to death.

The guy whose brain I'd just put a hole in was still just standing there so I swung the shield back at him, chancing a step off course and catching him in the jaw with the whistling shield.

The mummy caught fire and disintegrated, the last of the salt within carried swiftly off by the storm.

I kept my mouth closed this time.

I grabbed the dropped and buried compass, then checked the arm of my Crye Precisions. The black area was spreading and the cold was starting to get white-hot against my skin.

Knife out, I cut the forearm sleeve without cutting myself, then sliced it down the underside, peeling away that portion of the shirt with the naked blade and letting the devil winds carry away the mummy-diseased fabric.

I was totally expecting to see burnt flesh and exposed bone on the other side.

Nothing.

"I'm good," I said, mumbling to myself as I turned my arm over and over, stunned that the pain hadn't been real.

As I reeled in the compass I saw the whiskey-barrel shape of Sergeant Joe in sand wraith form coming out of the depths of the storm.

"Got two groups. They're fanning out over there. Might be others," he gasped over the storm, his bellowing voice mightier than the scream of the wind. "Let's squirt for the top of the dune and see if we can get outta their net, bro. Time to hustle, Ranger. Got the course?"

I held up the compass and followed him, the two of us tethered as we ran for the dune and began the near-vertical climb through the shifting sand that tried to swallow us whole.

"Go left two steps!" I yelled to keep him on course. I wasn't sure if he heard, but the flying sand ahead of me adjusted left and it was clear he did.

A quarter way up the dune I heard the grinding of stone. It creaked and groaned titanically, and I looked back to see if we were suddenly going to get a flood of Thunder-Punching Salt Mummies on our six.

"C'mon, Talker. Time to move, bro!"

Behind us, on the platform, an opening had appeared in the stone. A gaping black hole in the storm. A pit down into the desert. From out of the storm, I heard the papery rasp of some great thing deep down inside, whispering through the wind at us as we fled up the dune and into the desert.

"Come and see my treasures, strangers. Come and seek your dooms far below," the thing grave-whispered in my mind. Or out across the storm. I couldn't be sure which. *"Come... come and sleep... forever."*

Then a dry raspy chuckle that might have been the sound of sand scouring everything forever. Dissolving the worlds in its relentlessly acidic grind. An endless white noise drowning all noise, all life, everything in a howl that consumed even time itself.

It was like listening to other horrors through the walls of a motel lost in hell forever.

I shuddered and felt a cold river run right through me. I knew that pit was no way of escape for us. We could only go forward, south, and farther away from the Rangers.

So I turned and followed Joe into the sand, knowing we couldn't go back. And also knowing I never wanted to meet what, or who, was down in the pit beneath the sinking sands of this endless desert that might be endless in more ways than I understood or could even imagine.

It was March or Die.

CHAPTER NINE

WE cleared the next tall dune, quads screaming, hamstrings on fire, and bonus, my feet felt squishy in my damp boots. That was either a result of blisters popping, or blood. My toes had gone completely numb and I'm sure that's not good, and we ran for our lives across the next flat. Tasting ammonia in my mouth a while back ago was amateur hour. Now I was pretty sure I was spitting up small amounts of blood as my lungs screamed blue murder and my abs began to contract and fail to release. Either from the caustic dust or more likely the body saying mind over matter didn't matter anymore. Good luck, total system failure imminent.

You could hear the Lost Elves hunting us in the storm out there, getting closer by the second. What was more disturbing was the sound of the large spiders their knights rode, spindly legs beating on the sand like some muted distant set of rolling tanto drums of disconcerting doom. Rushing to and fro in the wild storm as we halted, crouched behind lower dunes we found between the massive sand mountains we still had yet to climb, and waited for the storm to swallow them... or for them to come and take their chances with us.

In the small distances we could see flying sand, dust-cloud-wraith images of these monstrosities passing us by as we hunkered low, digging ourselves into the sand and getting ready to deal as much instant murder as we could with what remained to us.

"Four mags left," said Joe, noting the situation. Doing the endless NCO work of a quick ACE report while escaping and evading. Counts and accountability. The pulse and heartbeat of every Ranger patrol.

I followed with my own count of the little I had to work with.

"Sixteen rounds in the G19. Four more mags topped off... Sar'nt." My mouth was so parched and devoid of water like some lunar landscape of craters and dust that I had to swallow just to get enough moisture to finish with *Sar'nt.*

"Don't forget... got that shield, kid. It's loaded, effectively. Breathe, kid. Fighting is fire. No air, no fire. No fire, no fight. You go black, save the last mag and work the shield like it's Friday and the smaj is recommending three-day passes to whoever's meaner than it."

"It's something..." I murmured as a squad of Lost Elves trooping behind the surreal black behemoth of a black widow the size of a small bus passed us by, running off through the storm and horizontal to our line of march. Our line of escape lay just beyond the dust of their tracks.

"How many Malvesties to go?" Joe hissed beneath the constant banshee scream of the wind that now for some reason was whistling and hitting high-pitched witchy trills. Off to the west, Lost Elven hunting bells and drums competed with the blast.

Joe had taken to calling the dunes we were climbing *Malvesties* after the RAP week obstacle course from Ranger School that kicked everything off.

"Two, Sar'nt."

"You know, back in the world the RIs let their wives run that course on Jane Wayne Day. They do it easy. My wife had a blast. We got this, bro. We got this. They're hunting us like prey. Beating the bush to spook us and get us to make a run for it. Best guess… they got three groups to our east, spread out and waiting for us to try and break through the net that way. Thinking we're gonna panic. But we ain't gonna panic, are we? We're gonna hunt a little now that they think they got things wired. They're organized now, so we gotta disorganize 'em some before we make our final move. We'll wipe out one group and get 'em to head that way while we squirt for the south and make one last push to reach the… what is it?"

"Obelisk, Sar'nt."

"Right, that thing. Looks like the Washington Monument but all leaned over like it's got no base support. We get there, we can make a stand and see who wants some. Hunting's the ultimate sport because you don't get no trophy. Your trophy means you get to eat today, make medicines, and have enough hide to dress warm. Hunting down a target for intel is the same. Hunting the hunters is a great way to make them think twice about hunting the boogey man." Then he looked out there into the flying dust of the violent storm. "And tonight… I'm your boogey man, losers."

I checked our azimuth, noting the direction we needed to move if we needed to move fast.

"So… if my guess is right, bro," continued Sergeant Joe, "that driving line of hunters, the one beating the drums and jangling the Christmas bells from hell… they're gonna move toward the west from the east over there. And we're gonna ambush 'em, get 'em to go silent 'cause we made 'em dead and all. Then we fade south while their buddies come looking for why all the noise stopped. Roger?"

I rogered.

"How we gonna do that, Ranger?"

Well… it seems I'd be participating in the planning. I'd gotten used to this in Ranger School. All Rangers, every rank, lead and plan patrols.

"I guess L-shaped ambush is out of the question, Sar'nt."

"Yeah, that would be great though, wouldn't it. Those losers come along and we just light 'em up with the two-forty and work 'em over slow and violent-like, enjoying every eight-round-burst second of it. But yeah… we ain't got the Death Machine, bro. So here's what I'm thinking, and you call foul if I got this wrong. We're both tired. That's got to be acknowledged. So if I'm getting wacky and setting up something beyond our capabilities, individually and collectively, call me out 'cause we can't get into something we both can't go all the way on. Feel me?"

I nodded.

Then he told me what we were gonna do. He wasn't wrong, but I drew the Judas Goat in the Game of Death we were about to play. That's what he meant by asking me to call foul.

I didn't. It was my job, and I wanted to do it.

Here's what the murdered Lost Elves saw in the last roughly six seconds of their lives when they came wandering along, doing their job, and trying to spook us out of hiding like we were frightened prey.

First thing they saw, swirling out of the storm of sand and wind, the unearthly howl thankfully picking up so hard at that last second before we sprang the ambush, they just saw a plain old linguist—they had no idea I was a linguist, but they knew I was their prey—standing there in the storm looking as lost as one can possibly get.

I even gave them a little wave at the same moment they spotted me, as though communicating that I might just try to surrender, lost and all alone out here in the storm, and make things easy for 'em. That was the linguist part of me ad-libbing and kicking in with a little non-verbal communication to effect our ruse. So, because they're clearly psychos, instead they came rushing out of the storm, knives out and letting go of these short bell-laden poles they were holding. The wind still causing the constant clang of the dancer's bells mounted there. The poles were hung about their necks and waists almost like the Lost Elven version of a Vickers Sling, but made of rich fabric and finely woven in blue, purple, crimson, and little metallic stars that were barbed and painful to the touch. The Lost Elves were dressed almost like the bedouins of our time. As though they wanted to be shielded from all light, even that of the stars.

As they let go of their bell-poles they drew curved long daggers off their chest sashes. They'd spotted me, these bell wavers, and gave bloodcurdling ululating cries as they ran through the desert chalk, sand flying away from their heavy boots and being carried by the sudden thunderous blasts of the storm whipping through the desert trough here. Marring the smooth wind-sculpted sand between us.

Behind these first to attack waited two drum bearers and what looked clearly to be the squad leader of this troop carrying a large forked spear. The latter group readied themselves to join the attack. The not-big drums were too unwieldy to make a sudden attack and so had to be dealt with.

They would live a couple of seconds longer than the first group of energetic psychos.

The three homicidal Lost Elves rushing through the sand at me probably ran right over the buried Sergeant Joe thinking he was just some lump in the sand. They didn't catch his perfect explosion from underneath the sand. He was carrying a spare dry bag as he did so. The spare dry bag had come out of his ruck of never-ending stuff, and he'd shoved his carbine in as we'd hastily buried him just under the sand, using a nasopharyngeal tube for him to keep breathing. Barely in the storm.

We'd been working on this up right until the last second, seeing the shapes of our soon-to-be victims coming through the storm from the west and heading east.

As they got close, almost close enough to spot us, I'd dropped back twenty meters and waited to trigger the attack while Joe lay under the sand in line with where we wanted them to advance.

Our goal was to break the main group of the beaters into two smaller groups so we could deal with them better.

The three ran by, but the last one was a few steps behind the first two, and when Joe exploded out of the sand, without even needing to assess the situation, he grabbed the straggler by the throat, holding the bagged carbine with one hand, and choke-slammed that one straggler right onto the sand. He followed the elf down in the same motion, driving one knee right into the elf's abdomen, and I'm guessing driving all the air right out of it, so he couldn't scream and warn the two runners that had left him behind. Bagged rifle pinning the victim's arms, knee not allowing any breath to be drawn. Then in one jackhammer moment of automatically relentless termination, Joe pulled the knife off his belt and drove the small blade into the elf's neck in three unbelievable rapid-fire savage blows. He was moving so fast, there might have even been more.

If the Lost Elf wasn't dead, I bet it sure felt like it was.

That was a lucky break for us, and Joe had capitalized on it with some Ranger SOP violence of action. My job, as I stood there waving at the three and getting them to lock in on me, had been to draw all three and start running, separating from the main body, as I slipped on the dead sorcerer ring that made me invisible and pulled a quick dogleg so Joe would be out of my line of fire once I started engaging. Then I could start ventilating them with the Glock.

But Sergeant Joe, sensing the opportunity to nail one of the three I'd drawn for the kill, made my work a whole lot easier as I stopped waving at them and started "running away," slipping on the ring and pulling my own special magical fade.

I was backpedaling on the fade, shucking the Glock from an issue T-shirt he'd given me to protect it from the flying sand in the storm. Along with the suppressor now screwed to the threaded barrel, once again produced courtesy of the Rucksack of Never-Ending Wonders.

I faded, backpedaling and invisible, while keeping an eye on the slaughter going down on the sands in front of me.

What I saw, three seconds into the fight, was Joe skin the carbine from the dry bag, sand still pouring off him, dying elf bleeding out under his powerful knee, and begin to shoot the follow-up drummers pulling small bows and the squad leader getting ready to advance under cover with the forked spear.

Line of sight clear for me to engage on my bad guys, I slipped off the ring, called, "Over here," in Hindi, maybe, I also might have ordered a spicy curry, at both Lost Elves, and watched them turn in bewilderment as I started shooting them both a lot. More than I should've but things were fast and we needed everyone dead immediately in order to quickly pull our fade to the south.

Three rounds on one, five on the other because he wouldn't fall down. In the storm's fury I had no idea how many of my rounds actually hit my intended targets. It would be impossible to tell in the dark and the wind what with all that was going on. And I'd be lying if I said different.

I may lie in the course of my position within the Ranger company as some kind of intel-gatherer-slash-personal-retirement-counselor-for-the-smaj. And I may even lie to myself about... stuff... on occasion.

But I don't lie in this record.

This record is the truth. And the truth is sacred.

So, within the fury of the storm I had no idea how many rounds hit both elves. The only thing I knew is the first one took fire, ragdolled into the sand, and lay there dying or dead. The other turned, didn't move, but didn't fall down after I shot him.

And I needed him to fall down to keep up my end of the hit.

So I shot him again and he went to his knees as I advanced on him, and once I was close enough, my grip solid enough on the weapon, I blew off the side of his face and he went over in the sand, blood and brains drooling out into the thirsty dust of a forever desert. Looking like black ink at midnight even as the storm sent more sand to cover what had been done.

By the time I confirmed my bad guys as down, I turned to Joe and saw he'd dusted all three of his.

I studied the dead bodies for a long moment. Fascinated by them and their strange gear. Wondering what kind of civilization they came from. Doing intel.

I felt like they were strangers here in the desert and I had no reason I could identify for having that feeling. I just felt it... like... like a thing that could be felt. That's some pro-level writing there, Talker. Even here in this lost howling desert wilderness of madness. That was my takeaway from the few seconds of intel consideration I had with them before it was time to pull our fade.

That they too, like us, were strangers out here in the desperate night.

Sergeant Joe saw me staring at the dead we'd been faster, smarter, and meaner than. "Like I said, you don't ever get to choose the battle. The best you can do is pick the spot for the graves, bro."

He proceeded to wrap his old socks in a grenade and gently place a rock onto the spoon while he pulled the pin, right there in the middle of the our dead enemies. "Pretty sure those spiders also act as scent dogs for them. This'll make 'em think hard about pursuing us once they investigate it... and we'll also have a few less of them on our tail."

Then he was hustling through the sand and we were off to the south once again. "Watch that point, bro. We got one shot to stick the landing and find it out here tonight."

I acknowledged that I was on the compass and had the correct azimuth.

The last two dunes.

The last two dunes were a flat-out run for our lives. Yeah, I've run a lot. Ran a lot to get in shape for this whole army adventure before I knew it would be the adventure it turned out to actually be. Ran in Kurtz's Ranger School everywhere and a lot for RAP week. Which I had to do twice.

That was nothing. All that extra duty back at the FOB for disobeying orders and getting busted down to private had made that easy. Running. Most of the NCOs in charge of my fourteen days of extra duty had simply decided to make me run the crag with them for PT and then start some mind-numbing cleaning task, while getting quizzed on the Ranger Creed, which I had to recite on command and sometimes over and over.

Memorizing's always been easy for me.

Running is a more recent development.

Kurtz of course made me run the leg-killing crag beneath the FOB twice. Him right there setting a grueling lung-capacity-destroying pace that made me wonder whether I was going to die of a heart attack or a broken leg given the uneven stones and constant vertical ascent and descent within that narrow canyon beneath the old fortress.

Then there was the Cloodmore Mile, as some of the younger Rangers now called it. Our run through werewolf scout forces and wetlands to reach the river where we met Vandahar for the first time. All to avoid being crushed by a Godzilla-sized cloud giant lobbing indirect fire in the form of one-ton boulders at us.

The older NCO didn't like it when the younger Rangers called it this, the Cloodmoor Mile. They felt it disrespected the Mogadishu Mile.

But the sergeant major let it be, saying, "It a young man's world, boys. One day they're gonna be the hardcore, grizzled, ruck-hump-miserable son of a guns you all sergeants are now. One day they're gonna need to have something to hang their hats on so the next generation of young Rangers can stand in awe of and respect them. Maybe even aspire to be like. You had the Mog. They got this one."

So let it be spoken by the smaj, so let it be done. No one bothered to question the sergeant major on where we were gonna get more new Rangers. It was enough that he'd said it. His NCOs believed it as though it were prophecy.

Of all the runs, the Cloodmoor was the toughest. I carried Sergeant McGuire through that one. He is still alive last time I checked, which was the morning of the attack on the citadel. He was leading a rifle squad securing the bridge head to cross over.

He'd nodded at me in the pre-dawn darkness as the snipers worked over the massing orcs trying to get ready and retake our foothold. They were expecting a big push and I was with Sergeant Joe's demo team, carrying a dangerous load of high-ex. That's how it always was with Sergeant McGuire. I'd carried him, crushed chest and all. He'd gotten hit by a troll-hurled boulder back at Ranger Alamo. I carried him down the river through the hills from the burning witch's hut and vineyards, and then across those sucking mud wetlands full of rivers and stagnant pools, under indirect fire from a giant.

That was the toughest run for me, by far. Easy.

But the run over the last two dunes made me feel like we just got started right at the end of the Cloodmoor.

ANSPACH/COLE

We had no idea if we'd outpaced the Lost Elves, if we'd somehow threaded the trap, all we knew was there were now more enemy forces in the area than we could handle.

"Right now, Talker," said Joe, who was breathing pretty heavy for him as we ran down the back side of the next dune, the storm beginning to die down, or experiencing a short lull for the moment. "Right now... they've figured out their beaters ain't makin' the noise like they used to. They're moving on that loc. In a few they'll figure out we did 'em, and now we're catching a bad break because the storm is dying and our tracks won't be fading."

Silence and the muffled sound of our hot boots being swallowed by the deep sand we slogged through. Our breathing ragged. Some piece of gear that could be silenced a little better if we had time, made noise. There was high-speed tape, I was sure, in the Rucksack of Many Wonders. It felt like all the rolls in the world were in there on my back.

But there wasn't time.

The wind moaned out there and it sounded like a ghost looking for a forgotten house to haunt.

"But I got somethin' for 'em," muttered Joe as we ran, knowing we would never, ever stop. That there was every possibility this would never end for us.

All things end, you lie to yourself just to keep moving. Just to take one more step.

"I got something for ya..." whispered Joe to all his enemies out there in the desert tonight.

We're hauling across the bottom of the next trough and I'm feeling like I lost a moment of time. Like I actually fell asleep while running or something if that's even possible. I'm gasping and coughing, using the shield to pull myself forward to the next step. I tear the shemagh off because I need more air. *Some* air. Some oxygen to fire the engine within just a little longer. But… I'm on the point. The needle on the compass only wavers when I stumble.

There's an explosion to our rear, dulled and muffled by the dunes, and Joe just says, "That's the something. Enjoy my last grenade, losers. I hope you choke on it."

We gotta be close, I lie to me. Lying like some sidewalk Three-Card Monte hustler. *Next one's the one, kid. You're due for a win. Place your bets. Follow the queen. Watch the Lady in Red.*

We topped the last dune and saw the obelisk rising above it even as we climbed toward its zenith. The slate-gray monument leaned awkwardly in the late night and now the moon was out and shining down in silver shafts through the fading storm moving off to the east. The wind was still there, but it too was fading. And yet still dragging ghostly sheets of sand off the desert floor and pulling the covers over all the crimes committed there. Cleaning it. Smoothing. Swallowing everything. Making it like a painting to be admired and nothing like the reality it was.

"No time to stop, Talker," gasped Joe. "Run now!"

Behind us, spider cavalry, at least ten of them, were coming down the far dune.

Arrow fire erupted from the mounted riders, and it wasn't totally inaccurate.

A chaotic mass of raven-like arrows began to fall along the crest of the dune where we gasped for some air, any air. Arrows sank into the sands, whistled overhead, and one came whistling in and planted itself in the back of the Ruck of Many Wonders. Barely missing hitting me right in the shoulder.

I swore, and Joe laughed. But we were tired and didn't have much more to give to the effort.

There was no way we were gonna make it. We were outta gas and they were that close, with ranged weapons to boot.

So we ran for our lives. Because sometimes when there is nothing left to do but run... you run.

"Run like you just drank all the devil's beer and he just pulled into the driveway!" shouted Joe.

The obelisk rose up out of what was clearly some sort of temple in the fashion of something from the ancient Egypt of long ago. Two giant stone sphinxes guarded a long stone walkway past crumbling columns, leading to a narrow but tall dark entrance into squat building that sat just in front of the leaning obelisk.

That was all I could see in the dark and the moonlight as we ran down through the sand, trying not to tumble, break our legs, or get nailed by chasing arrow fire. The most disconcerting aspect was that the ground trembled as the massive arachnids thundered up the other side of the dunes. The ululating cries of the Lost Elven raiders were muffled by the dense sand in between our two groups, hunters and hunted, and made creepier by that effect.

We hit the bottom, and after that there was a good three hundred yards of open sand to make the complex for hopeful cover and concealment.

The geometry of distance and salvation with variables for getting jammed in the back by the mounted knights' lances didn't solve for escape. I could tell that, but I ran anyway.

The ruck felt like a million pounds. My legs were burnt, my ankles felt like rubber from fighting the sand,

and I knew that was bad because it would be easier to turn an ankle now and that was what was absolutely not needed at this moment.

I told my mind, along with all the other things it was managing, just to keep an eye on the ankles and never mind the incoming. I could get hit, right, and keep moving. My arms were smoked from holding the compass. And the shield.

At least I could stow the compass now, but I didn't even have the energy to. So I just held on to it.

Joe, having been through everything I'd been through, ran like it was his first time around the airfield. I felt like a hobbling, waddling old man, just trying to hang on and suck his dust.

I am significantly younger than Joe.

"Come on, Ranger," bellowed the NCO. "That building in front of the temple... looks like the place to set up a sweet... kill zone. If we can't do it there... we can't do it... anywhere. C'mon, man!"

We reached the sphinxes guarding the column-lined entrance to the temple complex as the spiders came down the last dune, their long delicate black insect legs picking their way through the sand almost delicately, and of course quickly. The twanging bow shots went wide in the dying wind, but it was clear they'd close the distance and probably improve their marksmanship.

We made the sphinxes and went for cover behind one, each of us taking a side of the sphinx. The incoming was too heavy to stay in the open. Too heavy to continue our fade to the temple.

We were close, but not close enough to make the entrance to that strange and silent structure beneath the obelisk rising in the night.

CHAPTER TEN

WE hugged wall against the base of the towering sphinx carved in some darker stone other than the granite and limestone of the desert and what we'd encountered so far. Obsidian, I think. It felt cool and solid. It was ancient and there were many strange hieroglyphs carved across the base. A towering, winged lion with the enigmatic lizard face of a Saur rose above us, and its eyes, as we'd run toward it for cover, had struck me as half-dreaming. I was reminded of some passage by Poe describing a demon. Like ya do when you're running for your life from psycho killer elves hunting you in the night, lost in the desert ten thousand years from anything Poe ever knew as normal.

Most people don't know that Edgar Allan Poe was an artillery officer. I always thought that was interesting about him, and there was something in that that had led me to join the army. I remember thinking, as I was trying to make my decision... well, if Poe, a drug addict and manic depressive, could do it, I certainly could.

To be honest though, Poe would have been a horrible Ranger. The nightmares of battle that Rangers face and don't seem much phased by would have sent that man running for the laudanum, or absinthe, or whatever mind-altering poison he could get his trembling hands on.

Probably some hairy poem would have gotten penned though, and in that I am a little jealous. So far my writing consists of little more than a report of what has happened and my yearnings for coffee and wayward elven princesses who have broken my heart.

It's best to be honest about these things. Poe, I am not.

The sphinx's twin, wind-marred and missing its wings but otherwise basically identical, sat proudly on the far side of the grand sand-washed paving-stone entrance of the mysterious temple complex to our rear. The identified chokepoint we'd tried to make and didn't before the enemy got too close for us to move without getting pin-cushioned by multiple poisoned arrows.

This was as far as we were going without a fight. And it was clear Sergeant Joe was more than happy to give them one since they'd come looking.

Shots fired from the carbine sounded definite and even filled with anger and rage. Sharp and murderous.

The Ranger NCO wasn't playing.

"We ain't lost, we're just getting acquainted with the neighbors, bro. Watch the right. How far we got to reach the choke? I ain't dyin' here."

I was counting easily thirty rows of the grand desert columns we needed to pass along the stone paved entrance road to make it into the gaping black-hole entrance of the low and fat temple behind us. Sand dunes had crawled over the stones and columns but not high enough to give us any kind of cover from enemy fire.

Joe might not want to die here, but it wasn't like they were giving us much room to squirt. I couldn't count the mounted giant spiders out there but there had to be at least twenty, with tons of foot troops moving about. Green fire torches sprang up and to the rear of all these strange gathering forces, and spells erupted into the night, turning the desert a ghostly green and casting long shadows from the columns and the sphinxes that danced and moved.

"They're putting up illum to try and spot us," grunted Joe as he scanned the developing attack. Then he spotted one of their wizards out there, called his location and distance, squinted hard into the reticle, synced up the sling on his carbine, raised it up a hair, let out his breath, and sent a round, muttering, "Yahtzee, loser."

"Take that, Gandalf!" he swore a second later as the Lost Elven wizard took one in the head and tumbled down the dune. His apprentices and acolytes rushing to his side. But my eyes had picked up brain-matter spray casting along the dying wind and painting the clean surface of the dune to the wizard's rear. That guy wasn't gonna be doing much spell-casting in the future. He was dead.

As I shifted along the wide base of the monument, the strange Saurian scrawl of the hieroglyphs marked and stamped there seemed to twist and move on its own accord. But really it was from the eerie green sorcerous illumination that had been cast up below the cold night stars above our little fight for our lives. A cold chill ran up my spine as more of Joe's firing rang out clear and sharp in the silence of this strange and abandoned place. The Saur, in my opinion—and that opinion was due to many hours spent listening to the old wizard Vandahar—were, as Jabba would say, *Bad Bad Bigga Bigga Juju*. We didn't need to add them to our currently getting-worse-by-the-second situation.

There was a reason the Rangers had decided to get involved in the geopolitics of the Ruin. The old wizard had indicated there was a great war coming between the forces of darkness and… everyone else, basically. We were throwing in for humanity. And good, of course. The true threat was a being called the Nether Sorcerer. But the Saur had once conquered, and enslaved, most of the known world long ago, in the days just after we jumped forward through time. They were the perennial foes of humanity, and they ruled from the Land of Black Sleep.

They were allies to this Nether Sorcerer.

But as Vandahar had said, "That is no easy alliance. Both want the prize, and neither wants the sharing."

So the Rangers had decided to go for the kill shot on the Saur pharaoh. Sût the Undying. Destabilizing the throne might mean we could eliminate their vast army from the battle against the Nether Sorcerer most of the other races on the side of good would be facing imminently. But it would be no easy feat, and the Rangers had planned like they were going for grizzly. More supply ships would load us up with big weapons once we took the port of Sûstagul at the entrance to the Land of Black Sleep.

Then we'd assault the Valley of the Lich Pharaohs and face Sût himself.

Sergeant Thor had indicated to me that that was as far as he was going. The Valley of the Lich Pharaohs. After he "smoked old Sût" with *Mjölnir*, as he put it, then he was discharging himself. He wanted to see the rest of the Ruin. There was no strange tale of mysterious societies and lost temples, ancient ruins, and mythical lands that he didn't want to know more about. Fables of monsters he wanted to try his hand against were like a siren's song to him. And that—a siren's song, that is—is a powerful thing. I was almost been killed by one, and he was too, back on the beach at the citadel after we'd first come ashore.

The way Sergeant Thor figured it, he was ten thousand years overdue for discharge. And there was a lot of Ruin he wanted to explore on his own after that.

I hoped to be a part of that battle and maybe talk the Ranger sniper out of his quest to go do extremely dangerous stuff on his own.

But first…

To our front, the spider cav swarmed forward and Joe responded with the carbine. I couldn't tell who was getting hit from my loc as I watched my flank and got ready to pop any that tried us from that direction. I reminded myself I'd need to wait for them to get dangerously close to ensure I abided by the *every round is a kill* task, condition, and standard my NCO had set. The G19, a sidearm, wasn't much good past short distances.

Seven yards was my kill zone and I marked it in my head out there in the sands. Challenging myself not to waste shots beyond that range on any enemies that wanted to flank us from that direction.

We'd need every round to get back to coffee. I mean *the Rangers*. Yeah. I can't scratch that out of the parchment. So… Freudian slip.

I know I have a problem. The first step is admitting you have one, right? But if I'm honest… it's not really a problem… for me. You've got to have a reason to kill the enemy. And yeah, there are lots, like they're trying to kill you and all… but my favorite, and the one I'd been running over and over in my head as we buddy-ran through the dunes was… *kill enough of them and you'll get to coffee, Talker.*

I dangled that in front of my aching body and fatigue-slopped mind like a dirt farmer dangles a carrot in front of a mule. And it worked.

You do you. I'll do me. Whatever it takes.

A skittering behemoth arachnid went wide around the sphinx we were fighting from, crossing the sands on my side of the base of the monument out there and approaching my kill zone. About twenty yards out and closing, scrabbling sideways at the direction of the mounted knight in the wicked black saddle. The Lost Elven knight had thrown back his dark purple cloak and held a short bow with an arrow nocked and ready to fire once he had a clear target.

I peeked out and saw the knight pull on the bowstring…

He fired just as I ducked for cover. The arrow streaked past the corner of the monument and off into the grand paved stone walkway behind me. Acrid smoke and the taste of sour wine and something even more foul coming along in the wake of the missile's flight.

Yeah, they had to be using some kind of poison.

I crouched down and leaned back out behind the angle of the monument's base, keeping the barrel of the G19 low so as not to telegraph my shot. The mounted knight had kicked the giant black widow forward into a charge, and in the moonlight his breastplate flashed like a silver target, clear and bright. I landed the front sight of the G19 and waited as the knight nocked another arrow and drew the bowstring back to fire.

This time I fired first. One shot, square in the chest, punching iron or steel breastplate with a distinctive ring I will never forget. He didn't drop the bow after I shot him, but it was as though he didn't know what to do with what had just torn a gaping hole in his chest. The spider skidded to a stop, and I fired again at the mounted knight now that I had a more stable target. Not a head shot, but probably upper thoracic region. The pipes of the pump, as Chief Rapp might say. The knight clutched his throat, looked mournfully groundward, and feebly jerked the slavering spider off from the attack, riding off into the darkness like the strangest thing I'd ever see.

I turned back to Joe who was already swapping in a new mag from his corner of the defense at the base of the sphinx.

"Looks bad, bro. You're Bravo. I'm Alpha. Fall back two columns and cover me. We'll withdraw using the columns as cover. Go. Go now."

He inserted a fresh magazine with a push-pull to make sure it was seated, pressed the bolt release, calmly raised the rifle from retention to on target, and let fly another dose of M855 into the heart of another cracked-out elf. All of it efficient and fluid, mindless zen almost. The zen of calligraphy transformed into pure lethality, but zen nonetheless.

I don't know if someone died out there as he began to return fire, but if I had to bet... then yeah, someone died each time he pulled the trigger.

I hustled under the heavy ruck to our rear, using the steady covering fire as my cue to jump to the new position. Enemy arrows whistled hideously in the hot night, and I raced two columns back to the rear and called out, "Bravo covering!" as I took up cover behind the ancient stone pillar.

I fired into the mass of enemy troopers getting danger close to Joe's side of the monument's base. No idea at this range and in this darkness if rounds were effective.

Joe used the base of the sphinx to cover his retreat and make it to the columns and then back to the pillar I was covering from. He handed me the carbine.

"Fifteen rounds left. Keep 'em back for a second, Ranger."

Then he was digging through the Ruck of Many Wonders on my back, muttering to himself as he did so.

"Block. Check. Time fuse."

I landed the red dot on one of the Lost Elven foot troopers leading the others in a charge forward. Two scimitars out and trailing his weapons as he came. Dark-purple-almost-black cape flying in the dying wind and the late night like an image of what insanity is. It was surreal and bizarre and the very stuff of nightmares. The whites of his red eyes stood out in the night dark and silver moonlight gray sand.

I adjusted for mechanical offset of the sight and shot him once in the heart as he closed. He stumbled, kept moving a few steps forward, and then faceplanted in the sand. Scimitars flying away from his akimbo arms. I selected another target and shot to kill. Spider knights advanced behind their psychotic foot troopers, content to stand off and fire arrows when opportunities presented.

Kneeling and using the column for as much cover as possible allowed me to present little opportunity.

"Talker, gimme the carbine," said Joe behind me. "Here's the charge. Drop back three columns. Plant it on the outside face, and hook the caps to the det cord tail I rigged on the back. I got the wires. Once you got that done, call out *covering* and I'll link up there."

I swapped the MK18 for the brick of C4, didn't bother to skin my G18, and ran along the columns, keeping them between me and the enemy.

More arrow fire in the night came whizzing in at me. Almost sizzling in the dark like bacon frying. Some shots hitting columns and exploding in sprays of wood and arrowhead. Bits of brittle desert limestone cutting my face, and that foul sour-wine smell filling the night as I ran. I made the column, went over the instructions once more in my head, and placed the brick of C4 at chest height, facing outward on the column, away from the road leading toward the temple.

Then I yelled out, "Covering!"

I tried to find someone to shoot at, and fired a few rounds at a cluster of Lost Elven archers stalking forward in a combat wedge. They scattered, one returned fire, and I hit him. He didn't die, but he wasn't going to be shooting anymore. None of his buddies came to get him off the sands.

A moment later Joe was there, running fast as he threw himself to the ground and shouted, "Suck dirt!"

I went down as several arrows whistled through the night. Many shattered against the column.

Joe returned fire just to keep their heads down as we readied the IED.

"Two mags left. Talker, here's the M81s. I'll cover. Push quarter turn, pull one at a time. If it goes on the first one don't bother with the second. Tie 'em off on the caps. We det the outward side and it sends the blast inward across the road there, and hopefully lots of frag in a killing arc toward their avenue of approach. Feel me, bro?"

I had a roll of one hundred feet of NONEL shock tube rigged to the C4 block. I holstered my pistol and took the M81 firing devices. There were two of them side by side taped together with the safety pins both facing upward for a clean release. Push, quarter turn, pull on the pins. That would send a small pulse down the tubes into the blasting caps connected to the det cord, which was then connected to the C4 block. Explosive chain, that's how it works. I stood back, grunting I was good with whatever. Explosives training had come with time in the Rangers and some practical classes in Ranger School, twice even.

I got the idea, but... nerves. I'm working with something that can make a bad day infinitely worse. Some of the Rangers call it spicy putty. I think of it as Adult Play-Doh. Tanner calls it Killy Putty. That's probably the most accurate. And all three elements that make it go boom are already in place and just waiting for me to connect it all and activate the firing pin plungers on the M81 firing device. The pucker factor is real.

"Connect those caps to the det cord tail. It's a raptor clip connector so just use it like a hair clip. They're gettin' ready to push. That's just what we want."

Knots had also been a big thing in Ranger School. And because it was a class and something I could memorize, I'd enjoyed knots and had gotten good at them. And then the Portugonian sailors, and especially old Santago, had master-classed knots for me. Those old tars were endlessly tying knots with stray pieces of rope they carried with them all the time. Something to do with their constantly nervous hands. As though even when not working and worrying, they needed to be working, and worrying.

Joe fired again and I secured the caps and NONEL tubes to the charge.

"They're getting close, bro. Don't wanna rush you and all, but I'm black on mags."

Two magazines left. Sixty rounds.

"Got it, Sar'nt. We're good to go."

Sergeant Joe produced a ChemLight from one of his pockets, snapped it, and threw it down at the base of the column where we'd planted the charge. Marking the explosive for us as the chaos of the battle and the ensuing push began to develop. We'd know where the charge was, and when they got there…

… *Killy Putty* for the win.

Hopefully.

"No time to ask you if you're sure. *Es loc que es. It is what it is.* Play out the shock tube until we're out. Tell me how many columns back once you get there. Then no covering fire. I want 'em good and close on my heels."

I played out the NONEL shock tube, keeping low as arrow fire slammed into stone and sand all around me. When I hit the end of the roll, one hundred feet, hearing the steady fire of Joe and unconsciously counting the rounds left, I called out the number of columns in the night.

"Four!"

"Moving!" shouted Joe from near the collapsing battle line. He fired twice and made his way back, moving through the incoming and turning to fire from the columns as he did so. All at once I heard the spider cav rumble forward, many sets of eight legs thundering across the desert floor and broken stone as though it were some muffled hollow great drum on which they beat. Lost Elven foot troopers gave high-pitched screams and bloodcurdling shrieks as they made their final charge ahead of their betters, racing to kill the Ranger.

Joe fired a few more shots to get their blood up, dropped two fast movers who'd gotten within ten meters, waving blades, then turned and ran, throwing himself down in the sand. He worked fast, connecting wires and muttering, looked up once and spotted the ChemLight and the mass of the enemy in relation to the blast zone.

"It's close and we're gonna take a hit to the gut from overpressure. But hey… suck sand and do it. Put your fingers in your ears and shout. This one's gonna be loud. Fire in the hole…"

The heavy column ahead of us, which I'm guessing weighed eight thousand pounds easy, exploded in the night as the spider cavalry and elven foot swarmed forward, knives out, ready to kill us.

The primary blast wave caught some of them. The flying stone shrapnel ruined a lot more of the rest. When I looked up, I saw one of the bodies, or at least most of it, of a Lost Elf, lying in the sand nearby. The guy was still alive and trying to scream, but nothing was coming out. Forty-plus PSI had probably collapsed both lungs, so no air in and no air out to scream in horror with. Serves him right. We were not your average prey. Body parts of elves and spiders littered the grand walkway they'd passed along to reach us out here. The fatal arc created by Joe's withdrawal and the blast impulse of the charge against the column had had an incredible effect, blasting inward across our retreat, tearing them to shreds. They'd died suddenly. And very badly.

He'd led them right into it during a battle in which, if I'm honest as I look back at my part in it all, I'd thought was nothing but a running firefight for survival and that the only plan had been to do whatever it took next to survive to the next minute and not get hacked to pieces or pin-cushioned by a dozen poison arrows.

But Joe had been playing chess with them the whole time. And they'd lost.

My ears were ringing, and I was a little dizzy when I got to my boots, but it wasn't the worst.

The smoke was still clearing. One of the dead knights lay a few feet away. He was still alive and crawling toward the desert. Crawling back to their cave far to the rear. He swore and bled in Hindi. They were not good phrases. Curses. Promises. Anger. Revenge.

But my Hindi isn't that good and like I said, maybe he just wanted a nice curry before dying.

Joe raised his rifle automatically, pure predator getting the killing work done good and tight, sighted… and then muttered, "Can't waste good rounds. He'll be dead soon enough. And we got a long ways to go."

A moment later one of the massive spiders stumbled out of the smoke and ruin, its spindly and long legs wobbly, the body of a headless knight still in the saddle, upright and all. The huge beast wobbled forward toward us, almost bewildered but still seeming hungry, poison dripping from its horror-show ruined face and the one fang it had left… and then it collapsed over on its crushed legs.

For one long minute there was nothing but silence and the ringing in our ears. Even the desert wind was gone, as though so shocked by the sudden violence and carnage of Joe's plan that it had taken itself off for better vistas and lonelier places out there in the vast open and undiscovered places it guarded and wanted no one to find ever.

Forbidden oases. The rotting bones of ancient civilizations sinking into the sands. Dark demons that never slept, waiting near fires that never died. Waiting to ask riddles that could not be answered. Guarding treasures and gems beyond the dreams of the greedy.

In that moment I felt all that. Felt it was all out there in the night all around us. Felt the call of the desert trying to lure me into its depths, its promises of solace and pleasure. Even its curses.

And maybe I understood Sergeant Thor a little more than I had before.

The opposite of the ruined corpses of murderers dying in the sands all around our boots.

There are only winners. There are only the quick and the dead. The sand takes everything else.

In the distance, more shrieking cries from other Lost Elves rang out in the night. The sounds signaling to each other they knew where the battle was, where the slaughter lay. They would find an outcome different than what they expected. We had slaughtered the first to run us to ground. And we'd kill them too. But they would come anyway.

Joe swapped out his last mag and muttered, "Winchester."

Then...

"Let's go, bro," he said. "There're more out there. Take your time, but always make the enemy hurry."

CHAPTER ELEVEN

WITH Joe leading and me watching our six, we'd nailed our land nav point as we stood on the sand-covered road leading to the temple and towering crooked obelisk looming above us. Which, in anyone's Ranger School, is a *go*.

Take that, Kurtz.

"Good job, kid. The *obe—obelish*, whatever, looks deserted. What time do you think it is?"

He was shaking the Timex on his wrist.

That happened here in the Ruin. Our gear would fall apart fast, and even though the Timexes the Rangers loved held up longer than most things, they didn't last forever. The Forge had to crank them out by the big-box-store pallet. I'd lost mine in the river. Perhaps the blast had pushed Joe's over into inoperable.

That had happened before.

"My guess would be not midnight yet, Sar'nt."

"This one's done," said Joe, giving up on the watch and returning his attention to the temple as we closed on the dark angular opening that led inward at the end of the sand-covered and column-lined way.

"Got another in the ruck. But… let's secure this place first. If they wanna fight some more tonight, then we're gonna need to find a place to make our last stand in."

I smelled smoke.

Then I saw the body in the sand.

"You smell that?" asked Sergeant Joe.

Rangers are big on what they call *SLLS*. Stop, look, listen, and smell. You do it before every patrol and during short and long halts. I do it automatically now, and we'd both smelled that scent in the night.

Maybe it was the explosive or the burning flesh or gear all around us. But it didn't smell like those things.

The wind was mostly dead now. The night was hot, dry, and silent all around us.

I sniffed the air and smelled smoke. Barely. Then I heard the soft and melancholy tinkle of wind chimes somewhere in the night. Just for a moment, as though some last-gasp breeze had stirred them to life for one last haunting song before calling it an evening.

"Wind chimes on the objective..." whispered Joe to himself, then laughed softly.

I had no idea what that meant and now was not the time to ask.

"There's a body over there," I noted in the silence. We'd stopped. Doing our SLLS. Both of us taking a knee, covering by the columns that led down the grand walk toward the looming low temple complex and the crooked obelisk rising in the night. Now that the storm was gone, the moon was out, turning everything bone and silver under its cold glare.

"Spotted that. Others too. Some are buried in the sand. There, there, and there."

"From the blast?" I asked.

"Negative, bro. These have been here before the storm. Not long—they don't smell yet. Maybe twenty-four hours or less, which is saying something in the average daily desert heat during the day. Bodies get ripe fast. That's why desert tribes bury their dead by sundown. Someone didn't bury these because they couldn't. There's danger here. Too dangerous to bury your own dead."

The scent of smoke was gone now. I tried to recall it. Tried to think of what kind of smoke it had been. We'd smelled a lot of smoke in our time here in the Ruin. Many different kinds. And that was something you didn't think a lot about back in the world we came from. Smoke. The different kinds of it. But in a world gone basically Bronze Age... it's important. Even the source. Wood, dung, bodies. A smoke has characteristics, and the different kinds of its... *flavors,* let's call 'em... all mean something. Now that I was the smaj's intel monkey for the Rangers, I'd begun to think in those terms.

There was the smoke of cooking. The smoke of fires for heat. The smoke of battle. The smoke of a torch held by a goblin out looking for you in the night. The smoke a whole village of some enemy going up in flames in the night makes. I'd smelled many kinds. Many, many kinds of smoke.

I could tell Joe was waiting on what I thought as we knelt there in the short halt position on one knee, watching the night like hunting animals. But I wasn't sure if he was waiting on me to work out the equation I'd started.

"Whatcha think, Talker?" he whispered in the desert silence, scanning every possible direction we could be attacked from.

"Smells like... a watchfire, Sar'nt. Like we'd build on patrols in Ranger School when the temperature dropped and even Kurtz knew we needed to stay warm as tired and as hungry as we were. He didn't want anyone drowning in the bogs he was going to get us into in the morning. So we got fire instead of sleep and calories."

Joe said nothing and watched the night.

"Sergeant Kurtz... I mean."

"Yeah. That's what it smells like to me too. Feels like someone's watchin' us. Tryin' to figure out if we're friend or foe. Depends on who *they* are. Check that body over there," he said, pointing the carbine at the nearest lump in the sand. "One man's trash is another man's intel source."

I hustled forward, keeping an eye on the low angular temple in front of us. Still about ten more rows of columns to go before we'd need to decide if we were going in there.

I crouched over the body, pulled out my tanto, and made ready to stab it in case it was a ruse and someone was just playing possum like Joe might. It wasn't. The guy was dead. I brushed some sand away, but even before I saw the death rictus of the Lost Elf I had a pretty good idea who the dead were. Purple cloaks. Dark chain armor. This one wore a necklace of crescent moons and black widows.

He looked like he'd been strangled to death. A purple tongue, swollen and thick, lolled out from between his Joker's-smile sharpened teeth. His bulging eyes were frozen wide with final terror or psychotic fury.

"Lost Elves, Sar'nt."

Joe waited motionless. Then...

"There are broken throwing spears. Some shattered weapons. Looks like they tried to assault the temple and didn't make it in. Main body pulled back and left their dead for the vultures. Whoever's in there don't like 'em neither. So we got that in common, know what I mean?"

Silence.

"Maybe, you know… just… maybe…" Joe began, almost to himself.

From within the darkness of the opening to the temple, a figure emerged. I alerted Sergeant Joe with a quick, "Someone's coming out."

"Got him. Might be a friendly. Get ready to do your thing."

Joe kept the carbine lowered, but I knew a quick jerk of the barrel would bring it up and into action. I stood and walked forward, putting myself to the right and in front of Sergeant Joe. I held my hands down, palms open. Communicating we were interested in talking first. Violence later.

The figure wore a cape and a helm, like something the Spartans used to wear, except this one had a horsehair crest. It was dark and because of the moonlight and the night, I couldn't tell the color.

He wasn't tall. He wasn't small. He was ordinary and normal-sized. Which, even then, struck me as an odd observation and I'd think about that more later. That my first impression of the captain of the Accadion Legion, or what remained of them, was that he was an unremarkable man.

Which was so ironic.

CHAPTER TWELVE

"*GRANDINE estranei*," said the unremarkable man in the night who stood before us. Among the cracked and ruined columns leading the way through the lonely desert. Leading to the strangely ominous temple and the leaning obelisk out here in the middle of nowhere as far as I could tell.

Bingo. This one's gonna be easy. He was speaking Italian, and Italian is just plain fun for me. I'm not gonna lie to you, the Hindi the Lost Elves were speaking was iffy at best for me. I didn't *really* think they were ordering curry, or I was, but that was mostly because of context. Not exactly a curry-ordering circumstance we'd just been through. But as for the words themselves… I couldn't really say.

I'm a perfectionist. That bothered me on levels I can't even begin to communicate. But let me try a metaphor to indicate how it makes me feel when I cannot faithfully and accurately translate. Dive into a boiling hot Jacuzzi in August at noon and then, without drying off, put on a heavy wool winter suit that has spiders in it. The really itchy wool. The really small spiders with lots of itchy venom that makes you scratch, knowing it'll do no good. That's how it feels when I can't translate accurately. Oh, and the spiders bite you a lot and that's itchy and hot too and you scratch but you can never get rid of the itch. But I already said that.

Because that's what it feels like.

But Italian, now I could work with this!

"It's Italian," I told Joe. "He's greeting us as strangers."

Sergeant Joe sighed.

"Just this once, couldn't it be Mexican?" Joe muttered. "At least I could have ordered burritos. Tell him we're cool."

I turned back to the man standing there in the moon-light and didn't start with *Ehi, siamo fantastici. Hey, we're cool.* But I did tell him we weren't with the Dark Elves.

"We aren't a threat," I said in Italian. "We're not with those…"

I pointed toward the body of a dead Lost Elf half-buried in the sand nearby.

The man in the crested helmet moved forward cautiously. It was clear he was a warrior. By the light of the moon I could see more of him. He wore what I would call Roman armor, which makes sense with the language he was speaking. Vandahar, during his Forgotten Ruin world intel downloads I'd been sitting in on, had indicated that the world's foremost human civilization centered around the powerful city state of Accadios, which, according to the rough maps we had looked at, seemed to be located in Italy, near what might have once been Rome.

The boot of Italy had been badly marred by the ancient comet strike, "when the stars fell," or so we theorized, and the Adriatic was now much more of a lake than a sea along the eastern coast of Italy.

He wore a simple breastplate of gray iron. No fancy scrollwork of lions or eagles stamped on the gleaming face. He wore similar arm guards, shin guards, and boots instead of sandals. A soldier's kit. Nothing fancy. All of it made for battle. A pleated kilt made of hard leather strips and reinforced with iron completed the uniform. The helmet, as I have said, was more Spartan than Roman, and now I could make a guess that the horsehair crest was a deep blue and not the red I had expected of the Ruin equivalent of a Roman Centurion ten thousand years in the future.

That is, if the future hadn't gone all J. R. R. Tolkien and PFC Kennedy's game of Dungeons & Dragons.

His face was in shadow, but I could see a livid scar that ran down one cheek in the moonlight. And his eyes. They gleamed in the night like he was watching us intently, a predator ready to fight at a moment's notice. Like Sergeant Joe. On his leather belt waited a small sword.

I think the Romans called that a *gladius*.

"If you are not foe… then what are you doing so deep in the No Man's Land?" asked the man, in Italian once again.

I waited, unsure how to answer exactly as I translated all of it to Joe. But in the meantime, the captain of the Accadions asked another question.

"And identify yourselves. I am Tyrus, commander of the Eighth. Dogs of War. Soldier in the legions of Accadios. Servant of the emperor himself."

CHAPTER THIRTEEN

THE Lost Elven hunting bells and war drums suddenly changed in the desert night out there as we talked with the Accadion Legion captain. If the hour wasn't midnight... it had to be close. I felt empty and run out of gas. Dry and hollow. But I wasn't tired. I was past that. I'd just keep doing what needed to be done to get to a place we could call safe.

We stood there in the waning moonlight, the storm moving off to the east, the hunting parties moving now to something more martial. Or urgent. They knew where we were going, and they were coming for us now.

The strange Accadion Legion captain watched us, unbothered by the enemy summoning itself to another fight tonight. And though he didn't move, I sensed he had the power and speed to move fast, suddenly, and dangerously when he needed to. He was military. I'd seen that enough among the Rangers and SF personnel since Area 51 to know he was, ten thousand years in the future, cut from the same operator cloth as those predators I had come to call my own. There was something of that black jungle panther I'd once seen, in this commander. Pure hunting machine, a predator like no other.

He reminded me of Captain Knife Hand. Except, at least right now, there was no look of permanent indigestion. Just a commander weighing a desperate situation somewhere past midnight, lost in the desert and beyond any means of help or allied support. Finding no easy answers, no easy road, no easy fight. Just more combat and more struggle until there was death and the dead who had ceased their questions.

He'd fight to get his men to peace. You could tell that, just waiting there under the moon and listening to the enemy come.

And I understood that now as I waited there, barely wobbling back and forth in my own fatigue under the weight of the Ruck of Many Wonders. Just trying to keep the blood moving in my numb feet, on fire in my rode-hard boots.

Like ya do.

I'd been translating the introductions and the situation between Sergeant Joe and the Accadion Legion commander when the Lost Elven hunting parties out there in the shadow-filled night, dark shapes on the distant dunes, suddenly became war parties and made it clear they were coming for us now, tracing out of the desert wastes.

The night was young to them. There was still time for another fight.

There were horns calling out one to another. Formations suddenly coalescing down among the two sphinxes at the entrance to the temple complex or whatever this place was. On the map I'd mark it as the place of the Crooked Obelisk. Scanning the desert dunes to our rear, we could see lines three deep of Lost Elven foot forming into squares five to ten deep. The war spiders to the rear were rumbling about, coming out of the desert with more troops as the enemy made ready to advance against our position. Other darker shapes moving quickly about the formations as the horns from each unit erupted, busy about some diabolical business. Signaling readiness and other communications unknown to us at the moment.

Yeah, I might have made up my mind to die in my boots out here regardless of how little energy, food, sleep, and of course coffee I hadn't had... but I did have a very bad feeling about what was gonna happen next.

So... I had that going for me.

"They'll try again tonight then," muttered Captain Tyrus in his grim Italian that didn't quite have the accent of a native Italian, or even the comic Italian spoken by the gunner Soprano when he wasn't doing his *Hey, it's-a me, Mario* voice that drove Kurtz nuts. But maybe the accent Tyrus speaks with *is* native Italian, or whatever they call it, ten thousand years in the future.

I translated.

"Ask him what the situation is..." muttered Sergeant Joe, scanning the distance with his tactical monocular. The NVGs were low on power, so we were saving those. Plus the moon was good and the desert sand was so bone-white that shapes and shadows seemed broadcast into clarity out among its curves and slender snake-like features in the dunes.

I asked the Legion captain and got the answer. Then I told Joe.

"What remains of this guy's unit holds what they call the Forbidden Library, Sar'nt. They have forty legionnaires in there with two spears each. That doesn't sound like much, or good. One battle sorceress from Caspia, no idea on capabilities, that was sent with them on this mission. And *Otoro*."

"What's *Otoro?*" asked Joe, putting away the monocular.

"My sergeant wants to know what an *Otoro* is, or rather who. Is that correct, Captain Tyrus?"

The Legion captain stepped forward, his armor making little sound and quietened much like we do our own plate carriers and chest rigs. In the silver moonlight I could see that the horsehair plume was not just blue but aquamarine. The rarest most expensive color in the world. Or at least it was in our time.

I got my answer from the silent man who said little beyond what was pertinent.

Which is another non-native-Italian indicator.

"He says there's no time to explain, Sar'nt. Otoro is poisoned and will not be able to contribute to the fight. The samurai is using his skills to attempt to stave off the slow poison."

Samurai?

Stranger and stranger still.

Then...

"He says we are welcome, Sar'nt, to... *make the enemy pay...* inside their line if we are truly enemies of the Lost Elves. Then he would consider us allies of necessity."

Joe turned to the Legion commander in the silver moonlight, his face made like a granite statue by the light of the one thing that hadn't changed since we left ten thousand years ago. The moon. I guess the sun too. But hey, who expects the sun to change? Wasn't the moon supposed to crack in half in all those post-apocalyptic movies like *Thundarr?* That was actually a movie I saw here in the Ruin, not back where we came from, that one of the Rangers still had on their smartphone, and it was pretty good. The actress who played Ariel was smokin'. But I digress.

I watched Joe make his decision, but unlike any statue I'd ever seen in all those museums I'd gone to with Sidra, the Ranger's eyes darted, the jaw worked, facial muscles flexed and tensed as he wiped sand and sweat from his forehead. Everything telling me he was working the odds and the problem of our constant survival and imperative to return to Task Force Pipe Hitter and get back on mission to smoke the Lich Pharaoh.

Whatever was happening here… this wasn't our fight. We could let these guys pull the enemy and distract, and we could pull a fade while everyone mixed it up. Outrun the battle and head east following the storm. Come morning, we could hope the Lost Elves had faded back into their caves, or whatever, then push north and try to make the Atlantean Mountains, get over those, and hit the coast to link back up with the Rangers.

Back on mission.

But the numbers out there forming up beneath the desert dunes beyond the brooding silent stone sphinxes didn't look good for the Legion captain's numbers. Forty locals, some chick who could do spells, and an Otoro… against what I could tell was massing to about five to eight hundred foot and a bunch of supporting war spiders bigger than the knights' black widows. That didn't bode well for a bunch of Bronze Age primitives with spears. Give 'em some high-ex, a two-forty, maybe even just a SAW, and yeah… maybe… they could stack some Lost Elven skulls.

Oh my. I'm starting to think like Brumm. Everything lately for Brumm has been *Stack Skulls*.

But one thing the Ruin has taught me is that our weapons—state-of-the-art, war-tested, automatic weapons capable of copious death dealing on demand—didn't always mean we had the upper hand in a fight.

In everything I've written down in this fractured account I don't think I could make a case for that. The only thing our superior weapons and firepower did for us... was give us a shot in a series of very bad situations.

The enemy had numbers, and numbers mean a lot whether anyone likes it or not. Forbidden popsicle barrels had to be changed out. Magazines went black and then Winchester real fast when some of these monsters took a whole mag dump on full auto to... stack. Damn you, Brumm.

Sidearms jammed. MK18s got failures to feed even when you cleared them and kept them in good shape. The Ruin is a grungy dirty place and the remnants of the nano-plague break modern tech down over time. Got a Forge, great, you can replace. And then the whole slow breakdown process starts again. You can only carry so many Carl Gustaf rounds, and firing them gives you a mild concussion when you do so. All of these things combined, with always superior enemy numbers, had gone bad for us at many points. Weapon jam after you just double-tapped a fire team's worth of orcs, and there's still a platoon of the rest of 'em coming at you with war axes and bloody swords.

Then there was magic. Our sorcerer, Kennedy, could roast a giant, blow him off the side of a hill like it was the latest CGI mega-must-see movie, then shoot magic napalm over all the giant's buddies, the supporting troops advancing alongside the raging behemoth. The magic users we'd encountered so far had given us a run, but one day we were gonna run into the enemy's Kennedy, and plate-carriers weren't gonna do jack against magic napalm or sorcerous artillery strikes.

What made the difference if it wasn't firepower?

It was the fact that the Rangers had tactics, and training, *and*... they were Rangers. That creed wasn't just something you memorized and said to get a go. It was a way of life as much as any religion to them. The Rangers that owned it, believed it, relied on it, were the ones I wanted to be like. It wasn't always that way for me...

... but it was now.

Joe stepped toward the outnumbered Accadion Legion leader there in the desert before the Crooked Obelisk looming in the night above us and held out his open hand to our new ally for the moment.

"You had me at make 'em pay, Captain," said Joe. I translated. "These guys need to for sure," continued the Ranger NCO. "And Rangers are the best debt collectors you're ever gonna meet this side of Jersey. Where do we fight these losers?"

Captain Tyrus took Joe's arm with his, grasping the forearm like actors playing Romans once did in the movies ten thousand years ago, and shook.

And honestly... that was pretty cool.

CHAPTER FOURTEEN

THE opening into the "Forbidden Library," as the Legion Captain had called the angular, low, and squat building beneath the rising desert obelisk, was much larger than it had seemed as we approached through the desert. Getting closer, it was clear it was *much* larger.

In fact, the low building was not low at all. It was tall. And I wondered if we were experiencing some kind of magic, or just an optical illusion.

You never can tell in the Ruin.

The angular opening into the desert temple was a square that tapered at the top, rising high above our heads as we entered the deeper darkness of the place within. Ancient snake-like glyphs marked the lintel, carved and writhing away up the side of the imperious edifice.

I smelled smoke coming from within. A group of men dressed in similar armor to that of the Legion captain were standing around a watchfire inside the cavernous front entrance. Huge statues of animal-headed humans lined the walls, all carved out of the same black obsidian as the sphinxes, stretching off into the shadowy distances. The building must have stretched off into the surrounding dunes, given its massive dimensions once we were within it.

Some of the legionnaires were leaning on tall spears. Others squatted around the fire, wrapping wounds with fresh bandages. There was a smell of death here also. All of the men were watching the fire. A few turned to see the captain enter, some watching the opening as the sounds of the horns and marching army began to be heard in the distance.

The looks on their faces betrayed none of their feeling about the coming battle. If anything… it was Tuesday for them. Or whatever the Accadion equivalent of *Tuesday* is.

In the darkness, I'd missed two sentries standing in the shadows to the sides of the door. I looked back and spotted them when the dull stamp and quiet thunder of the approaching force of Lost Elves and spiders began. I was trying to see how much time we had and how we were going to defend such a wide opening with so few people. The silent sentries were there, waiting with spears they easily could have stuck me with had I been a threat to their commander.

I do intel. Sometimes badly.

That was when I saw the two sentries in the darkness. Barely. Joe had tagged them and shot me a knowing look as I caught on, identifying everything and making sure I was noting it also.

The Ranger task condition and standard of *Always be kind, polite, and have a plan to kill everyone* was in effect. And as Tanner likes to say, "And always carry a knife—in case there's cheesecake or you have to stab a fool."

The captain leaned close as one of the men, taller but not by much, ran up from the fire, coming to a halt and clearly ready to receive some kind of orders.

"Corporal Chuzzo," ordered the captain swiftly in Italian. "The enemy readies another assault. Shields to the center as before. Spears one deep. Scorpion teams Sun and

Moon left and right. Forward of the line of shields. Sound the call to arms now."

"Aye, *Capitano!*" shouted Corporal Chuzzo and then began shouting to the rankers of the Legion to organize into battle lines to defend the entrance.

At once, within the mass of legionnaires suddenly moving everywhere, one of them sounded an urgent call to arms three times, much like the army's "Reveille" but slightly different. Three times, but as we observed, it felt unnecessary. These soldiers knew their jobs. Tired, wounded, they were professionals and highly trained. They knew the stakes and they moved quickly to prepare for the killing work that would be expected of them soon.

Some of the legionnaires moved to form a line with huge bronze circular shields stamped and painted with wild-eyed three-headed dogs, tongues lolling over vicious teeth. Claws ready to attack and draw blood.

To the sides of this shield wall forming within the depths just inside the entrance to this place, one line of spear on each side formed. Hulking legionnaires, their faces dirty and scarred, many wearing blood-soaked bandages, made ready to defend against the impending Lost Elven attack.

Within two minutes the Accadion legionnaires were ready, standing in motionless perfect silence within their battle formations as they had been ordered to. The captain had told us to wait as he'd disappeared into the hustle, organizing men, giving last-minute orders to his junior officers, and making sure all was as he wanted it. Quickly.

"They know what they're about," muttered Joe as he had me drop the ruck. Joe took out the canteen, shook it, and took a small drink.

"Drain the rest, bro. I don't know that we're gonna walk away from this one. We're pinned in here with them and the odds ain't so good. I got about fifteen rounds left in the last mag and you got what you got. We'll need all the water we can do. If we make it, they probably have some, or this place has a well. I can smell water somewhere beyond their dead they got stacked in the corner over there, but we ain't got time to top off."

I drained a quarter of the collapsible quart canteen and Joe handed me two large pieces of his wife's magic jerky.

"Here ya go. It's Christmas, kid."

I shoved one piece in, chewing as I crammed the other piece in.

The stamp of boots and spider legs outside the Forbidden Library, out there in the desert sand and the grand walkway leading through the ruined columns, was beginning to rise to a low distant afternoon thunder reminding me of a storm I'd once heard. The ground shook and the sound of the bells and trumpets the Lost Elves moved with was arriving and echoing across the dark space we were going to fight in.

Which... didn't look like much of a library to me at this point. But to be fair, so far I hadn't seen much beyond the front entrance.

"The Legion is assembled and ready to give battle, *mi Capitano!*" shouted Corporal Chuzzo in the firelit darkness.

Captain Tyrus strode out of the shadows, moving quickly and economically to the center. He received the salute from his junior NCO, a crisp slap against the chest and a wave of the knife hand to signal respect. Then he turned, inspecting all three elements of his defense.

I had no idea how this military force ran their rank structure, but it was clear Corporal Chuzzo was now the senior NCO. Add the stacked bodies Joe had spotted, and that told me they'd taken heavy casualties to get pinned down out here in the middle of nowhere.

Sergeant Joe and I had moved to stand between the shields and the "Moon" element of the spearmen. From here I could see just the barest beginnings of the permanent look of indigestion crossing the Legion captain's face that I had learned marked all good leaders.

The look that said *I don't have enough to get done what needs to get done but it's gonna get done anyway.*

The Accadion legionnaires remained like statues in their formations and lines, giving away neither hate nor love to their commander as they waited for his words. Their expressions were inscrutable.

In the silence Sergeant Joe whispered, "These guys are some bad motor scooters. We 'bout to see some real live Bronze Age warfare whoop, and my guess is it ain't gonna be real pretty."

The captain, satisfied with what he saw, looked around one more time and I had that distinct feeling, as the drums and bells of the enemy began to grow and compete with the insane lunatic trills of their shrill disconcerting horns now that they were closing, that he was making eye contact with each and every one of his men. That he knew them by name, and more importantly knew their deeds. And that he was reminding each and every one of them of what he expected to be done in the next few desperate minutes that would mean life or death for all of them.

And seeing in return that they were ready to deliver as they had done before.

In the silence that followed, he gave no heroic or grand speech about what they were going to do now. Their actions somehow meaning something down the line in history books about the bloody dead. *Echoing in eternity* and all that jazz. He just nodded once at them and then said, *"Vere gli occhi più grandi dello stomaco, cani da guerra."*

Bite off more than you can chew, dogs of war.

Then the legionnaires roared with laughter, yelling *"Cani da guerra"* like lunatics in an asylum just set free and given all the whiskey and coloring books they could do. I had the feeling that what had been spoken between them was just some colloquialism they'd found funny. The part about biting off more than they could chew. Their captain had communicated to them in that moment that the situation was indeed grim and that what they were feeling was expected of men who were about to die bravely. Then he gave them some reminder that it was okay to forget all that, just leave it behind for someone else to take care of and kill as many of their enemies as they could before it was all over. One way or another for them. He knew they would do their best.

He knew that.

And they did too.

Maybe that's of no interest to anyone. The words that are used in certain moments sometimes seem not to connect, sometimes have deeper meanings than just what's on the surface. Strange to those who have never faced death in battle. Maybe. Maybe it's just interesting to me. But words. They are always fascinating to me.

Whoever reads this account... maybe that's interesting to you. I do not know.

CHAPTER FIFTEEN

THE psycho elven line hit us hard in the opening move. Joe and I had been moved to support the shield line by Corporal Chuzzo as the captain went to take command from the right, moving between the shields and the Sun Spears to get the best view of the battle. I could see he'd drawn his gladius and stood ready to deal some pain and death when the moment came. Its edge gleamed in the dark like a wicked razor made for the cutting work of death-dealing fast and close.

Then, just before the first psycho elves came running into the killing field, a lithe figure in robes, clearly feminine, joined the captain, standing just behind him. Making it clear she had come to do her part in the imminent fight. Slender alabaster hands erupted from the large sleeves of her hooded robe as I struggled to get my eyeful. I could see silver and gold bangles dancing along slender arms tattooed with delicate scrawls of dark ink.

"The *capi-tano*," Corporal Chuzzo had said to us. And I'm noting his words and dialogue style here in the account in almost comic Italian because his accent was clearly more Italian than Captain Tyrus's. More like what I'd expect of a native Italian speaker, especially someone from Sicily. Much more comic over-exaggerated mob-guy Italian than how the Legion commander had used the language.

Again it struck me that perhaps Captain Tyrus was not a native speaker, but that was something I'd consider later.

"I'm-a Corporal Chuzzo. *Mi capi-tano*, he... ah... he says you speaka the Lingua Accad?"

I told him I did, speaking back in Italian. *Lingua Accad.* Interesting. And I have to note that sometimes there were other words from other languages being used, mostly Romance, that crept in. Occasionally there was some English and even Gray Speech. *Grau Sprache.* That hybrid the Ruin now called a language. But Gray Speech was used rarely and often only in negative usage. As if to indicate something distasteful, or as an insult.

Autumn had told me Gray Speech was the language of the Crow's March. An evil place by all accounts. The realm of the Black Prince. A nation of vampires and werewolves according to myths and half-whispered rumors.

And yeah, as the enemy drumbeat increased, I smelled the oil on the weapons of the legionnaires, heard them muttering prayers to gods I didn't know, felt the ground shake, and I thought of Autumn.

Because maybe I didn't have too much thinking time left. And I knew she would be there with me at the end. If even it was just the good memory of her, and who we once might have been.

I was tired and ready for...

Well, I was okay with whatever came next.

Things the linguist does when there isn't coffee to obsess over. And yeah, I'll be honest. I asked about it. Coffee that is. And no... I didn't wait for the battle to be over. Just after Corporal Chuzzo, anchoring the right flank of the shields, told us the captain wanted us to support the shield wall and be ready to replace any gaps, yeah I asked about coffee.

Yes, with mad elves streaming into the opening of the lost library, racing forward with spears out in small clusters, dying as they attacked the shield wall and were stabbed to death, violently and relentlessly by the legionnaires manning the shields, or by the line of spear, using much longer spears than the other two lines to the side, suddenly jabbing forward and skewering these first invaders between the ribs. Or just impaling them on the hip.

When a wounded enemy went down the legionnaire working the spear would simply pull the iron tip back and jam it forward once again for the killing shot this time. Either going for kidneys or the throat.

They were pros, and I was impressed by the skill with which the Legion spear dispatched their downed enemies in those first few moments of the furious battle for the front entrance to the Forbidden Library.

But seriously, as I have said, I would be honest no matter what. Totally honest. So… here it is. Me… at my weakest.

"Hey, Corporal Chuzzo… is it?"

"*Sì*. Anrico Chuzzo from Salurn. You know it?"

"No. We're pretty much new here. But hey, do you guys have coffee? Do you know… coffee? *Caffè?*"

At least I didn't say Happy Go-Go Juice.

He looked at me bewildered for a half second as I tried to make it clear what I was seeking. Nonchalant and all right there in the middle of a battle like, *Hey… is there a Starbucks nearby?* But the Bronze Age equivalent. Something along the lines of "Do you have a fire, roasted beans, a grinder, and some…" I babbled on and on about *Amer-*

169

icanos, ristrettos, and *doppios.* I even said *quattro lungo* because if you're going to ask for an espresso why not ask for four?

It's not like I was expecting them to get a cold brew or even pour-overs going right there for me. But maybe someone had some in whatever they used for a canteen. I was sure they at least had some kind of rudimentary beans, a grinder, and hot water ability.

I mean, c'mon… they're not savages. They're not goblins. Goblin coffee has got to be bad. They probably brew it out of you don't want to know what.

But beans, grinder, and hot water…

Oh mama.

These legionnaires are from a Bronze Age society, and coffee is really old tech. And there were those Portugonian beans we found at the FOB. So chances were good… right?

I had to ask. Don't judge me. I had to.

Still, as the shrill screaming suicide elves ran right into the entrance and threw themselves directly onto the shield wall and died on the Legion's spears, as the Lost Elven archers began to enter and fire, making it clear that the ridiculous tactics of the enemy weren't actually so ridiculous, I asked Chuzzo for coffee.

I am a weak man, and I will never be a Ranger. If there had been coffee in Ranger School, I would have aced that camping trip, easy.

But that's kinda the point. Or so Kurtz white-lined me to near death over.

Corporal Chuzzo was bewildered, and it was clear he couldn't believe I was asking right at that very moment if they had something to drink. I was making drinking motions with a cup using both hands. I probably looked like someone trying to teach a monkey sign language and all. But I was a foreigner to him, and foreigners, in my experience, can get away with a certain amount of social impoliteness due to feigned ignorance if the subject is important enough. To them.

Even at the start of a battle which is clearly looking weird and bad from the get-go.

Also, clearly, we all recognize that coffee is really important to me.

Then, amazingly, a look of sudden awareness dawned in the corporal's eyes, and I could see he was generally excited to tell me that yes, they indeed did have coffee, *caffè*, call it whatever you want.

"Ah, yes! We have-a the *caffè. Sì, sì!*" *Yes, yes.*

Hallelujah, I rejoiced, and reconsidered my view of the universe and divine beings who are indeed benevolent to junkies. All I had to do was survive this battle and hey… coffee! Probably.

"I mean-ha… we did," said Corporal Chuzzo. "We started out from barracks at camp-a with many, many sacks. But… this-a mission has been very hard and as you canna see… out of-ah the five hundred that began… not so many now. *Sergente* Coluzzo, he runna the supply and carry all the *caffè* on his mule, Bessama. But the mule, *povera* Bessama… she got eaten by the desert kraken."

Poor Bessama with all the sacks of coffee. Eaten. And oh… there's a thing called a desert kraken that eats mules. And their coffee. Super. I bet that's pretty horrible.

"So we have-ah… no more of the *caffè. Sergente* Coluzzo, he went mad over it and started eating sand. Then the wights got him and we never found the rest of his body.

The desert is-ah very dangerous. But *caffè* is good. *Sì*. I wish-a we had some."

That close. I was that close to getting coffee.

I turned back to the battle, a grim fatalism overtaking me. Yes. The psychotic Lost Elves were going to pay. Dearly. And then some.

CHAPTER SIXTEEN

THE first of the psychotic Lost Elves to slam into the Legion shield line didn't exactly explode. But in a sense, they were a kind of IED. Improvised explosive device.

Even as I stood there asking my insane questions about coffee and the likelihood of me getting some, then being put right in my place where I belong, even I was thinking that what the enemy was doing at that moment seemed just mindlessly suicidal as they hurled themselves onto the sharp heavy spears of the Legion. Slamming into the massive circular bronze shields the wall held at the center. I was thinking that indeed these creatures, these Lost Elves that seemed the opposite of the almost tranquil Shadow Elves of Autumn's people, were just stupid, or instinctively psychotic, plain crazy as the day can be long.

And so far, given the battle back at the citadel, the underground river ride through the underworld of forever, the running from the Lost Elves, the sand dunes in the desert, the fight for our lives and killy-putty det at the sphinxes... days truly *can* be long. Especially if they're one long three-day... day.

This was feeling like one of those days... because it was.

Kurtz had nothing on this. I was surprised I was still going and for a terrible moment I had that brief fear that if you stop, your heart is gonna give up and call it quits.

But then I thought how great a long sleep would be, even if it was a dirt nap. I could at least dream of having a nice macchiato with just the right swirl of crema and burnt espresso.

Please, please, death, be that. Please let there be a coffee shop in the heaven of wayward linguists who were too busy to figure out an afterlife. Or a Starbucks in hell if that's where I go.

I'll be grateful for at least that. Pitchforks and lakes of fire and all the other sufferings.

But hey, that's every day in Ranger School. The three-day-long impossibly long day thing, I mean. Not the pitchforks and lakes of fire. Though then again…

So yeah I'd been there before, and other than the occasional fatigue hallucination, it was pretty much that brutal. Lack of calories, lack of sleep, and constant mission. But I wanted it and so I'd just started slapping myself and doing push-ups, air squats, or sit-ups just to stay awake and not get caught sleeping by Kurtz and cadre. Which was easier to do when you weren't in a leadership position and all you had to do was watch your sector during a short or long halt.

Easier to nod then. Easier to get caught. Easier to get recycled and smoked goodly.

I'd been here before, at the end of what I thought possible, I told myself. I'd done it then, I could do it again.

But yeah, one big three-day-long… *day.*

The first elves to die against the shield wall of the legionnaires died screaming and waving their wild scimitars or short wicked damascened knives. Like they were actually gonna do something against all that metal and muscle. Meanwhile, the Legion was just mechanically busy spearing and hacking at more and more Lost Elves seeming to fly into their shield wall through the darkness here in the entrance to the library. The enemy came streaking forward out of the moonlight to enter the fight, letting the bodies slam into the wall. Keeping the Legion busy with killing them. And the Legion, in turn, was more than happy to slaughter and let the dead lie at their boots to maintain the integrity of their impenetrable wall.

And then it happened. The strategy became clear.

The mushrooms the dead elves were squeezing in their death throes, hidden and clutched tight in white-knuckled fists, began to emit wisps of eerie green and necrotic blue smoke. Not a lot, but the vapors formed snakes of smoke dancing upward like charmed pythons groping their way over the bronze shields and up to the legionnaires behind them.

"Gas!" I shouted, not sure what I was recognizing but knowing I was seeing some intelligently planned aspect to the madness of the Lost Elven attack.

No one except Joe had any idea what I'd just said, because none of them spoke ten-thousand-year-old English.

Which is weird because the word is the same in both languages. Italian and English. *Gas.* But not necessarily in the same usage. And clearly, these legionnaires had no idea what *gas* was. They would, looking back, have known it more as *smoke.* Or *poison smoke* even. *Vapor* possibly.

Velenoso.

Poisonous.

"*Fumo velenoso!*" I shouted as soon as I figured out why no one was listening to me, comprehending my warning.

The first Lost Elven archers entered the battle within the entrance arena of the library from the open night-shrouded desert, working in small four-man squads, firing slender high-pitched whistling arrows at the shield wall now obscured in blue necrotic smoke. And the troopers behind the shields were beginning to cough and hack. One pitched over, and the legionnaires shouted commands to one another to close the gap.

Instantly a spearman from the rear surged forward through their close rank, grabbed the downed man's shield, and locked in with the rest of the wall.

Integrity restored, the men within shouted encouragement to each other to hold the line as more waves of suicide elves slammed into them like fleshy torpedoes seeking only salvation in death. The Lost Elves laughed as they were hacked and stabbed to death by spear and gladius, and I'll tell you right now... *that ain't right.*

"*Mantieni la linea!*" shouted Corporal Chuzzo above the clang of battle and the wild maniacal laughter of the dusky-blue-skinned elves. Golden hair like fire, faces like demons, eyes rolling with insanity, the foes of the Legion seemed to fear nothing, not even death.

Hold the line!

Another legionnaire went down, overcome by the strangling smoke pythons in dead-skin blue.

Sergeant Joe moved fast, shucked out of the Vickers Sling holding the dangling carbine, and shoved it into my hands.

"Tell 'em, Talker. Tell 'em now I'll take that guy's place on the spear line!"

I translated and Corporal Chuzzo acknowledged this was good, as reinforcements were starting to pull from the spears in the second rank. Joe disappeared into the seething mass of legionnaires ready to hold the line once again as more elves, whipped into a battle frenzy of dancing knives and death cries, flung themselves into the shield line, cutting where they could, hacked to death by the relentless legionnaires whose swollen biceps and huge forearms did the killing work and seemed not to tire in the least as the work grew hot and furious.

This was old-school Bronze Age warfare like no one from our time had ever seen, and it was incredible. And frightening. And… thrilling.

Think less of me… but it felt more like a football game. And… you *wanted* to get into it. Both sides had their own momentum and encouragement into the swirl of battle trying to break each other's lines. Both sides believed, not felt, but *believed* it was that willingness to… play… that was going to make the difference on whose line would break first.

And who would die next.

It was fascinating. And there was something about it that lured you into it even as you watched in horror. Like it was a spell, or a hot chick. Kennedy and his Ranger gamers like to say "Save for this" or "Save for that." "Save against extra duty. Save to clean your weapon." It has something to do with the game that's been explained to me more times than I've been interested in. But in this moment, I think I understand it a little better. Both Sergeant Joe and I were being forced to save versus getting caught up in Bronze Age warfare.

Joe had failed first, and I was about to.

It was like watching two opposing forces coming straight at each other. Neither fazed by the strength of the other. Neither giving out until there was nothing left to give. Immovable force, meet immovable object. Like me and coffee, but the opposite.

Then I remembered they had the numbers. A legionnaire turned and went down, his throat slashed. I hustled into the battle, pulling him out, but his throat was cut clean through, and he died staring at me, choking on his own rage that this had happened to him.

I held his head back trying to clear the airway and feeling powerless. There wasn't a thing I could have done for him. But that didn't make it any better.

"He's gone," said Corporal Chuzzo and we left him near the line. "We do not leave anyone... for them. Do not worry, my friend. We take care of our dead, for we are all we have."

Then he was back in the battle line, pushing his men to hold, picking up the ones who were knocked down, bracing them for next impact. Calling out the gaps, and at the last finally throwing himself in to take the place of a dead man, swinging with his gladius, grabbing a shield a cackling elf had stolen. The Lost Elf was missing a hand one of the other legionnaires had chopped away, the bloody stump pumping blood, but his free hand was carrying a legionnaire shield as more of his buddies came close and cackled, crowing like they'd gained some great victory prize in the middle of the relentless battle.

Chuzzo laid into them with his weapon and won the shield back, leaving some dead and others in disbelief at the rage of the tall, slender legionnaire who was the last NCO standing.

He would not let the shields of his Legion fall into enemy hands. Not the shields of his brothers.

Then Corporal Chuzzo turned, took his place on the line, and called out once more, *"Mantieni la linea! Mantieni la linea, Cani!"*

Hold the line!

Hold the line, Dogs!

I saw Joe drive a spear through the line and push it all the way through a Lost Elf trying to crawl over the top of the shield of the legionnaire in front of the Ranger. He shouted some primal war whoop and shoved the elf off the tip of the spear and down into the bloody slaughter on the ground. The next time I would see Sergeant Joe, he would be holding a shield and rallying legionnaires to stay in the battle when it was at its closest and it was everywhere, and there were no more lines. Just chaos and madness. Blood and slaughter.

One of the shield bearers on Captain Tyrus's side of the battle failed, overcome by the snaky mushroom smoke of the dead elves. He dropped his shield and took three poisoned arrows right in the chest an instant later. The man screamed and then instantly turned blue as all the oxygen seemed to leave his body at once. He died twitching and shaking violently.

The captain shouted at the man holding the spear behind him to move into place, but the gap was wide and two Lost Elves, eyes wild, raced for the sudden opening. The captain stepped forward with his own circular shield, large and round, and slammed the first in the chest, hitting that one so hard he rebounded into the nearest spears and was instantly impaled. Then he thrust his gladius forward in a sudden decisive moment, jamming his blade right into the second elf's chest, driving straight through armor to break the sternum. He shrugged the wide-eyed dead elf from his blade, checked that the shield wall had closed, and faded to his place in the line between spear and shields.

The entire business taking seconds. Little emotion was displayed, and it was clear Captain Tyrus knew his business in these situations. And whereas many of the legionnaires were going on pure violence and even desperate rage, the captain seemed the same as when we'd met him on the sands outside. Cool, calm, but a killer all the same. In every situation.

He cast his eyes across the formation and called out where he wanted his men from one minute to the next.

The necrotic tendrils of gas didn't seem to spread much. They only tried to crawl over the shields of the troopers they had died directly in front of. But the miasma hung there forward of the Legion's line of spear and shield.

Then the captain nodded at the hooded sorceress, and she stepped forward, taking a small bottle off her belt. I could see, by the light of the fire beyond the line, her image in silhouette. She looked good. Then the sorceress upended the crystal bottle into her mouth, looking like some beer commercial hottie in shadow, and threw back the hood of her robe.

Because of the watchfire behind her I couldn't make out any details regarding her obvious beauty. But her shape was decidedly pleasing. And of course... *me likey likey girls.* So she had that going for her.

She waved her hands, two giant windmilling circles, and suddenly a huge gale, just one, entered the area from the nether of nowhere I could tell, driving the necrotic gas snakes out of the entrance and back into the desert, rushing past the jihadi elves. And yet the smoke snakes didn't dissipate, and this is the creepiest part. Instead, they, the smoking snakes that came from crushed mushrooms and weren't really there, they just fled the entrance to the Forbidden Library, slithering off in smoky trails and out into the desert night.

Meanwhile the Lost Elven archers had managed to shoot down some of the spear elements in the Sun Squad element of the Legion spear.

More Lost Elven warriors, these carrying their own round shields, advanced against the Legion shield wall, beating their scimitars against their own shields as they approached the line. Some peeled off to go after the Legion spear on the flanks.

The organization of the battle was beginning to crumble.

The Legion spear line, both of them on each flank, jammed their weapons forward, impaling these new, more heavily armed warriors wherever they could. Still more Lost Elves flooded the entrance, pushing forward to take their turns with the Legion, trampling their own grinning dead for the chance to cut the enemy.

"Ready shields!" called out Captain Tyrus over the battle. At once, the shield line raised their shields at the command as Corporal Chuzzo echoed and added, "Ready…"

Long and protracted, like an NCO waiting on order to execute the command would do.

"Advance!" called out Captain Tyrus.

The Legion corporal echoed the order and suddenly the shield wall moved toward the entrance as one. Hacking with their swords at the dying beneath their boots as they did so.

At the same time, the corporal called out the next of the captain's orders which I didn't hear over the din of the battle as now the elven warriors, more heavily armed than the suicide skirmishers, had begun to hack back at the Legion's shield wall. Swords and shields rang out with exchanged blows, and the yells of men and elves fighting, grunting, and dying sounded beneath it all.

One of the first war spiders entered the Battle of the Forgotten Library at that moment. This one was bigger than the black widows the knights rode, hairy and wider, with two huge fangs hanging beneath its scary face. As if the slaughter needed a real nightmare to witness the carnage, the monstrous spider obliged. It was definitely some kind of gargantuan tarantula bred for battle. A small wooden tower, covered in bronze Lost Elven shields, was mounted to the back of the monstrosity, and two archers fired down into the Legion spear ranks.

Arrows struck the burly legionnaires, but they held the line, getting hit by plunging arrow fire and driving their heavy spears into the unprotected flanks of the warriors now being crushed by the advancing shield wall.

That was when Corporal Chuzzo echoed the commander's order I didn't hear.

"Shield spears pronto in avanti!"

Shield spears forward ready!

The trap, or a response to the elven attack of warriors and spider-mounted archer support, this counterattack was brilliant in its sudden execution. Instantly the tide turned as the more heavily armored Lost Elven shield-bearing warriors were caught by spears on all sides while being driven from the building at the same time.

The Legion had waited for them, had slaughtered them, and were now throwing them out like drunks and whores at the end of a long night of drinking.

I brought the carbine up and drilled the first archer leaning over the parapet on the back of the tarantula. And yes… Joe's rifle was so zeroed that I domed that guy good and proper.

The other guy ducked, figuring out that whatever I had just done that made the head of his Ranger buddy's skull turn to Lost Elven bone matter and red mist was something worth ducking over.

The Lost Elven warriors on the killing floor were hacked to death by the advancing shield line while the spears continued on against the giant spider who stood there stupidly dripping poison from its huge fangs. It reared up on its hind legs as the threat got close, and, I'm not kidding, *roared* before lunging forward faster than I thought possible at the shield wall, biting through two shields, killing one of the legionnaires instantly, and taking off the arm of another who wouldn't live through the night.

I lowered the MK18 carbine sights to the giant tarantula's head, intending to start putting the last of the fourteen remaining rounds into its giant dumb insect, or was it an animal, hard to think of an insect that big, brain. My psionics wasn't even getting any kind of *reading*—and trust me I really don't know what words to use for this stuff—from it. That's how stupid it was. Usually when I'm focused on something, the psionics kick in and give me an indication of how mentally active a subject is.

The tarantula was just plain old bull stupid.

There was every chance the precious remaining amount of five-five-six I'd use up would just go to waste and the thing would keep raging against the shield line, literally biting legionnaires in half as I shot it.

But before I could make that bad choice, the spears from all three sides of the Accadion inverted defensive square rushed forward and entered the giant arachnid from about thirty-six different points.

"Bastardi in avanti strike! Uno, due, tre, quattro!" cried Corporal Chuzzo as the Legion spearmen drove forward as a single unit against the gargantuan tarantula.

Forward strike, bastards! One, two, three, four!

Then...

"Ritirare!"

Withdraw.

As one, the Legion spear withdrew their brutal weapons that had impressed me in ways a sharp stick with a pointy end never could have, or so I thought.

The spider died, crawling away and bleeding.

Then the next wave of elves came on, their own spears supported by arrow fire. And everything fell apart.

For a time, it was just mindless slaughter. Elf to man. Weapon against weapon. Tooth and claw to the end.

Last man standing.

CHAPTER SEVENTEEN

SERGEANT Joe woke with a start, G19 clutched and ready to do instant murder, but not pointing at any targets, including me.

I was glad for that. I'd seen Joe kill. He did it in the blink of an eye the moment you presented a threat to his continued existence, or the mission.

And I'd seen him kill a lot last night. Wading into the press of the hot battle against the Lost Elves at midnight, carrying both a spear and a gladius. Slaughtering with both hands.

Covered in blood, wiping sweat from his eyes as the elves went running off into the desert and the dawn, he'd turned to me and said, "The only thing in life you should fear, Talker, is mediocrity. The only thing."

Now he was awake after being lights-out dead for four hours.

"Bad dream?" I asked and watched him put the G19 down next to the ruck we were using for a base camp. Bad dreams and nightmares would be no surprise after what we had just gone through last night. And pretty much most nights here in the Ruin.

There was always some new horror to whistle over and say, *Well, I hadn't expected that.*

Now I was standing over him with five rounds in the carbine. My watch over. We were active now. The last five rounds we had left waiting in a magazine that didn't feel heavy enough for all the things that needed to be done to get us back to the detachment.

"Yeah… real bad. Just the usual nightmare," muttered Joe, rubbing his shaved head. "Dreamt I was back in Ranger School."

Then he groaned and spat in his hand, looking at it for a second.

We had each gotten four hours' sleep. Joe ordered that I go first and after putting up a total lie that I was good to go and could take the first watch, I quickly fell down next to the ruck, and using my FAST helmet wrapped in what remained of my Crye Precision shirt, I'd racked out and had my own nightmares about the battle we'd fought until the moon went down and the Lost Elves pulled back.

There was something about Autumn in those dreams, but it might have been the dead girl from Portugon I was gonna run away with. Or maybe it was just me wanting something other than my mind trying to process Bronze Age slaughter during that defrag phase we humans call sleep.

I don't know.

After the battle last night, we'd watched the darkness, the Legion dragging their dead off the field of battle inside the entrance to the Lost Library, Captain Tyrus and Corporal Chuzzo organizing a new defense to hold the next massive room within the Forbidden Library with what little they had to work with.

The captain decided to pull out of the broader entrance to the temple, or Forbidden Library, or whatever this creepy weird place is. The entrance where we'd fought was now a bloody mess of corpses and when the heat of the day came it would stink to high heaven. Lost Elves lay hacked to pieces and giant spiders with broken legs, oozing gore and noxious poison, remained in crumpled heaps like festering sores. The Lost Elven magi that had tried to turn the battle had ended as badly as the ground troops. Joe had made sure of that. Capabilities-wise, the only thing we'd brought to the fight that the future ancient Romans didn't already have was the spear that killed from long distance— the MK18 carbine. Joe had spotted the magi about mid-way through the fight and dropped back some behind the shield wall, got some elevation via climbing a broken statue with his carbine, and then proceeded to give them high doses of five-five-six to the head. Rounds we'd once taken for granted that were probably becoming Ruin myth as the Rangers spread out through it. Many of the rest of the sorcerous mages got spears driven straight through them by the desperate legionnaires, who rushed them quick before they could fire their arcane magics. Now the husk-like wizards, wrapped in their purple robes adorned with moons and stars, stared with dead eyes at the carnage within the library in horrific disbelief. As though the impossible, impossibly, had happened to them.

The look on these was different than the psycho foot troops who'd died grinning like drug addicts overdosing on death.

It was one of the worst battlefields, in aftermath, I'd ever witnessed. And yeah, it was the stuff of nightmares, if just for the grinning dead.

And one other note. Bronze Age warfare, with its shield walls, spears, swords, and bad-breath-distance violence was much more mutilating to people… and things… than gunfire. Modern warfare looks almost polite compared to this kind of fighting. I've seen people shot to death that I couldn't even tell were dead. Sometimes, even the monsters almost look peaceful.

Fighting with swords is much worse. Orders of magnitude worse. Trust me on that.

The Legion, along with both Sergeant Joe and me, had remained on our feet until dawn. If they came, we'd fight them again because there was no other option I could see.

"With the sun it will be safe soon… for a while," Corporal Chuzzo told us in the pre-dawn silence. Even the birds didn't come this deep into the desert. Out there the dunes looked cool and sculpted, except for the tracks of our retreating enemies. "The *demoni profondi* do not walk under the glare of the sun. They hate it."

Deep demons.

That's what the Accadions call these Lost Elves we'd just fought.

I spit on one of the corpses and at the time I had no idea why'd I'd done that. I just hated them. Hated them like no other monster or race we'd fought here so far.

Joe looked at me and said, "You been hangin' 'round Kurtz too long, bro. That kinda hate'll eat you up."

But honestly, I hadn't planned to spit on a corpse. I'd just had some bad taste in my mouth, and then I spit on a dead elf nearby. And as I did, it felt good. Maybe it was the dying legionnaires I'd helped last night. Helped to get them out of the battle so they could die in peace for a minute, muttering their prayers to gods I didn't know. Say some name over and over.

I understood that.

Maybe it was that. Maybe that was why I spit. I know so little about myself. Only I'm not who I used to be anymore.

"I take it these guys don't have a lotta love for each other," said Sergeant Joe, indicating the dead elves and the living legionnaires watching the dawn and the horizon, ready for another wave of psychos to come over the dunes and ask for some more of what they had to give. "Ask 'em about that."

I did.

Then I got the story from Corporal Chuzzo.

"Until this mission into the No Man's Land, if you woulda ask-a me…" began Corporal Chuzzo as we watched the first strands of light turning the morning purple in the east. The desert out there was graveyard silent and if the Lost Elves were out there, waiting among the sand dunes, we couldn't see them.

The silence was the purest and deepest silence I'd ever heard. Like you could say words out there into the sand and dust and all that seeming endlessness and they'd be lost forever.

I thought about that. Wondered what I'd say. What I'd tell Autumn that I never could. Maybe that's what the desert is made for. To say all the things you never can. Maybe.

"Until this mission, if you ask-a me, *mio amico…*" continued Corporal Chuzzo. "I woulda tell you they just fairy stories made up to frighten the children and make them come-a home from playing in the alleys of the Last City, which is our beautiful home. I heard-a the same when I was just a little boy with no shoes and no shirt. Then, *hey presto*, I became a legionnaire. And someday I might be a centurion and have a building in Accadios to collect-ah the rent and watch the streets and the children playing ball dreaming of being a legionnaire, you know? But… that's-a if we survive this one, which, I gotta tell you boys, don't look none-ah good for that. So, I guess no being an old leej for me."

I delved further because in no way had the corporal answered Sergeant Joe's question for intel on the enemy laying low out there in the desert who'd just made every effort to kill us and had done surprisingly well at it given our current head count.

There were now fifteen legionnaires not counting the captain and the corporal. The battle sorceress and whatever an Otoro was were also accounted for. And that was about it.

Supplies and ammo, spears, didn't look so hot either. Spears break and there were a lot of them shattered and driven straight through spiders dripping poison and dead Lost Elven wizards, and none of the legionnaires seemed too keen on retrieving those. Like they knew they were un-clean, whether that was due to poisons, dark sorceries, or just the curse of the bad luck that had gotten them march-ing into the desert.

Fifteen legionnaires had died fighting hand-to-hand against the agile Lost Elves who, though armored almost equal to the Accadion legionnaires, moved faster and made almost double the number of attacks in hand-to-hand combat when things had finally gone that way.

The Lost Elves were like PCP freaks, and my guess is there was indeed some drug-usage aspect to their military. That's actually more common than most people know in many militaries throughout the world. Hell, the forty-five was invented to knock down drug-addicted Filipino tribesmen who weren't getting killed by the thirty-eight. And yes, I learned that while spending some time learning Tagalog.

But the Legion armor, and the sheer muscle and ferocity of the Accadion soldiers wearing it, plus their well-practiced tactics of fighting formations and intelligent leadership, had made the day, or the night, last night.

Still with all that, the battle had eventually dissolved into a brutal brawl just to hold the entrance. The three elements of the shield wall and the two lines of Legion spear had broken into smaller teams as the battle lines got ragged and more Lost Elves pressed the attack. Captain Tyrus had assigned priority to taking out the enemy archers mixing among the ranks of foot soldiers who were keeping the lines of spear pinned and unable to move to hit the massed attacks from the flanks. Hit-and-run raids by four-man Legion teams fought their way forward and destroyed the archers wherever they surfaced in the battle line. Corporal Chuzzo and Captain Tyrus, rallying the line while keeping the Legion fighting there as their strength waned, ultimately allowed the legionnaires to pull these hits and maintain a battle line.

It was pretty amazing soldiering. And leadership.

Looked like total chaos to me.

The dead were dragged away. The dying also, so they could have some last moment to settle their souls before moving on.

This became my job because I just decided to start doing it since it needed to be done. Carrying the dying off the battle line. Legionnaires shouting at me hoarsely to take Anrio, or Marca, or Fuzio now to the rear so they could die.

Shouting, "Take him now! He's-a going! *Metti una moneta sotto la bocca!* So his mother can sleep." Tears in their eyes, these swarthy fighting men, bloody faces and sharp weapons in their hands. Turning back to the battle and hacking at the next charge as I carried the dead out of the chaos of the battle.

Put a coin under his mouth so his mother can sleep. That's what they'd said. What they'd demanded I do.

I still carried some of the strange coins taken from the dragon hoard. Part of the divvy the captain and the smaj had made sure we had. Our pay here in the Ruin. Last night I had just enough of the enigmatic coins I'd often studied, and a few to spare.

In the end, as I went into the battle myself, my shield out and a dead man's gladius I was holding in a reverse grip, I hoped there would be no more death for our side because I didn't have many more coins left.

Yeah, of course I fought too. The legionnaires shouted at me that I was holding their weapon wrong. One of their weapons from one of their dead. But the reverse grip had worked for me when using the large knife Brumm had taught me with, the "chopper" as he called it.

"People say it ain't good for much," Brumm had once muttered as he taught me a four-pattern cutting combo with it. "Even Kurtz hates it. But I say… gets the job done, know what I mean, Talk?"

I advanced behind the shield, right flank at the tip of a wedge. Moving forward like some multi-segmented turtle to nail two archers who were taking shots from behind a line of armored Lost Elves.

There weren't many archers left at this late hour. Even the psycho elves seemed ragged and worn. And there was a fear in their eyes as we faced them now and got ready to exchange killing blows and cuts. Fear, and there was anger there too. They knew what they were doing wasn't enough. They'd never faced a foe like these legionnaires, and as we'd learn later from Corporal Chuzzo, the daylight was no friend to them. They needed to be deep underground by the time the sun rose in the morning.

And for them that clock was ticking.

When I went forward with a team to kill the two archers harassing our spear, morning wasn't far off by then. The night beyond the entrance to the library was as dark as it gets. The deepest part of the night. Next comes morning.

The desert air was cool out there, coming in short breaths through the bloody chaos on the library floor. When it came and dried the hot sweat beneath your clothes, you felt like when this crazed night was finally over, you'd just take off your clothes and walk the desert in the night. Feeling cool and alive. Alone. The opposite of the moment of battle.

Reverse grip.

The first Lost Elf I killed came in at me, swung wide with his ornate and even gaudy scimitar, and connected with my shield. The Sharpie-rune-scrawled defense seemed to force my arm into just the right position to effectively, and effortlessly, block the incoming blow.

So maybe it was a magic item, I wondered. Maybe.

Reverse grip on the chopper, the gladius, blade edge outward, I swiped up and to the left, cutting right through my opponent's tendons on his exposed arm. Pushing myself inside his defense immediately. At the end of the first cut, the first form in the pattern for working the chopper as I'd been taught, the blade was high over my enemy's right shoulder. I jammed it savagely down, driving the tip between his clavicle and his scapula. Punching the tip down through mostly soft tissue and right down Main Street to the heart.

The thing about the "clavicle drag" move is that not only do you kill your opponent pretty reliably, but then you also get to control them like a puppet. The reverse grip on the gladius now turning into sort of a joystick for the dead elf on the end of it. Then I did it two more times because the gladius was sharp like a razor and it went in and out with all the ease of something cutting butter. A knife I guess. Good job, Talker. That's some pro-level writing. Something cutting butter. Yikes, sorry Tanner. You'll do better when you find this account and take over. You'll be funnier.

I used the joystick controller to pull the elf down and behind me. He slid off the blade, and the legionnaire in the second rank was more than happy to stick a sword through the enemy's eye. Most likely unneeded at that point, but one can't be too sure in the Ruin.

Now that I had lost my lost elf meat puppet shield I turned my attention back forward. Who wants to be the next contestant on "High Score Ruin"?

The archer I killed one minute later. The first swipe was as I'd done before, a cross-body slash across his exposed throat. The chopper made the cut savagely, but it made it. He was dead and ruined.

We withdrew and a legionnaire named Kaius told me, "I needa to teach youze how we fight-ah with the gladius. You fight like a drunken bull. Dangerous. But you could be more so, know what I mean, my *amico*? Plus you exposed your side, and I woulda stabbed you twenty times by the time you made-ah the second cut."

I told him I'd like to learn, and he smiled grimly as once more we made it back through the spears and Corporal Chuzzo redeployed us to a weaker part in the line to sustain the next push.

An hour later the battle was wild, and man-to-elf single combat was what it was all about as we drove the last of them from the library and they pulled back into the desert early morning, running away silently over the dunes that didn't seem to care about the mess we'd made here.

Not even bothering to fire arrows or lob insults in Hindi as they went. Insults that really might just be orders for a spicy chicken tikka masala with naan bread and maybe some okra.

I don't know. I have no idea. My Hindi is tragically inadequate, according to my standards.

Meanwhile, back to trying to figure out why the legionnaires were here and interrogating, passively, their NCO.

Fail.

Corporal Chuzzo made gestures feigning not really understanding what I was asking and then started getting busy with NCO work as the post-battle operations among the Legion seemed to follow some SOP we didn't know.

I turned to Joe and told him they were being coy about why they were out here.

We waited until the sun rose while the Legion pulled back to the inner sanctum within the library. Guards were posted and Joe found a place to set up our small base camp consisting of his Ruck of Many Wonders. The Legion gave us two leather bags full of water, we ate, and I passed out.

Four hours later, Joe grunted at me that nothing happened and told me he was going down for the count. I took the carbine and watched over him for his four hours of wonderful sleep. Of course I talked to everyone, it's what I do, far too much of it as the Rangers like to remind me. Even Tanner says so from time to time, and he's not short on words himself. Or wasn't, before he died. He talks a bit less now. Death has had an effect on him.

As it does.

I made short forays to whisper to Corporal Chuzzo, and the captain, and one brief encounter, a very weird one, with the sorceress.

I also spotted the Otoro.

Imagine an eight-foot gorilla in samurai armor with big ninja swords. Sitting cross-legged, eyes closed, in deep concentration.

Corporal Chuzzo told me he'd been wounded and poisoned in the running battle across the sands to reach the library. "He's-ah… tryna to heal-a hisself."

When Joe awoke, telling me he'd had a nightmare about being back in Ranger School, I downloaded all the intel I'd been able to scavenge.

CHAPTER EIGHTEEN

"SO, what's the dope, bro?" asked Joe as he drank water and gnawed on his wife's recipe for special beef jerky. Nearby, some of the legionnaires moved about. Off in the distance of the massive hall we'd fallen back to, I could see the hulking Otoro sitting before a small brazier, surrounded by more of the animal-headed statues that lined the walls and reached from the floor to the high ceiling. These all had wings that crossed over our heads, touching in the center of the high hall. Delicate wisps of smoke rose up from the dark brazier in front of Otoro.

The sorceress was not to be seen at that moment, and the captain was with the sentries near the narrow entrance that gave way to the outer entrance we'd fought for, that was really much more of a covered courtyard.

"Situation is this, Sar'nt," I said after getting nothing from the corporal other than a status update. "They came ashore along the Lost Coast, dropped off by a galley during the night after a week at sea. They crossed through the desert, skirting the eastern edge of the Atlantean Mountains, and then came down into the desert the maps call No Man's Land. That was when they encountered the Lost Elves, Sar'nt. They were two hundred strong when they started out and they fought a running battle against spider-mounted archers on all sides. Some of the NCOs wanted to turn back and even Chuzzo said this was a suicide mission. Many of the men suspect the powers that be sent their captain on this mission because they want him dead and out of the way."

"Then why'd they come with?" asked Joe.

"Corporal Chuzzo says the captain is the best soldier in the Legion and has already been hailed *Imperator* on the field of battle, whatever that means, three different times in three different wars."

Joe rubbed his jaw, taking another piece of jerky out for both of us to eat.

"It means, bro, if these guys are anything like Roman legionnaires from back before our time, well… it means this cat has earned the equivalent of the MOH on three separate occasions."

MOH. Medal of Honor.

"It means he's a stone-cold killer in this world," Joe continued. "And yeah, if the politics are as Bronze Age as the warfare, a guy like that evokes a lot more threat than just jealousy. So yeah… they probably sent him out here to die."

I digested this and continued with my intel dump.

"That jibes with the rest of the story, Sar'nt. The captain told them they were sent on this mission, and they were going to get it done. Even when they were taking casualties right and left out there, fighting a running battle for three days in the sand, he kept them headed toward the objective."

"We can feel that," whispered Joe.

"Solid copy, Sar'nt."

"So… why are they out here… *officially?*"

"The corporal's real OPSEC on that, Sar'nt. When I probed a couple times, he just told me to ask the captain and said, '*La Legione non parla fuori dalla scuola.*'"

"Lemme guess… The Legion don't talk out of school?"

"Nailed it, Sar'nt."

"So you went and talked to the captain?"

"Copy, Sar'nt. I was on my way but first I got intercepted by the chick. I mean the sorceress with crazy eyes."

"Yeah. She smokin', yeah? Looks like she could be a heartbreaker from what I could see."

"Yeah. All that, Sar'nt, and then some. But as PFC Tanner likes to say, *I shoulda seen crazy coming, twice.*"

"Tanner," sighed Joe. "That guy. Okay, go on. Crazy eyes."

"Real crazy, Sar'nt. And get this, she 'speak-a the English' as the Accadions might say. Not as good as we do. Kinda ornate and crazy. Like Vandahar. So that's weird. She just came up to me and started speaking in it like she knew I knew it."

"What'd she say to you?" asked Joe.

"She just looks at me and she says, 'You're not supposed to be here, Rangers.' Her voice is all husky and deep. Kinda sexy if that's your deal. Then I said something stupid because I hadn't yet figured out she was crazy. Like, 'Hey, you speak English.' And she shakes her head like I'm too stupid to understand her, or even speak to her, real dismissive like I was a time waste, and says, 'You have no idea the powers of my sugars and syrups, lost little warrior.'"

"And…?" prompts Joe as I try to imitate the look on her face. He'd like me to get on with the intel.

"Well, clearly she thinks she's smarter than me, Sar'nt. So… that bugs me. She has that same vibe I've seen among ivory tower hotties during my time there. Too good for anyone, you know? But crazy girl too. Dangerous. I know that kind."

In other words, as I don't tell Sergeant Joe, the kind of girl that turns a severely damaged individual like myself, on.

I have problems other than coffee.

Sidra. Need I say more?

"Then what?" asked Joe. "She just takes off after that?"

"Yeah, but before she does, she says, all witchy like she's doing her best Chuckles Manson, 'You'll die here. You and the short one might wanna just go ahead and take a long walk off in the desert before tonight. All gonna die. All... gonna... die.'"

Joe laughed and muttered, "Short one? I've run with all kinds of tall babes. Never had no complaints."

I cleared my throat, drank some of our precious water, and continued.

"Then she just leaves me standing there, Sar'nt. She smells like sandalwood too. That's not important and all. Red hair, curly. Crazy eyes, I already said that, that really suck you in. Nice body though. *Nice* body. All kinds of potions, I'm assuming they're potions, on this bandolier she wears. Lots o' crazy psychedelic colors in there. Feels like a witch, Sar'nt."

"The one Kennedy torched. Like that, bro?"

I thought about that for a second.

"Yeah, but hotter, like... you'd go out with her even though there was a good chance you were gonna get turned into a toad and all."

I have problems.

Joe thought about that for a second as he reached into his ruck and took out some pairs of issue socks. One for him. One for me.

I changed out of my other pair and told him about my conversation with the captain.

"I went direct to Captain Tyrus after that and told him what we were doing out here."

"What'd you tell him, and what'd he say?"

"Told him we got separated from the rest of our unit during a battle along the coast. We ended up in an underground river and on the other side of the mountains. We're trying to make our way back to the coast. Told him I couldn't speak for our leadership but that we were working with an ally of Accadios who indicated that we might have mutual interests that align us with Accadios."

Sergeant Joe digested this. "That's good. Well said. Now we just need to figure out why *they're* out here. Because I can't think of any official mission that would serve any purpose out in this sandbox of suck. Seems like a great place to die badly."

"Believe it or not, Sar'nt, the captain actually told me. And that's something because… he's a man of few words. Real few. He indicated they'd been ordered by the 'High Command of Accadios' to find the Lost Oasis and bring back something called the Witch's Eye. What he didn't say, Sar'nt, though it's clear it's what the rest of the legionnaires think, is that this is a one-way mission to smoke him and everyone else is just along for the collateral damage ride. If he knows that, he ain't sayin'. For him it's the mission. Even if it is a suicide mission, it's still the mission.

"So apparently, they, the High Command, know war is coming with the Nether Sorcerer soon. And this Witch's

Eye, whatever it is, to me, as explained, barely, by Captain Tyrus man of few words… would be some kind of combat multiplier on the battlefield for the forces of Accadios. It would let them see the enemy's movements—according to legend. When they started out they had a sage in their party, Ascapius, who had studied its lore his entire life. He knew how to find the Lost Oasis, which is apparently unfindable, and somehow this here library is the actual gateway. But Ascapius died out there on the sand and all his scrolls were burned in the battle and lost to the enemy. The enemy even managed to drag away his body.

"So now they have no way to find their objective. They've fought their way to the library. They've lost their supply train. And going back is not an option for two reasons according to Corporal Chuzzo. One, they have one day's worth of water left, and it would take at least a week to cross the desert, exposed to enemy attacks they don't have the numbers to repel. And two—"

"That's already two reasons there, Talker," interrupted Sergeant Joe. "But I can guess what Reason Number Two is. Tyrus is a no-fail guy. He wouldn't turn back even if he could."

"On target, Sar'nt. He'll search the whole desert to find this unfindable thing until they're out of water, troops, and everyone is dead. Then he'll keep searching."

Joe paused for a long moment and rubbed his head. "This just gets better and better."

"Uh… Sar'nt…"

"Yeah?"

"It gets worse. Or better because I guess that was sarcasm and all, Sar'nt."

"How's that?"

"The Lost Elves who normally hate the daylight… they showed up about an hour ago. Right now, they're moving massive piles of flammable debris—old wood, books and scrolls, wagons—toward the entrance, pushing in behind the piles and shielding from anything the Legion can do, which ain't much considering how few are left and that they really don't have any ranged capabilities. Apparently Tyrus had a platoon-sized element of archers to begin with but they all got smoked out there in the sand. The captain thinks the elves are going to start fires at nightfall near the entrance, use spells, and smoke us out. Which… seems very possible."

Sergeant Joe considered. "Any other way out of here?"

"Negative, Sar'nt. Just the one entrance, which is also the only exit. And the Lost Elves out there, they came back with all their friends. And I mean *all* their friends. From what I can see, it looks to be a couple thousand. In about three hours they're gonna storm this place and wipe us all out. That is, according to Corporal Chuzzo and the way the betting is going with the rest of the legionnaires. They're currently betting on their own demise."

Joe laughed once, but his heart wasn't in it.

Then: "I get that."

I nodded, but I didn't. I try to always bet on me to win.

"That ain't gonna happen," the sergeant said. "Is it, Private Talker?"

"No, Sar'nt. It's not."

I meant it.

"All right then. Let's see if we can bail these jokers outta this mess they got themselves into."

CHAPTER NINETEEN

"OUR mission is a… one-way mission."

Captain Tyrus was near the sentries. He'd been watching the Lost Elves out there, busy with their bonfires and mischief. The afternoon wind was up and that wasn't going to be good for us if it kept blowing right into the entrance. The smoke and fire would come soon. We'd asphyxiate before we burned.

Then they'd still come in and chop us up. Their plan was brilliant and there wasn't much we could do about it.

But there was something about the desert wind, and I didn't, or rather couldn't, put my finger on it at that moment. We were too busy watching the dark-robed shapes out there in the fading afternoon, Lost Elves combat engineer types pushing more and more flammable material forward toward the entrance. Prepping the battle space for the final assault.

And like I said, the Legion didn't have the numbers to do anything about it. What was gonna happen next, was looking like it was gonna happen.

The Legion captain had stepped away from his constant watch of the enemy to talk with us for a moment. Still, he kept his eye on the enemy, watching them do their evil work. I could tell he was trying to figure a way out of this, and he wouldn't stop until he had, or was dead.

The other legionnaires, hard as they were, seemed resigned now to what was about to happen. They'd figured the odds and had bet accordingly. Literally. The tougher ones promising corpse piles at their feet. Other soldiers of Accadios praying silently and looking skyward. Making their peace or offering some deed or service for salvation rendered.

They were open to all offers.

Corporal Chuzzo went about cheerily reminding everyone to keep their gear ready in case the legionnaires who came to find their bodies needed more gear.

"It's-a the least we can do for our brothers, *Cani*."

Some smiled at this. Others laughed and slapped the NCO on the back, telling him it was good someone would be with his wife now that he was going to be dead soon.

"That's-a fine," Chuzzo said. "Franchessa... she is too much beautiful to ever be the alone-ah. Plus, I'd killa them if they were still alive. And I don't want to be flung from the rock for murder. That would break my family's heart."

So yeah, the mood was grim. And thus like all soldiers... jokes in the face of death were made.

"It's a one-way mission," continued the captain as I translated for Sergeant Joe. "I knew that. There was no other choice—for me, or for the men. They would have crucified us all if we hadn't gone. But it is a mission, and there is an artifact to retrieve. And war is imminent. Someone had to go. Why not us? And Ascapius was clear about the Eye's usefulness. So there was a chance we could make it back, if only because the High Command needs such a thing."

"Ask if there's any way back to the coast, bro, once they get the artifact," Joe had me ask the commander.

"If we could get there, we could get back," answered Captain Tyrus after a moment's consideration. "The Oasis, whatever it is, has water, for that is the nature of oases. So we would be fine for the long march back to the coast. We could go wide, if we had to, and try to thread the Valley of the Kings in the Land of Black Sleep and come to Sûstagul. There was once an old Legion garrison there, and pirates who would take us back to Accadios for pay. But with only one squad of fifteen... that valley of traps and tombs after dark would swallow many of us whole, if the old legends are to be believed."

"So what was your plan?" I asked.

The Legion captain grew silent for a moment and watched the desert out there. The first bonfires had been lit by the Lost Elves and the smell of burning wood had begun to drift into the library.

"The Stairway to Hell. We would try that."

"I have no idea what that is," I said in the silence that followed.

"Northeast of here by reckonings of the stars," answered the captain, "there is a pass called the Old Atlantean Road. One of the Old Ones' fortresses guards the pass, but the defenses watch the Lost Coast to the north. The Guzzim Hazadi scouts say the desert side is undefended— if they are to be believed. The Stairway to Hell comes out of the back of the fortress and down to the desert floor. It is lightly defended by a series of watch towers, and we could take those by surprise. We could go that way and take the fortress from the rear, fighting our way to the main gate."

"Would that be... difficult?" I asked stupidly.

"Nothing is ever easy," said Captain Tyrus. "The Lost Elves hold the fortress. But an attack by stealth and a running fight through to the other side while starting fires within the fortress itself to cause confusion… might let us make the gate. And then turn for the coast. Once we're there, the Lost Elves won't come down out of the pass. Survive the coast and we can get the Eye back to Accadios and the generals."

"Does he have a map?" asked Joe once I'd translated all this back.

I confirmed with the captain, then said, "He does."

"I'll bet that fortress would put us out near the line of march for the task force. That's the way we get back, Talker."

"True that, Sar'nt. Problem is we're pinned down in here on top of which it sounds like we'll need an attacking force to take the fortress from the rear. Rangers can do anything, Sar'nt, I embrace that, but…"

"I read you. Honestly it still sounds like a suicide mission that way. But his force, us, and some long-range scout skullduggery might just get us a chance for that run down to the coast, where we know we have friendlies."

"Copy all that, Sar'nt. How do we get out of our current predicament to… let me get this straight… attack an entire enemy-held fortress from the rear with fifteen guys? Plus the captain and Chuzzo. And a hot witch who might be, and probably is, crazy."

Sergeant Joe mused about that for a moment. "Don't forget that ape samurai guy. He seems like a wrecking machine. How much you wanna bet, I hit him with an atropine injection, his poison clears up. That or he throttles me. Never fought an ape, but hey, there's a first time for everything. Still, if he straightens out, that thing's build like an Abrams, so we got our own main battle tank goin' for us. And maybe we got a force multiplier, too, if this one-way mission is all it's cracked up to be. Ask Tyrus why the sage... is that what their Gandalf was called before he got wasted in the sand? *Escapus?*"

"Ascapius, Sar'nt."

"Yeah, that guy. You told me Ascapius thought this library is the gateway to the eye thing they're looking for. Ask Tyrus what the hell that means. Specifically."

I did.

Translating is so glamorous. It's like having three conversations all at once while participants stare at you impatiently. But the captain seemed to get that we could be of value to the survival of his men and success of his mission, so he let us work through all the info we needed.

"Apparently, Sar'nt, Ascapius said that, and these are the captain's words, *by maps and reckoning on foot, or even the eagles of the air, the ancient legends say that the Lost Oasis is not just lost, it's hidden, and that there's no way to find it.*"

"Well, that doesn't seem helpful," noted Joe.

"There's more, Sar'nt. Apparently this library, and there are others out here in the desert, has books that show the way to the Lost Oasis."

Joe looked around in the hall of animal-headed obsidian statues with wings that covered the ceiling above. Each statue seeming not to even see us. Unconcerned that we were about to get roasted and then hacked to death in here. But they were just statues of what someone thought a god was. What do you expect out of rock and stone?

Near the door, one of the sentries began to cough, and the captain ordered everyone to don their Legion version of the shemagh.

"Books ain't exactly a gateway," Joe said, looking around. "More to the point, I don't see no books here."

"Yeah. Me neither, Sar'nt."

I asked the captain if they'd found any books here. He summoned Corporal Chuzzo and spoke rapidly, telling the junior NCO to lead us into the inner library.

Corporal Chuzzo led us through the waiting-to-die legionnaires and past the silently mumbling Otoro with a beatific look on his face. Whether he was aware of us or not I don't know. But I can tell you this: getting near an eight-foot-tall gorilla sheathed in samurai armor... was unsettling. Sergeant Joe was right about the beast being like an Abrams tank. Infantrymen get very nervous around tanks. They have five weapons and it's the last two that are the worst.

A main gun. A co-ax seven-six-two. A fifty.

And a right and left tread.

That's the part infantry hate.

Otoro felt dangerous. Like he was the warm knife that did go through warm butter.

Hey, I nailed the metaphor. Look at me writing and all.

Raw power, like that of a dangerous animal that had learned to control itself, barely, emanated from the creature's very presence.

For a moment the samurai smiled as we passed, as though drifting in some pleasant sleep, and revealed animal gorilla fangs, short and vicious. Reminding you what it really was deep down inside. I don't know if that was even its smile. It just seemed like it as we passed near the smoke of its brazier and meditations as it tried to control the runaway poison. Perhaps it wasn't a smile at all but just a trick of the lighting, a shadow thrown from the flickering ancient torches the legionnaires had ignited along the walls.

Dangerous. That was the word in my mind. Psionics? Or just plain old common sense. But something was warning me to be *very* careful around it. I was glad Joe didn't suddenly jab it with an atropine injection. It felt like fifty-fifty between helpful or murder spree.

There wasn't one of us that could have stood up to that beast.

The corporal led us to two doors I hadn't noticed before. The entrance to the inner sanctums was hidden between two of the tall animal-headed statues. Corporal Chuzzo pulled on one that was already half open, and beyond the portal we saw the most fantastic library I've ever seen.

That anyone has ever seen.

CHAPTER TWENTY

THE ceiling was impossibly taller than the building we'd witnessed from the outside. The low temple and the rising crooked obelisk the Lost Elven army was currently surrounding. Shelves of old books, archaic scrolls, and all manner of curious objects rose five stories tall above the stone floor we were standing on.

Empty braziers waited around the center of the room, and at all four corners stood statues of cat-headed humans, each one different, carved of that gleaming-in-the-dark obsidian and acting like flying buttresses to the room above. But really it was as though they were watching us. Staring down at us. Waiting to devour us. Waiting for us to do the wrong thing.

And we had no idea what the wrong thing was.

The sorceress was here, too. In the dark. Immobile. Watching the shelves. Her back to us. Wrapped in her hooded robe. She was tall. And through the robe you could see her shapely hips and rear by the light of Corporal Chuzzo's torch.

Very shapely.

I have problems. But hey, she might be the last girl I ever see. So...

We're about to be burned to death. Then chopped up.

The corporal took his torch and lit one of the braziers.

She'd been standing here in the dark before we came in. No… that's not creepy at all. A totally not-witch thing to do. Perfectly normal.

She turned as we entered. Then spoke like a normal person. Not the crazy witch I'd dealt with before, early in the day.

"Ascapius said the books would show us the way… but…"

Her voice was now that of some frightened soprano. Tiny and high. I fully expected her to start talking with her little finger next like some total psychotic. Totally different voice than the one I'd heard before. If her hair had changed color, I was gonna freak out. But she left the hood of her robe up and I couldn't see if it had.

There was… here… a clear silence. I don't know how to explain it any other way than that. And there was one other thing here. In the center of the room, before the stories-high bookshelves where uncountable manuscripts ancient lay, was a lectern. Right in the center of the braziers, just before the wall of ancient tomes.

But that silence. It was clear. Startlingly clear. True. The opposite of the muffled heavy silence of the desert beyond these walls. A desert one could lose oneself in. Forever. It was as though the molecules were—in here in this inner sanctum—*lighter* here. The air somehow cleaner. Something… *other* was the very definition of here.

Gandalf… I mean Vandahar. Or even Kennedy. Either one would have been really helpful right now because I was feeling like this was the kind of place that was their specialty. A place where the magic was loose and wild.

The fire in the brazier grew and then fluttered from some breeze that had followed us in past the fires of the

Lost Elves, the waiting-to-die legionnaires with their determined commander, and the wide-open desert out there turning to evening.

"But I do not have time… to read…" mumbled the sorceress like some creepy lost little girl you find alongside the highway and then find out later is a ghost or something.

She turned back to the wall as though in a trance, her gaze traveling over the shelves, cluttered and littered with leatherbound tomes and fraying yellowed piles of parchments.

"This place is an inferno waiting to go up. Bet we could use that if we need to," said Sergeant Joe, still trying to figure a way to kill our way out of this one. Like Rangers do. Or at least kill our enemies as they killed us. That was always considered a win in Ranger culture.

Then…

Then I got this really weird feeling. Like I wasn't there, right there, at that moment. Like the molecules were just light enough… for me to be somewhere else right now if I really wanted to.

The air felt… *slippery.*

It was psionics talking this time. Had to be. And no, it didn't give me the magic answer or point me toward the right book that told us the grid coordinates to go find the Witch's Left Shoulder or whatever. And even it had… we still had to fight our way out of here.

That was looking less likely by the second.

Smoke was starting to come into the room now. The fires of the Lost Elves were growing and getting bigger out there in the desert night.

"It'll be dark soon," murmured Corporal Chuzzo as though reading my mind, or maybe I was broadcasting my thoughts à la psionics. He too was staring in awe at all the books rising above our tiny little existence. It felt like ten thousand years of books in here. "Not much time left now," whispered the Legion corporal.

But that *otherwhere* feeling… it was everywhere now.

It was the same as… and the opposite of… and better than… *I know, weird, but that's how it is and that's how I'll describe it…* it was the same as the moments where death had been close since… since Autumn married the king and became Queen of the Shadow Elves.

These were the moments when I thought my last was at hand… and I chose to think of her. Because that's all I had left.

The moments since the dream of the Cities of Men, and the two of us in a rowboat that had a patchwork sail, just the two of us starting over… I'd had those thoughts every time death was close. Thoughts of us.

Even before the battle last night. Before the Lost Elves smashed into our line and all the dead and dying that followed.

I was in my body as I stood there in the inner sanctum of the Forbidden Library. But I swear I was listening to some old Jimi Hendrix song. Except, turned into a hymn now in the Ruin. And I could see Autumn in the place of the secret Shadow Elven chapel to the Hidden King. There, in the *Tumna Haudh*.

It was evening there too. Fortress Hawthorn.

Evening prayers.

What did the Catholics call it? Vespers.

I could see Last of Autumn, no longer dressed in armor. The plain robes of a woman like the other Shadow

Elven women of the fortress. Some of whom had come to love some of the Rangers.

But there was still something... royal about her that had nothing to do with her being just a queen.

She was kneeling in front of her stone cross deep within that chapel no one who was not a Shadow Elf had ever seen.

Praying to her god.

And I could tell, for just a moment, there in that library lost in the No Man's Land, surrounded, the molecules feeling so light that I could just slip right through them and be with her now...

I couldn't hear her whispering her prayers.

But I could tell... she was praying for me.

"Are you crying... bro?" whispered Sergeant Joe.

I swallowed hard.

I might have croaked "Yeah" as I began to walk forward now. Following the barest of desert drafts as it came into this inner sanctum.

A tear had run down my dusty, bloodstained cheek. I wiped it away and continued forward. Trying to hold on to the vision of her praying... *for me*. It was gone. Fading. As was the old music made... Ruin now.

But now, this slippery moment in the cosmic universe of everything I don't understand... had given me a clue. And even that wasn't important to me.

The knowledge of what I'd seen. What it meant. *That...* that was everything to someone as lost in the desert as I was.

But their sage had said the books would show them the way once they made it here. The Legion. Captain Tyrus on his suicide mission beyond the maps only marked as No

Man's Land near the edges of yellowed parchment. There had to be, what, five million books in here? But don't quote me. I'm bad with numbers. I do words.

"Talker..." said Sergeant Joe from far away as I walked into the books, staring upward, not really knowing what I was looking for and knowing it was impossible to find. Knowing that what I was really doing was more like... stalking. Following the trail to the answer.

I followed the breeze to the foot of the massive stories-tall bookshelf.

I wasn't crying anymore. I'd only cried once. Heaved a sob and let a tear fall. I thought she'd scrubbed every memory, and even the existence of me, from her mind. When I'd been near her... her face had betrayed nothing. I no longer existed for her anymore.

But what I had seen in that brief vision...

... was true.

Just listening to the silence at that moment. Listening to the universe. Hearing within the vast silences of it all... the delicate flap of ancient pages. Somewhere here... somewhere along the shelf.

Just barely.

Current events whispered that we were surrounded and knowing where to go next didn't matter. *Time is running out, Talker. We aren't getting out of here. What does it matter?*

But she was praying for me under the first stars of evening in a place the Rangers had begun to call home now.

We could never be together. She was the queen now. But in the quiet evenings, first stars out, first stars I see, wish I may, wish I might, when the tired king who'd been the dragon's prisoner of war, his body and mind ruined, had gone to bed to sleep and dream without pain and suffering, she went to the chapel of a hidden god and offered something for my safety.

Prayers. Promises. What can you offer the gods that they don't have? What can you offer a king who remains hidden? I do not know the Shadow Elf god.

But…

Sometimes you can love someone, even if you can't anymore.

I looked to my left, then my right, scanning the shelves. Waiting for the breeze off the desert floor to show me… what we needed.

To my right, three shelves above my head, just within tiptoe's reach, an old book's pages fluttered, and my breath caught just as it had during the sob.

Sergeant Joe was next to me.

"I smell water, man."

I took the book down. Held it. Felt the power within it. Smelled that smell of water, smelling like lead, coming from it. It was like a weight in the universe. A stone you could throw into a pool.

I walked to the lectern at the center of the room, stood over it for a hesitating second… and then placed the book there.

Nothing happened.

But you could feel the power.

"Open it, bro," whispered Joe in the reverential silence of this place.

Something dangerous was about to happen. But that had been every minute of this day. And for a long time before that.

"Stand back," I croaked. Closed my eyes. Saw the last image of Autumn rising from her prayers, everything dissolving into the forest mists and the stars and night above. Knowing I still meant something.

And that you can love someone, even if you can't anymore.

And then I opened the book.

CHAPTER TWENTY-ONE

"IT'S a stargate..." mumbled Joe from behind me.

I had no idea what a stargate was.

"From the movie, except without all the future stuff," explained the NCO.

No idea there was a movie called *The Stargate*. I was probably too busy learning Chinese, in all three of its forms. 'Cause I'm a player like that. Chicks dig me. So...

... apparently, once again, I am woefully under-prepared for the actual world I ended up in. Silly me, I thought I'd be doing languages for diplomatic functions that involved cocktail parties and hot foreign spy chicks in little black dresses. Not trying to survive in the kind of fantastic worlds that schlock movie directors and hack sci-fi writers think up just to keep themselves in comic books and collectible movie memorabilia.

Who knew the future was gonna get weird? If I had, I woulda been more interested in Ren faire stuff and longswords.

So call it the stargate. Sure. To me it was more like a bubble in time and space, filled with the clearest, most effervescent water ever known, that kept bubbling and expanding within the volume of the whatever it was.

It didn't even look real. More like a movie special effect. But... there it was.

I looked over at Corporal Chuzzo. His mouth was hanging open. Like comically wide open.

For the Bronze Age legionnaire, things had just departed the norm.

He looked like a deer in headlights.

I'd opened the book, and the space-time bubble had suddenly sprung into existence right there in front of the five-story bookshelves filled with rotting tomes and aging parchments from ages lost. Some shelves were even stacked with precarious piles of scrolls.

It's important to note at this point that the sheer volume of knowledge there in front of us… was probably irreplaceable by Ruin standards. By any standards. That was not lost on me. Everything that had ever happened to the world, or in the world, since we'd left, all of the accumulated wisdoms, histories, understandings of magic, and even how *the Ruin Reveals*… even those scrolls the old wizard Vandahar sought everywhere we went, like *The Book of Skelos*… even those must be in there somewhere in that mess, or at least fragments of it… all of it was probably in there. But it would have taken a lifetime to even begin to catalog all of it, much less read it.

And to understand it? I wasn't stupid enough to even try to put a timeframe on that. Except… well maybe never.

In other words, there was a lot of knowledge lying right there in front of us.

And better than knowledge, I realized… there had to be a vast amount of languages just dribbling off the yellowed crumbling parchments and massive tomes. You'd need a Me handy just to understand it all.

Someone that I once was drooled at the possibility for a moment, standing there in front of all those beautiful words I could discover. Words that had been lost to time. Forgotten. Understood. And used once again. But then the space-time bubble, and the world we could barely see on the other side of it—or through it, or within it—appeared, and the new me, the guy who'd run, and hung, with the Rangers, the most elite fighting force the world had ever known...

... wanted to go in there instead. Inside that world. Explore it, scout it, and fight whatever was in it to get the mission done.

It was like I could see two Talkers there watching the whole scene for a moment. The boy I once was... and who I was now.

I wasn't that kid anymore.

"What's a stargate, Sar'nt?"

I mean... I could figure it's obviously a gate to other worlds, or stars probably, by the name of it. But from what I know about stars, how hot they are... it's probably not a gate to stars. And I bad idea if it is.

"It's a bridge to another world," mumbled Joe, destroying my theory about stars.

"Seems like a way outta here, Sar'nt."

Behind us, the Lost Elven war drums were beginning to beat out there under the stars of an early desert evening. Soon it would be full dark. Time was running out. Their shrill horns would soon start, indicating their call to attack.

"Yeah. That's what I'm thinking, bro. And someone's got to go through first. I volunteer me."

I stepped close, and Joe put out a hand like a small tree trunk to stop me.

"Is that... an oasis in there, Sar'nt?"

Through the bubble in space-time, we could see white desert sands. Then crystal-blue waters. A small oasis ringed with beautiful palms, a small quiet village made of odd-sized square buildings like something you'd see in Greece on the island of Mykonos.

Again, another Sidra memory.

It was like looking into a snow-globe world. The waters in the oasis were crystal clear and you could see the bottom of the pool beneath the water. Ancient carved stones were fitted together there showing scenes I couldn't quite make out from this side of the bubble. But it was clear all of it was one giant mosaic like something from ancient Roman and Greek times, lying there beneath the clear blue waters. More like a pool than a lake.

And more like a picture-perfect resort than an oasis. That is, if the Ruin did resorts.

Near the far end of the small kidney-shaped oasis lay a tent pavilion that looked like something out of *1001 Arabian Nights*. A giant white tent trimmed with gold. It was grand and eloquent in its pristine beauty, and again it reminded me more of the picture-perfect Madison Avenue version of what a desert oasis should be than the actual real-world version.

So... maybe this was an illusion. Or a trap.

Through the bubble in space-time, it looked luxurious and inviting, and to me that smelled like a trap of some kind.

I said as much.

"I don't see any threats in there, Sar'nt. But... maybe the whole thing is one giant trap made to look so good we get sucked in. Especially now with our options running low."

Joe had already decided. As I knew he had.

"I don't see another way, bro. We buy the ticket and take the ride. Feels more to me like a jump. And I'm just the guy to do it. Plus, we outta tickets and the fun zone's about to close. I say we jump."

Everything the two of us were adding to the decision tree was on point. But in the end, it came down to one thing: there were no other options. In about ten minutes, those shrill Lost Elven battle horns were going to start up and then we were going to fight room-to-room and see how many corpses we could stack, damn you Brumm, for the win.

"Should we tie you off with some cord, Sar'nt?"

"Yeah, good idea. Run and grab our gear, I'm gonna do a few tests. Tell the commander this looks like our way to his OBJ. Tell him if this is good to go, then we pull back to this inner sanctum and exfil through the bubble. Once I'm in, I'll give you the visual thumbs-up it's good to go in case it's one-way. I'll establish a security halt, then we'll set up a patrol base once we get a recon going. We're gonna treat these guys as a patrol, so you're the ASL and I'm the team leader. You got your duties down, Ranger?"

"Roger, Sar'nt. Once I get the visual, I'll start moving them through and brief the corporal on the security halt and which positions along the clock they're gonna occupy. Then I'll start sending them through, Sar'nt."

Again, I'd learned stuff in Ranger School. For me that was a pretty okay backbrief.

Which is what Rangers do when a leader gives them a mission and they repeat back everything expected of them so it's clear they understand next steps.

"Good to go. Do that. Also, I want you to be the last guy through, Talker. You carry that book. But first…"

He reached down to his battle belt and pulled off an ANS-14 thermite grenade.

"NCOs always carry one extra to det engine blocks or sensitive info, bro. I got two because—"

"Because if you got one you got none, Sar'nt."

"Copy that, Ranger. Pull the pin, deploy the grenade onto the shelves. It doesn't explode, it just burns. And it burns hot. Real hot. Why are we doing this, Ranger?"

"Burritos, Sar'nt."

He smiled and slapped me on the shoulder.

"Rangers lead the way, kid. I hope the bubble doesn't collapse when you pick up the book, but that's the chance we gotta take. Run, get the ruck… we're goin' through. Det the library and make 'em think we burned up inside."

"Then burritos, Sar'nt."

"Macho-size, bro. Macho-size."

CHAPTER TWENTY-TWO

I popped the spoon and rolled the thermite grenade against the bookshelves. Before it exploded just a little, throwing sparks and flame against the dry tomes and dusty ancient parchments stacked five stories high, I grabbed the book that had opened the bubble. I kept it open, holding it out like some reverential high priest from some lost age of long ago, and I strode toward the bubble and saw the rest of the patrol of legionnaires and Sergeant Joe waiting on the other side. The sorceress and Otoro were there too.

Flames grabbed the books all around me and turned them into living breathing torches within just the few steps it had taken me to walk from the lectern to the bubble. Updrafts sent burning manuscripts up and away, catching other shelves on fire instantly, as the desert wind from outside suddenly gusted through the old temple, past all the carved idols and dead, sucking up more oxygen and creating more fire. The Legion had stacked their dead and set fire to the pyre in the last moments before we surrendered the outer hall, the Lost Elves storming the front entrance and looking for a fight we could not give them.

The legionnaires told their dead "*Ave*" until they would meet again.

Then they grabbed their gear and followed Chuzzo through the bubble. Captain Tyrus and two sentries held the rear guard and came through at the last. The elves were now in the inner hall and howling for murder.

"I'll go when you go," ordered the Legion captain.

I shook my head. "Go now, sir. I think the one with the book can close the portal, or at least keep it open, as he goes through. You might not make it if you go through at the same time as me, sir."

The captain nodded, understanding the situation, understanding my untested logic that was only a hypothesis, and then strode through the bubble with none of the hesitation the rest of his men had indicated.

Even the giant gorilla in samurai armor had sniffed at it and growled. Then Chuzzo had said, "This is the way, *mio amico*, our only chance now."

That was when I heard it speak. It was a low deep rumble, and the cadence and tone were clearly... Japanese.

Man, the Ruin gets stranger and stranger.

It spoke Italian first. But like some old movie actor like Toshiro Mifune might have spoken Italian. Grim. Determined. Hard. A growl made by an eight-foot murder machine. Death personified.

"I do not like this. This is not the way."

"I understand that it is not your quest. But it'sa the only way now, my big friend. Go."

Then, in Japanese, the gorilla samurai grunted something as it drew one of its massive ninja swords off its back. It was the longest sword I have ever seen. It held it out and to the side, straight up and down, and I had no doubt it could cut anything in half that it wanted to.

"If this gets me to Axe Grinder... then it is what it is."

And the huge thing went through.

But the Legion captain, to him it was just Ruin Tuesday, and strange space-time bubbles, or sand krakens, or one-way suicide missions into the desert didn't matter at all. All that mattered to this one was the way forward to accomplishing the mission. That was his thing. Stargate or not. That was what he was made for.

Now, with half the wall of books on fire, the shrill horns ululating within the temple already, it was clear the Lost Elves were fighting their way through the heat and smoke outside to follow us so they could kill us. Soon this room would be an inferno and there was no way they could follow us any further, much less stand the heat.

There was every chance they would have no idea what had happened to us. The heat would be too intense for them to enter this area of the burning temple for days.

I stepped through.

I felt myself turn to bubble gum for an instant, and then I was standing on a dry desert dune, warm sand beneath my feet, looking at the beautiful resort oasis in real time.

It was bright noon here.

It had been evening where we'd come from.

Corporal Chuzzo had sent his men to the various stations of the patrol clock just as the Rangers ran their halt. They'd even taken one knee like we did. Everyone watching their sector. Joe was low on his belly and watching the oasis through his monocular. The Ruck of Many Things on his back.

I'm sure in his constantly teaching whirlwind, he's shown them exactly what must be done.

Now they were learning how much the short halt on one knee sucks. But how vital it is when stalking.

I turned, saw the bubble in space-time, and saw the burning library only by the firelight cast from the wall of shelves. Saw the door we'd closed and spiked against the mad elves. Soon they'd be through.

I closed the book, and the bubble popped out of existence.

Now we were here.

Wherever here was.

CHAPTER TWENTY-THREE

WELL, the sorceress took the Witch's Shoulder. Correction. Eye. The sorceress took the thing we, well really, the Legion, came for. The Witch's Eye.

So, that's on them.

Bet you didn't see that coming.

Apparently neither did we.

"Don't you have *psychics*, or something?" muttered Sergeant Joe to me in the catastrophic aftermath of the witch's magical disappearance. "Isn't that what that nerd PFC Kennedy said happened to you here and all? Like the guy in Third that got turned into a bull?"

Minotaur.

Psionics.

"Copy, Sar'nt. Negative on my ability to predict the future. I can... mind-blast stuff and see while I'm blind. So far that's all I've figured out."

"Well, that's your excuse. I don't know what mine is, but she sure did pull a fast one on all of us."

We were standing in front of the genie whose oasis this was. The Legion captain wasn't shaking with rage, exactly. But there was a dark storm cloud of death-wrath hovering over all of us. And it was coming from him.

The moment was dark and uncertain. Very dark. Very uncertain.

"You have used one wish," said the genie in his booming, perpetually friendly voice. Interrupting our stunned silence at having been tricked by the witch. He smiled, and his teeth shone brilliantly against his crimson burnt cinnamon skin. "You have two more left, Master."

He was talking to me. I'm... *Master*.

"I think... Al Haraq..." I began. "That will be all for the moment."

"Most excellent, Master," boomed the perpetually happy genie. "I truly live to fulfill the last two of your wishes. Make yourself at home in the oasis, but mind the rules as I have explained them to you. I wouldn't want you to get more than you bargained for."

Then he laughed thunderously, turned to smoke, and once more entered the great ruby-colored bottle we'd found inside the pavilion tent at the end of the oasis.

A lot has happened. I'll explain.

The genie was speaking English. And apparently, I was his master now and I'd been granted three wishes, one of which we'd just used to get the Witch's Eye. Which the witch from Caspia, the sorceress, promptly took hold of, cast a spell on herself that made golden sparkling circles like hula hoops surround her, spinning madly faster and faster, then connect at points as she just disappeared.

It was clear by her taunting laughter that this had been the plan all along.

Now the Legion captain was speaking to me in Italian. His rage was barely controlled. But it was controlled. So, despite having my own genie and being a *master*, I was still working for everyone else. Plus, I felt that Sergeant Joe wasn't too happy with how I'd phrased the wish, which we'd spent the better part of an hour crafting just to get it right.

To be fair, I had taken charge of that task because words are my thing and all. And so... I'd left the door open for her to just grab the prize and run. Or disappear. Which is exactly what she just did.

Fun, huh?

"The generals sent her along to make sure," began the Legion captain, his face pure murder, his voice controlled even though the teeth were gritted. I had the feeling he was about a hair's-breadth away from going murder o'clock on someone. "They made sure that even if we survived the desert, and this one-way mission that had to end in death, that she would take the Eye and leave us stranded here. This... is their design. I bear you and your sergeant no ill will. You saved my men."

A lot has happened since the last entry, but it's only been about four hours. The sun is going down near the oasis. The fifteen legionnaires are lying in the sand in a rough circle, and they can't keep their eyes off the three fantastic beauties that came with the aforementioned genie.

Taraia.

Smyra.

And... Asamina.

Imagine three smoking hot Middle Eastern beauties with Instagram followers of about thirty-two million worldwide back in the day ten thousand years ago. Cat's eyes. Lithe. They're wearing silks that don't leave much to the imagination. Taut bellies you could crack an egg on. Rich, lustrous, dark hair. Huge eyes and long lashes. They know how good they look and it shows.

There's just one problem.

Touch 'em and you stay here forever with the genie. Those are the rules Al Haraq outlined as the terms of the wishes and the service of the genie. He's very businesslike for an ethereal being that can grant fantastic wishes and all and who, it seems, lives in an alternate reality that ain't Earth. Also, according to the rules, you can't have any of the treats they, the three deadly beauties, have offered us. Dates, spiced meats, fruits so luscious and juicy you didn't think they made fruit like that where we came from. That also gets you a prison sentence here.

They've offered to dance for us. Or massage the muscles of the legionnaires, and by the way they cast their huge eyes and long lashes, it's very clear they're interested in more, as the personal ads like to say.

Nope and nope. Touch 'em, or let them touch you, and you're trapped here forever.

And still you can't help but weigh whether it might be worth it.

There are Middle Eastern drums playing somewhere and it's quite nice, but we can't figure out where the music is coming from.

"This place is-ah cursed," Corporal Chuzzo said in a whispered aside to me. "It's-a nice curse. But… it's-a cursed. Plus, Franchessa would kill me. So…"

He motioned zipping his lips.

They, the legionnaires, may be Accadions ten thousand years later. But they're still Italians. And Italian males at that. Without putting too fine a point on it, many of them are very much considering eternal genie damnation.

Corporal Chuzzo, who can barely keep his eyes off the three beauties himself, is barking at them and reminding them they are legionnaires and to attend to their weapons and gear, even if they are far from home and whores. And also, that the Legion expects them to do their duty.

He clubbed the one called Jocoma who couldn't close his mouth or wipe the drool string away as one of the beauties stretched and arched her back.

"Jocoma, tanto va la gatta al lardo che ci lascia lo zampino."

Which basically means... *Curiosity killed the cat.*

"Sì, Corporale, ma alcune cose valgono la pena di morire."

Which means... *Yes, Corporal. But some things are worth dying for.*

So they have their problems too.

When the witch disappeared, the giant gorilla samurai drew his blade in one swift, faster-than-I-thought-possible motion, and cut nothing but air as the witch's disembodied voice giggled and disappeared, her taunts fading in the ether all around us.

The samurai gorilla muttered in Japanese, "Faithless whore."

It was a long tense moment after that as everyone tried to figure out what exactly had happened. Everyone, that is, except the fifteen legionnaires who couldn't take their eyes off the feminine IEDs even if the universe collapsed in on itself with the greatest fireworks show ever.

Those dudes were gonna get every eyeful they could. And the silken beauties didn't seem to mind.

"Al Haraq..." I had said just before we made the wish, uncertain what would happen after the wish-request went off. Knowing we needed everyone in the game. Even the legionnaires. "Can you make your... slaves, concubines... I don't know... I don't want to offend you... but girl-friends... go away so we can concentrate on the wish?"

The genie is about seven feet tall and built like some Mr. Universe bodybuilder, and no he doesn't have a smoky lower torso. He looks like an average, perfectly built seven-foot-tall bodybuilder movie star. Yes, he's bald. Topknot. Golden earring in one ear. Goatee. Just what you'd think a genie would look like. Except with legs. He's friendly, too.

"Oh, them…" he said, not really even noticing the girls were there. Clinging to a nearby palm at the pristine water's edge and making eyes at the dying legionnaires as they stretched and simpered. "I can't tell them anything. They're half the problem around here. But that does not concern you, Master. Have you thought about your next wish? I am very excited to see what we can fulfill. Or what may go horribly wrong."

Well… that makes matters worse.

Here. On the subject of *here*…

Before I tell you about the wish, how I became Master, and what's gonna happen next, I need to tell you about *here*. Because *here* is real mind-blowing. It's so weird that you have to keep your mind off it. Especially when you're trying to make a wish in which things could go… horribly wrong.

As Al Haraq said just before we began trying to make the wish to get the Witch's Eye, "I am not responsible for what happens, Master. And I cannot warn you from folly. What you wish for… will happen. Be careful, Master. Be very careful. I do not know you well, but I sense that you are kind, Master. It would be a shame to see you wish yourself into the Abyss of Sah-alhir for all time where you would know sufferings few mortals have ever experienced."

I have no words for that.

So…

Here. As in where, when, and how, we are.

And the answer is: *I have no clue.*

But we ain't on Earth. So maybe it was a stargate, like Sergeant Joe thought it was at first. Kennedy would probably have some ideas, too. But between me and Joe, we got none.

So let me describe *here* for you.

It's an endless desert. So that's like where we came from, except it feels… more. Like time might not mean anything here. Distance too. There's a distinct smell of sulfur in the air. A whiff really. It comes and goes, and the palms, the dates, and the beauties smell really nice. The water smells nice too. But occasionally you get those acrid drafts of sulfur. So… that's unsettling. The heat is incredible. But hey, it's a dry heat. It's like a furnace though.

Oh, and this is fun in a really disturbing way… there're three planets in the sky. Maybe they're moons? I don't know. But they're huge and close. And they move fast. Most of the sky is taken up by them when they pass overhead. The legionnaires think we're in Hades by what I've heard them darkly muttering among themselves, and I might not totally disagree with them that we seem to be in some sort of… hell-adjacent place. Maybe.

The moon-planets passing overhead are freaky enough.

Add the genie… and it's a trip, man.

We explored the whole area before we met him. We found strange artifacts and treasures within each of the buildings of the Mykonos-like village. Machines that even Joe and I had no idea of what they did or where they were from. Entirely alien. Piles of gold, but the coins were stamped with images I had never seen. Horned demons. Tentacled things. And that was nothing. Piles of lustrous pearls the size of your fist. Chests full of finely cut rubies that dazzled so brightly it hurt your eyes to look at them for too long. Ancient weapons that are clearly magical. Some sing. Others shimmer. One blade sticking out of the sand seems to generate fire along its length. It just sits there in the sand, burning.

"No one touch-a nothin'," warned Corporal Chuzzo.

We maintained our patrol and swept the entire area, and thanks to the enforced restraint of the captain and Joe, we didn't touch anything. Then we made it to the tent and cleared it, moving in just like Joe and I would clear a building.

He spotted the lamp lying there among the rich thick carpets on the floor of the tent in patterns that bothered the mind to look at.

"Check it out," he ordered while covering me.

There were a lot of pillows here. Curtains and silks. We weren't totally sure we were alone. We had the feeling someone was watching us. So we were playing it safe.

And also trying to keep our minds off the fact that we might not be on Earth anymore and we might have just made getting back to Task Force Pipe Hitter impossible. Forever.

"I said to just check it out," said Joe when I pulled the delicate jeweled stopper from the top of the bottle after I'd picked it up.

Red smoke erupted out of the neck of the bottle like from a marking flare. It just poured out. I dropped the bottle and we pulled out of the tent quickly, thinking it was gonna detonate and blow us to hell.

Which we were probably already in.

We hit the sand outside and a moment later, out walked the genie and looked down at me.

"I am Al Haraq, Djinn of the Bottle of Flames, Master. And you have three wishes for me to fulfill now."

CHAPTER TWENTY-FOUR

NIGHT fell in the oasis, and according to the djinn Al Haraq, we were safe as long as we minded the rules. The beauties disappeared as a soft blue evening fell across that desert. The dunes looked cool and peaceful and the palms surrounding the oasis began their white-noise hush in the evening breeze. It was cool and pleasant. The epically beautiful girls went into the ornate tent, but I had a feeling they lived in the bottle.

I didn't know. It was just a feeling. This place was so strange and weird, and that was saying something for the Ruin, that it might as well be that way.

Captain Tyrus had the legionnaires roll out their kits on the sand and he set a watch as they built a small fire against the night. Rations were shared, and apparently it wasn't against the rules to drink from the pool, so the legionnaires went down to the cool water, dipped in, and filled their bottles. All while trying to catch some glimpse of the cursed beauties of the djinn. Walking as close as they could get to eternal slavery.

Sergeant Joe walked me out to the dunes, and we discussed our options, as we saw them, for getting everyone out of this mess.

"No way I can see out of this except that genie guy. Out there looks like a thousand miles of suck in every direction and it's anyone's guess which direction you take 'cause we got no intel on which one is the right one. And don't get me started on that up there." He gestured skyward. "Freakin' moons give me a headache. So no celestial navigation."

The marble-blue moon, cold and glaring, crossed overhead, bright and shining like an angry face in the night glaring down at us.

"Go speak with your genie, bro, and figure us a way out of this one."

Twenty minutes later, I summoned Al Haraq at the entrance to the tent. You know… 'cause I'm the master and all.

And yeah. I too was thinking about those beauties. To be specific, I thought I might ask one for some coffee. But ten thousand years of slavery, just to start, chilled even me. So—on mission, Talker.

The djinn walked out of the tent, smiling as usual. Arms folded across his massive bare chest. The whites of his eyes and teeth brilliant in the night against his dark reddish skin.

"Yes, Master. Have you decided on your next wish? Perhaps wealth beyond imagining? Or would you like to become an ancient Red Dragon with your very own pile of gold, gems, and empire to sleep on? Anything is possible, Master, if you use the right words."

I took a deep breath.

"I need to explain my, I mean our, situation to you… Al Haraq."

"I am listening, Master. But I cannot—never, ever—help you with the words of a wish. You understand, Master?"

"I do, Al Haraq. But since I am your... master..." I paused. "I'm not totally comfortable with that term. Can we just be friends?"

"No, Master."

I sighed. Then I explained the events that had gotten us here and clarified what our intentions and mission were. That we needed to return to where we came from.

Inside the tent, behind the djinn, a lamp had been turned on, and I could smell barbecue. It smelled delicious. I could see the forms of the lithe beauties moving about in silhouette. It was... distracting.

Hey. Back on mission.

"Okay... master and servant then. Can I ask you stuff? Non-wish stuff?"

"Certainly, Master. You can ask me anything. I know many things. But you must ask. And..."

He looked around and crouched down. He looked back once again at the tent as though making sure the beautiful girls within could not hear him.

"Don't tell them. But once every moon, you, Master, can summon me to do a task for you. And if I can accomplish it, then I shall. I see that you are warriors. I once fought in the Wars of the Wayste during the Golden Age of Throm. Against the Saurian priests themselves at Night Valley and Varg's Rift."

He laughed deeply.

"I slaughtered many, Master. Many, many indeed. I would be more than happy to slaughter your enemies when the time comes, Master."

"That's good, Al Haraq. I think... we could use that sometime. But right now I need to get everyone back to where we came from."

"Yes. Yes you do, Master. Here is not a good place for you. It's only a matter of time before one of those Accadions makes a mistake he will regret for ten thousand years. And that's just the beginning, Master. Believe me. I know of what I speak."

"I do, Al Haraq. So… is there a way out of here?"

"Oh, yes indeed, Master. There are two ways."

He folded his arms and stood tall. Beaming at the night and the strange moons crossing overhead.

"And what would those be, Al Haraq?"

"Well, Master. The first would be to wish. I could take you anywhere you wish. It's just that you'd need to be very specific. Very specific indeed, Master, in ways most mortals don't understand. Because of course, Master, I could take you to the very Morghul Fortress itself, or even the Jade Ponds of Kungaloor and the Court of Sayam the Wise… but if you don't tell me where exactly to take you… and I mean *exactly*, Master… well, you could end up in a wall. Or underground without air to breathe—which your kind need to go on. So. Where would you like to go, Master? I am ready to fulfill your wish, my noble master, and take you anywhere your heart desires. Speak, and it shall be done!"

I swallowed thickly. One, I was parched. And two, the more I understood about wishes the less I wanted to use them. Or really have anything to do with them. They felt dangerous in ways high-ex only began to. You could have a bad day, for about ten thousand years of bad days.

I cleared my throat.

"You said there was a second way."

"I did, Master."

"And…?"

"Ah. You wish to know of it, Master?"

"I do, Al Haraq."

"Then all you must do is return the way you came."

So…

"I just open the book and we go back?"

"Well… yes, Master, if you want to do it that way. That's the way those kinds of books work, Master. But it's boring. I could make you appear in the Treasure Houses of Sung, or the Temples of Akazong with smoke and fire and dragons flying in the sky to announce your very presence. It would all be very, very grand, Master, and you would make quite an impression. The queen of Akazong is both wealthy and beautiful, Master. You would want for nothing if I gave her your hand."

The djinn beamed proudly with the offers of all he could do.

"That's good to know. But for now, let's save that wish and use it for something fun. Whaddaya say, Al Haraq?"

He laughed long and almost disconcertingly like someone who doesn't know when to stop laughing.

Then, "That sounds like a *lot* of fun, Master. Yes. Let's wait for something really special indeed."

"I have one last question, Al Haraq. Are there weapons and supplies we can take from here? You know… without violating the rules? Without getting cursed to stay here for ten thousand years?"

The djinn looked across the oasis as though looking at everything contained within it.

"You have explained your mission to me, Master. And I can tell you that almost everything here would be useless against the *asnan musfara*."

The *stained*. He meant the Lost Elves. Those were his words.

"And why is that, Al Haraq? Why won't they work? The weapons we find here?"

"That is very easy to explain, Master. They are all cursed. They would work for the *asnan musfara...* and against you. Everything here is here because of a curse. That is the nature of the contract here."

He smiled at me, and I felt a cold chill crawl up my spine.

"There is one thing though... Master. And I can do this. I can remove the curse that brought the thing here. This would be... a *special deal* between you and I, Master. *But...* I would have a price for this. Because it is not a wish. It is merely... something I can do for you. For a price. And having said this, Master, I know of what odds you face against the *asnan musfara*, and they are not good, even with these things I could help you with. But... perhaps..."

Pins and needles. I'm on them.

We've got a way back with the book. And now a weapon, or weapons, to waste those Lost Elves with. Probably the equivalent of a magical nuke or an eldritch flamethrower. Some fabled Blade of That Guy, or the Staff of Some Dead Wizard. If we had Kennedy's dragon-headed staff and we could use it... game over. Anything to take that fortress. Because five rounds of five-five-six, a bunch of legionnaires and all the good intentions in the world...

Like I said, I'm a words guy. Not a numbers guy. But even I know that ain't enough numbers to do what needs to be done to make it through the back door and out the front gate of that fortress at the top of the pass. Plus you have to go up a winding stairway in the mountains called the Stairway to Hell.

That doesn't sound good.

"Walk with me, Master," said the djinn. "Let me show you the thing I can do for you."

We walked in silence, under the strange moons passing overhead and along the quiet oasis pool, into the silent village full of cursed weapons and strange artifacts. We took a small and dark alley that was close and tight, then came out behind the back of the low white stucco houses.

"Is that what I think it is, Al Haraq?"

"It is, Master, what it is. If you desire I can remove the curse and you can take from it what you will. But they are weapons that would, I believe, suit your task at hand. Give you the chance you need. That is all I can offer. In exchange for my price."

A CH-47 Chinook transport helicopter sat in the desert sand beyond the quiet cursed village.

There are a lot of strange things in the Ruin. Strange and wonderful and terrifying. And downright weird. Your brain never gets used to it, not entirely. But after a time, a part of you—eventually and, yes, reluctantly—does learn to *expect the unexpected*. Still… what you don't, ever, learn to expect, here in the Ruin…

… is a CH-47 Chinook transport helicopter.

I walked up to the back ramp and peered into the darkness within, taking just a few steps.

I saw weapons crates in there. Ammo crates. But not like the Rangers used and were deployed with. These were from some older era of American military power. I walked further into the aircraft, stunned into utter disbelief. The djinn followed, creating a small red flame in his palm as I peered close and tried to read the markings on the crates.

AKMs.

Twenty per crate.

XM177 COMMANDO, U.S. Military.

Twenty per crate.

V40 Mini Fragmentation Grenade.

Fifty per crate.

There were other long flat boxes. Ammo cans on a pallet. Supplies.

"What happened to them?" I asked. "To the soldiers who used these. Did they come to the Ruin?"

I turned to see the djinn smiling down at me in the dark. The red flame hovering in the palm of his large hand making him look sinister and malevolent by its hellish light.

"They did, Master. And they chose... unwisely, Master."

CHAPTER TWENTY-FIVE

THREE days later, we opened the book and went back to the Ruin, leaving the world of the genie's bottle. The resort desert oasis of untouchable temptations.

Believe me, the legionnaires were happy to go. The constant torture of the lovelies, and eternal damnation if they succumbed to it, made them more than willing once I opened the book. We threaded the bubble and entered the burnt remains of the Forbidden Library.

The vast halls and charred corpses cemetery-silent.

In the three days before we did so, we offloaded as much gear as we could do from the old Vietnam-era Chinook twin rotor transport helicopter.

CH-47. The workhorse of the Vietnam War. It was still in use during my time. The only clue we ever found in it of what had happened, how it had found some unfound QST long before the one invented at Area 51, was the two crew chief's helmets placed near the loading deck. Two sixties mounted nearby and loaded with belts of ammo and seeming ready to go right now.

Each helmet was marked in white chalk.

Joker.

Thief.

We had no idea who they were. The only thing the djinn Al Haraq would say on the subject of the chopper was, "They chose unwisely, Master."

Meanwhile, Sergeant Joe was like a kid in a candy store. That is, if that candy store had high explosives, guns, ammunition, old-school rations, and vintage special-operator Vietnam-era weapons in pristine condition.

That you could play with even!

"This is MACV-SOG gear, bro!" he said, holding up one of the gun-oil-smelling RPDs like he was in love or something. "They cut the barrels down on these Russian light machine guns so they were lighter than the pig for jungle ops. Feed some seven-six-two in and you've got the ultimate ambush bush-cutter. Total beast mode."

There were a lot of explosives besides just the mini-frags. Crates of old-school C4 packed in sawdust. Along with that came all the gear a MACV-SOG team would need to go out into the jungles of Southeast Asia and cause as much mayhem as possible. Rhodesian-style chest rigs. Canteens. Claymores. All of it. Standing there in the late evening under the surreal moons, Joe laid out our plan to get back to Task Force Pipe Hitter.

Two weeks later, we were ready to execute as we hunkered in a wadi just before dawn, southeast of the Stairway to Hell. Behind us, in the long halt patrol base formation, the legionnaires were arrayed in all their proper positions. I'd moved among the team leaders as the assistant squad leader, letting them know what our orders were. Ahead, Sergeant Joe was positioning the one-sixty we'd taken from the Chinook, orienting it to the most likely avenue of approach if the enemy came down the wadi in the next hour before we conducted the attack at dawn.

When the Lost Elves would be at their weakest.

We'd stealthed in all night, moving between patrols of Lost Elves looking for other patrols in the past week that hadn't come back. Patrols we'd smoked as practice for the legionnaires. The legionnaires had quite enjoyed this as we stood over the dead bodies of the psycho Lost Elves in the night. Clearing the objective, stabbing the dead, and collecting intel.

"One man's trash is another man's intel source," Joe was saying as we rifled the dead elves, looking for anything that would help us breach their fortress at the top of the pass.

"Hey, this is-ah much easier than stand-up fighting," whispered Corporal Chuzzo in the darkness. "I been in a lotta battles with people who get hacked to-ah pieces and broken bones while you gotta stand there and take it. Much better just to shoot them in the dark from hiding. Very smart."

Which is what we'd done to the Lost Elves that night as we taught the remains of the Tyrus's Legion force how to run a classic L-shaped ambush.

They liked it a lot and wanted to do much more. There were other enemy patrols out that night. Instead we taught the Legion the discipline of the hit-and-fade.

"Be the thing they fear tonight... and dread tomorrow."

In other words, make them unable to sleep, and when they do, the nightmares they have are nightmares about you. That is, if nightmares have nightmares.

Now, after a week of killing their patrols, we were going to hit them, hoping they were exhausted in the daylight.

But back to that night in the oasis, as we explored the lost Chinook, and Joe laid out the plan.

"This is what we're gonna do, bro. We're gonna kit these guys up into two heavy squads. We're gonna make four five-man squads outta what we got. Two assault, two support. Then we'll open the book and go back into the library to scout and see if the Lost Elves think we're good and dead."

He picked up a LAW rocket, mumbling, "I haven't seen one of these since..."

"Then it's burrito time, Sar'nt," I prompted, jumping the gun, trying to get a go regarding Ranger plans for promised revenge.

"Negative. Not yet. Their captain's map shows the location of the Stairway along the range. We're gonna fade deeper into the desert carrying all the gear and water and—can you believe this bird was even carrying a few boxes of K-rations? Crazy. I bet they could tell some stories. MACV-SOG was where Special Operations all began. These guys are legends."

I'd never heard of MACV-SOG.

"These were the ghosts of Vietnam. The real-deal killers. They went into the bush, outnumbered, and stacked commies shoulder high. Black operations, special operations... three quarters of the stuff they did is still heavily classified, bro. They used the enemy's weapons, unconventional weapons, special weapons, all the stuff that got it done, son. If that genie had given me the wish... I would have wished for something stupider than what we got here to do what we're gonna do to the Lost Elves next. This is *better* than we could have wished for. Seriously, bro."

"Looks old to me, Sar'nt. No red-dot sights. Night vision. Nothin', Sar'nt."

Joe was counting up the ammo. There was a lot.

"With this you don't need that stuff. This is old school and it's the genesis of all our modern warfighting, Talker. Once the army figured this out, we became the greatest war machine in history. So here's what we're gonna do..."

And here's what we did.

For two weeks, way out in the deeps of the desert, carrying all the gear we could, which didn't seem to matter much to the legionnaires who were used to humping everything on their backs as a matter of Legion SOP, we taught them how to kill with modern weapons. We saddled them with rucks, chest rigs strapped over their armor, rigs full of stacked mags for the commandos. The armor they would not give up no matter how much we tried to communicate that with an RPD no one was going to get close enough to them to stab them with a scimitar or a damascened dagger or the Magic Sword of Thogar the Whatever. With an RPD, they could grease an ogre easy-peasy. And then some. Even I thought that thing was brutal. And fun. We draped belts of 7.62 over their pauldrons and below their Spartan helms.

To be honest, they looked like total killers.

Then we marched them into the deeps of the desert and taught them how to patrol and move as a modern fighting unit. We ran ranges, and they weren't great with cover and movement, but they loved to shoot and got ecstatically excited about hitting things with the RPD. We suspected they just liked to make the sand fly up in small plumes. But, we reasoned, they didn't need to be accurate with the bush-cutter.

"If they're even close with that thing, you got dead elves to burn, bro," said Sergeant Joe.

Also, they didn't like using iron sights. They preferred to just spray bullets in the general direction of their enemies while laughing and screaming Legion hardboy phrases we barely understood. I guess that was their version of the Rangers' memes. They even had their own "Air Force," which we figured out to be the Accadion Navy. In time, the memes between the two seemed totally interchangeable. But they couldn't be made to understand that using iron sights would give them better aim on their enemies.

We didn't trust them with explosives beyond the minis, and even that felt dangerous to use. They weren't as great at gripping the V40 mini-grenade as they should have been. Too many of them liked to palm the grenade before they threw it. But eventually we ended up giving two each to the legionnaires, and explicit instructions on when to use them.

They could only use the minis when we told them to and had designated targets for them to destroy.

The captain took a satchel full and extra mags. We had no problem trusting him. Again, he seemed to have a natural affinity for the gear and weapons that even he couldn't explain, stoic as he was. It seemed to bother him on some level, though he never voiced it aloud.

We did teach them how to roll a grenade into a bunker. They liked that and equated it to some street game they'd played as urchins in the alleys of Accadios.

The gorilla samurai, on the other hand, would have nothing to do with our weapons. He considered them "dishonorable." The giant beast would say nothing more on the subject. Its martial presence defied any argument we could make that we were not, indeed, unclean savages in its superior sight.

"I will fight alongside you because needs must," it grunted in Japanese. "But I have only come seeking to face a foe named Axe Grinder. I was led astray on this folly into the desert, deceived that the ogre scum had fled into this accursed place. But I will find him. I will confront him. I will destroy the Axe Grinder."

I had no idea what that was all about. Gorilla business. But I worked with the teams to make sure we used the samurai in Assault Team Alpha and that the gunners didn't spray close to his position if he went forward to engage in hand-to-hand.

We had two elements. Alpha, led by Joe. Bravo by me. Alpha had a team of three legionnaires and Joe along with the samurai. Then a support team of four legionnaires and the Legion captain, who ran the sixty.

Tyrus mastered all the weapons we taught him almost effortlessly. Unlike many of the legionnaires. It was as though the Legion captain had been born to use the weapons we'd found. He also had no problems with us teaching and leading his men, and even himself. He had no ego. Once he understood that we were proficient at killing, he understood that was the best way for him to find the witch who had stolen his prize.

Bravo under me, the guy who failed patrols in Ranger school, was broken down the same as Alpha, with an assault support element. Except we went with the RPDs for the support unit, using two of them, instead of a sixty. One for Corporal Chuzzo and one for me. They were half as heavy, and we could carry more on the long fast hump up the Stairway to Hell.

The MACV-SOG gear came with an earlier version of the Vickers Sling. Made of leather, it was perfect for carrying the light machine gun. The rest of the legionnaires were trained with the XM177 Commando, which was really much like the M4—and according to Joe, it was the actual predecessor. Joe and I took one each of those, just in case.

Add as much C4 as we could carry, and it was a lot to hump, on top of the rations and gear and water.

The good thing for me was that among the found gear I managed to pick up some extra old-school fatigues that fit. They weren't desert. They were jungle tiger stripe. At night, in the desert, the tiger stripe broke up outlines enough to be effective. But most importantly, they were clean. Which... after the underground river full of bodies and salt mummy rot, and the slaughter at the front entrance to the library, dragging away the dead and holding the dying... *clean* was a good thing.

Never underestimate the power of fresh socks, or fresh clothes.

The legionnaires remained adamant about wearing their own gear, insisting it was a point of honor for them. We acquiesced and allowed them to Frankenstein their kits.

The RPDs were Frankensteins anyway.

For the next two weeks we patrolled them to death, and they ate it up. Especially the captain. Their level of endurance out there in the desert night was amazing. But then again, they'd spent their life marching across the Ruin and doing battle outnumbered in hostile environments. We learned some things from them. They learned a lot from Joe.

I was busy making it all happen, and everything I'd learned in Ranger School was put to the test, used, and became my every minute of my every day. What Joe told me to make happen, I did. Because of the language barrier, and because I... wanted to.

We worked at night just out beyond the range of the Lost Elves' patrols, away from the mountains and the fortress. Hunkering down in the day out of range at a new patrol base we'd set up that night. Slowly working our way to the northeast and scouting for the pass we'd soon assault.

One night, during the watch, the captain informed us that the Lost Elves were not locals to this region, according to his intel developed before their march into the southern sands. That within the last twenty years, rumors all along the Lost Coast indicated they had come looking for something specific to their belief system, preferring not to participate in the developing struggle between the dark forces of the Nether Sorcerer and the Cities of Men.

Not that either side would have them anyway.

The Lost Elves had several bases of operations throughout the Atlantean Mountains, but their main hub of activity was centered around the old fortress at the top of the Atlantean Pass. It wasn't the tallest part of the mountain range. It was, in fact, near the tail end that would be swallowed by the vast deserts of the No Man's Land west of the Land of Black Sleep. Still, from our reconnaissance missions in close to put eyes on our objective, it looked to be about two thousand feet up to the fortress from the pass on the desert floor.

We had to do that in six hours. The Stairway. Then we hit the fortress. We needed to be out the front gate and running for the coast before nightfall if we were going to succeed. Darkness would bring more Lost Elves out of the caves.

We took two PRC-77 radios—one for Joe and one for me. Once we reached elevation in the pass, we would try to make contact with the task force. If we got pinned down in the fortress, they would know our location and conduct a rescue to pull us out. We'd find a chokepoint in the fortress, turtle, and try to hold the Lost Elves off until we got busted out by the task force, according to Joe.

"The one thing we have goin' for us, Talker, is that for the most part they'll stay out of direct sunlight. We know these jerk-elves don't like the sun. That Stairway looks like it's all open-air to the top, other than the guard towers along the way which I count ten. We det those so we have no one on our six and keep humming fast. Any resistance we encounter, we roll 'em fast with the assault teams and suppressive fire from support. Hose 'em quick, then throw grenades and keep moving forward to the front gate."

It was a simple plan. And to me, it was the only plan that could be made given how little we knew and what we had to work with.

But it was a plan, and a plan was better than no plan.

As we hunkered in the dark in the wadi, one hour from dawn, I looked back at the legionnaires in the darkness who'd allowed themselves to be covered in old-school Vietnam-era camo sticks. They looked like demons in armor, strapping Frankenstein Chicom weapons and ready to do some serious payback for their dead.

They looked like Rangers.

We wanted to sneak in as close as we could to the Stairway so that we hit the first steps at dawn as the Lost Elves were forced underground. We needed all the time we could get.

One hour to go.

CHAPTER TWENTY-SIX

A week before the assault on the stairs, one night on watch, Joe and I had a talk. The talk I needed to have finally.

And by talk, it was mainly just me listening.

He started it off like this because we were discussing some of the legionnaires, a few in particular, and their problems understanding what we were asking them to perform.

Mainly the guys in Bravo Support.

"If you hold a dog's leash too tight, bro, he's not going to work for you," said Joe. "He's going to stay by your side. You want him to work... you have to teach him to work off-leash. Let Chuzzo make his mistakes. Let him learn. Then let him succeed. Kid'll get it."

He looked at me.

"Now you. I'mma ask, Talker. Linguist guy who's hanging with the Rangers but takes every chance to put himself down as *not good enough* to actually be a Ranger. What's your deal, bro? What do you want, man?"

I said nothing. I hadn't expected that. My mouth wanted to say something, because that's what I do. But honestly... I had nothing. I was out of ammo to defend my actions with.

"What do you wanna be?" he said after a moment when I couldn't think of anything to say.

Then… it just came out because I couldn't help it. Because it needed to.

"A Ranger… Sar'nt. I've… want… wanted that. To really be… one of you."

The wind blew on the sand that night and for a long minute we just sat there, watching the moon cast shadows along the troughs and silver crests of all those dunes out there.

"You know, the only thing stopping you, is you, Talker. That's it."

"I know that now, Sar'nt. Took a long time for me to get honest with myself. But… I know it now."

"Listen. You've hung with the Rangers. We have done some straight-up hairy balls-to-the-wall stuff here. Easily the equivalent of anything back in the sandbox. Weirder, too. And everyone, including me, has seen you right there in the suck with incoming. You have *Rangered*. You wear that scroll because we allow you to wear it, and the standard for wearing it—*our* standard—is that you pay the rent on it every day. You have, Talker. You are a Ranger. Regardless of that damn tab."

He pointed to the one on his right shoulder.

"This just means you're Ranger-qualified, bro. No easy feat. I'll give you that. But it ain't nowhere near as heavy as that damned scroll you're wearing right now."

I mumbled something about knowing that. I don't remember what. I was just listening because I was getting a whipping I had been avoiding for a long time. If you think it was like… *Great, you're a Ranger, welcome to Dreamland…*

… it wasn't anything like that.

What he was saying was… because he said it next, was this…

"Your inability to rise to the challenge, the challenge of accepting that you are a Ranger, has nothing to do with what you can do, and everything, and I mean everything, bro, with what you believe. I can say it, but you'll never *be* it until you stop trying to be liked by everyone and start being a Ranger because you believe that you are one. Got that? You tryin' to get that tab Kurtz is dangling in front of you, that's a game you're playing with yourself. You think... if you get it then maybe you can admit you're one of us. We figured that out and made sure, in fact the smaj himself even made sure, we made sure you *weren't* gonna get it. We wanted you to know it first. Believe it. And stop tryin' to con yourself because you ain't conning anyone else."

I nodded. My carefully constructed world was collapsing. And honestly... that was a good thing. Finally. I could let it go. All my bull. I started to breathe like I'd never breathed before.

Easy. Finally.

"Let me tell you somethin' about belief, okay? I know what they say about the Book of Joe and all. All the garbage that comes outta my trap. The young Rangers think it's gospel. Book of Joe. I heard it. Here's the truth. You could learn a lot by all the mistakes I've made. That's all it is. That's all I'm distilling for everyone."

He paused and laughed once like he was about to go somewhere he didn't want to.

Then he did.

"Let me tell you somethin' about belief. My wife..."

He paused and got silent. I waited.

"Seems like last year, man, but that's ten thousand years ago. And that's every deployment, bro. You feel so far gone that it might as well have been ten thousand years ago. We had this thing, her and I, we believed in. Just the two of us. Her, really. But for me... it's my whole system now ten thousand years later."

Silence again.

I waited again.

"Bein' a Ranger... there is every chance on every pump that you are going to die. Way higher than the average leg. Higher than airborne even. Rangers ain't super-soldiers. Maybe they are, who knows. They get smoked comin' off a bird. IEDs. Just like everyone else. Rangers get it too, Talker. Life is dangerous, and war ain't no playground. She knew that. So I made up somethin' that ain't in no Bible you're ever gonna read. Somethin' for her to keep going, you know, when I was gone."

I didn't. But I was keen to find out. This was the most he'd ever talked about himself. His life outside being a Ranger. Or his wife.

I thought about Autumn. Autumn praying at dusk. For me in a chapel in the dark.

Joe swallowed hard and looked off toward the moon.

"I told her there was this gate in heaven. See... there's this gate... and... well... in heaven when ya die, you know how it is... it's heaven and all. Time to go have all the fun that you never imagined possible. I could get behind that. And since we knew with me bein' a Ranger and all that I was probably gonna buy it first... I told her this gate was different than the pearly gate where everyone got through and went off to have fun and all. This gate... it's called the Waiting Gate. Ain't no pearly gate. It's where people who die, people who aren't ready to go on to all the fun there is there in paradise... well, they wait there for someone. Moms who love their kids more than they loved their lives.

People who bought it with cancer early, waiting for the one they had to leave behind. The one they couldn't let go, and who couldn't let go of them. The ones that really love each other. Couples who were together every day of their lives. See, to them, heaven just wouldn't be... heaven, you know. 'Cause the one that they love ain't there, yet.

"So I told her that no matter what happened to me... I'd be waiting at this gate, no matter how long it took for her to come along. If I bought it in some hellhole, I'd wait for her along with the rest of them there. And you know what that did? It did everything for her, bro. She was gonna leave me before that. Couldn't take the pumps and not knowing if I was alive or dead somewhere, one day to the next. But when I told her I wasn't going to enjoy heaven until she got there, that I was gonna wait with my face pressed into those bars at that waiting gate, right there with the parents of disabled children they had to leave behind, or you know... people who really loved each other, like I did her... that was enough for her. She knew I was gonna wait. I was gonna be waiting. No matter how long.

"It's been ten thousand years, Talker. I know. And I know right where she is. She's waiting there where *I* was supposed to. I don't just believe that, man, I know it. And one day I'm going to buy that ticket and... best day ever, bro. Best. Day. Ever."

CHAPTER TWENTY-SEVEN

DAWN cracks the sky as we watch the last of the Lost Elven patrol scramble up the stairs, heading toward the towers, calling it a night.

Seeking peaceful sleep from the nightmares they've been hunting.

Joe nods at me that it's time to move out of the wadi. Time to cross the LOA and begin the assault.

I turn to Bravo, the dark-faced demon legionnaires waiting to get their kill on, behind me in the wadi.

"Rangers lead the way," I say, and they smile back eagerly in the darkness.

I advance out of the wadi, carrying the RPD and forming them into a wedge, crouched low and breaking off from Alpha on our right. One hundred yards and we're gonna smoke the sentries.

I am a Ranger.

CHAPTER TWENTY-EIGHT

TANNER would later tell me that the dead we'd smoked, from the very beginning of our run through the desert at the start of all this, including the battle at the Crooked Obelisk, and finally the patrols we were ambushing out in the desert, were talking to him as they wandered the desert, searching for their salvation, and telling the dead Ranger our progress... in so many words.

Tanner and Sindamairo, the horse Autumn gave me, had been up in the Atlantean Mountains trying to find a way down into the desert so he could find us, or our bodies, as per the smaj's instructions.

He got into some stuff up there. But that's another story.

The dead came wandering out of the desert, telling him who they'd been killed by, their angers, their stories, and yes... even the Lost Elven dead have loves they mourn over, and they wonder what will become of the ones they have left behind.

Tanner listened and began to put his intel together.

In the brief conversations he heard and had, using the language of Damnation, Tanner was able to put together that the two "reaping demons," as the Lost Elves referred to us, might in fact actually be missing Rangers running amok in the Lost Elves' little sandbox down there on the desert floor beneath the Atlantean Mountains at the edge of the map, interrupting their hunt for the Spider Queen.

Tanner then rode back to the top of the mountains, deployed the comm gear the smaj made sure he took along for the search, and linked up with the drone being run by the pretty little ponytailed Air Force co-pilot, getting through to Task Force Pipe Hitter.

Once Tanner got a clear idea of the fortress, using the tracking info of the dead, he'd pretty much figured out we were going for the pass and that we'd try and fight our way through.

He could tell from the dead we were getting closer. And on the morning of the attack, in the dead of night, one of the ghostly dead elves we'd smoked sobbed bitterly that it had been cheated of all the evil it had planned to do in this life.

Sergeant Joe and I had no idea that just twenty-four hours earlier Captain Knife Hand had ordered a forced march from the coast, up to the gates of the fortress, and planned to hit them just after nine that morning when the sun would give the Rangers advantage against the night stalkers, according to Tanner.

The Rangers did twenty-two miles in total darkness and arrived ready to attack. They crawled to within meters of the gate and waited for the signal in the shadows and rock. Weapons teams set up on the two huge block towers that guarded that side of the pass. Mortar teams were ready to go as the fire support team made the calculations to start dropping indirect fire all over the giant fortress of the Ancient Ones.

There was comm traffic between the scout forward observer role Tanner was acting in, and the main body of the task force getting ready to mollywhomp the fortress and make a way for us to bust out.

What we also didn't know was there were about four thousand elves down in the fortress ready to go.

Alpha and Bravo, Joker and Thief, Sergeant Joe and Talker, we knew none of this as we crossed through the red dawn light, using the uneven terrain to get close to the sentries guarding the two massive columns that marked the stairs cut into the rock of the mountain. Sergeant Joe, working with Otoro, got low and crawled forward toward the two Lost Elves on the desert floor. Above them, the steep stairs twisted and wound their way upward. The gorilla samurai moved quietly and seemed to have no problems regarding honor when suddenly he came out of the low dawn light blasting across the desert landscape, catching both sentries turning away to shield their eyes from the rising sun.

All they must've heard were his steps—heavy, but not thunderous. Then the *snick* of the massive blade he drew. I'd heard it before, and it sounded like death whispering. And finally a gorilla's heavy breathy animal grunt as he cut through both of them in one terrific stroke.

Joe was nearby with the Commando, ready to pick up anyone who survived the targeting.

Nobody did.

The gorilla, satisfied with his assassination, actually used the hand signals we'd taught the legionnaires for non-verbal patrolling communication, to tell us it was all clear to move forward.

"That monkey's been learnin' the whole time," whispered Joe as Bravo moved into support position to take the first set of stairs below the first guard tower.

Alpha moved on the stairs, and I swore I could hear the legionnaires quietly giggling to themselves in the quiet dawn of first morning as they humped their new weapons and made ready to get their slaughter on.

We'd tried to break them of that.

But…

We bypassed the first, second, and third towers easily. At each one, the elves had gone in and gone deep, leaving one sentry near the door to wait out the accursed day. Joe or Otoro cut throats or strangled with a garrote, securing the access to each tower as we moved up, the two elements leapfrogging forward.

We only short-halted to allow Joe to generously use C4 and tripwire for detonation at the entrance to each tower. We weren't leaving anyone on our six.

Tower Four was when it all went to hell.

But that was a good thing that no one had planned for. Only Tanner, who was watching everything from a nearby ridge, could see how it was all coming together despite a lack of communication between the elements.

Still, that didn't make a difference.

The sudden series of detonations began to draw the Lost Elves, all four thousand of them, away from the defenses and barracks deep within the fortress atop the pass to address what was clearly an attack by twenty "reaper demons" coming up along the stairs out of the desert.

This practically opened the fortress for Task Force Pipe Hitter.

All we knew from our position was that one of the elves from inside Tower One had come up from out of the under-dungeon beneath the tower where they slept, found the guard missing, put on protective gear, and went out in the sunlight to look for the missing guard whom Joe had strangled and dragged outside. Placing the body around the side of the tower and out of sight.

Our recons of the stairs had shown that the Lost Elves rarely emerged in daylight. As long as we stayed outside, we had a good chance of getting right up on the fortress before having to fight.

We'd always anticipated a big fight. Everyone was carrying at least two LAW rockets and we hoped to create enough chaos with our own version of Kennedy's "magic missile" to bust through the main gate and beat feet. But the battlement that guarded our side of the pass was manned at all times, and the elves watched from a long slit in the building's up reaches. We knew we'd eventually have to fight it out.

We had something planned for that.

That plan went out the door, like plans do, when some Lost Elf guy tripped the wire and detted Tower One. It exploded in a sudden shower of rock flying out over the desert floor. One side of the tower was missing as the smoke cleared, and a second later the entire thing just collapsed along the face of the mountain below us in a dusty rockslide.

Did I mention the stairs we were climbing were nearly vertical?

Today was gonna be the worst leg day of all, humping a light machine gun, a carbine, ammo, and a PRC-77 vintage Vietnam radio.

But somewhere ahead, Talker kept telling himself... he was gonna get coffee even if every Lost Elf in the world needed to die to make that happen.

Goal-setting is important. Follow me for more Life Hacks.

Meanwhile, Tanner didn't know we had those radios and so he couldn't try the channels to get to us. Besides, we were keeping them off until we reached the pass to save the juice for transmission.

The brick batteries of those old antiques weren't what we had in the future ten thousand years ago.

So, over the course of the next minute, both elements froze in place on the stairs, watching the destruction of Tower One... and then Towers Two and Three as they went up and then down in similar fashion as, in each case, some stupid elf runs out to take a look-see and find out what's going on. We even see the guy on Tower Three run out, bust the tripwire, and set off the C4, cratering the base of that tower.

"Alpha, follow me!" shouted Joe in the next second, and they pushed forward on Tower Four.

I could already see elves coming out of the tower, running to see the commotion. I opened up with the RPD and ran a line of fire across them, stopping before Alpha gained the top of the stairs and started shooting at the Lost Elves up there, gunning down the ones coming out of the tower at near point-blank range.

When Bravo made it up, we were greeted by dozens of mauled and dead elves, while legionnaires secured the platform and Joe tossed grenades down into the darkness of the tower where the barracks were.

"Bravo moving on Tower Five!" I shouted as we passed Joe.

We took lead and hit Tower Five with gunfire and grenades.

The way Rangers have always led the way.

The elves came out with their arrows and began to fire. Captain Tyrus advanced with Bravo, murdering bad guys and taking incoming. One of the legionnaires was hit as they got close. Keeping low and working in two teams, Bravo took the platform cut into the rock around the ancient tower. The elves needed to lean over the stairs to fire, and that handicapped them. That was when the captain shot them down and pushed his men forward at the same time. He perfectly understood and executed momentum to take control of the battle space.

I came up behind the captain and deployed two minis onto the platform above, calling "Grenade out!" as the legionnaires covered. We waited for the explosions and then stormed the platform for Tower Five, the legionnaires judiciously spraying any elves that had managed to survive.

At the same time, or so Tanner would tell me later, the Rangers in the task force hit the front gate with Carl Gustafs and added to the mayhem inside the courtyard with indirect fire from the mortars. Sergeant Kurtz and the weapons team opened up on the rightmost tower, a massive chunk of sheer rock that watched the approach to the fortress. Soprano worked over the murder holes, sending fire in at the elves preparing to rain down arrows on the Rangers moving in assault teams on the demolished front gate.

Specialist Rico, now Sergeant Rico, and the other weapons team ate up the other tower guarding the approach in similar fashion.

The Rangers were getting a huge break from our attack. Most of the elves in the fortress and the five remaining towers had reacted to our attack first and were now pushing on the rear of the fortress, streaming down the Stairway to Hell and moving right at us with overwhelming fire.

We made it to Tower Seven before we got slowed to a halt.

We could hear the explosions coming from the fortress above, but we were pinned by arrow fire now.

It was clear we'd bitten off perhaps more than we could chew.

"Talker!" Joe shouted. "Get on the radio! I think we got help coming up there!" He was dragging a wounded legionnaire out from under arrow fire. Joe had an arrow sticking out of his own leg, but if it bothered him, he didn't show it.

We were about to get hit with everything the elves had.

CHAPTER TWENTY-NINE

EVERYONE was hit. To some degree. Even though the Rangers in the task force were blasting their way through the fortress, most of the enemy was racing down the stairs at us now, regardless of the "accursed" sunlight, in their typical psychotic heedless fashion. They'd kill us if they did anything else today.

And yes, they were throwing everything at us. Missiles, spells, arrows, Hindi curses—or orders for curry—and even rocks.

Legionnaires were bleeding. Knocked out. And fighting if they could. I moved among them, coordinating sectors of fire, dragging the wounded and unconscious to cover, and trying to stop the bleed on two guys who were hit bad.

I grabbed one legionnaire who was fighting with a Commando in one hand. "Here," I said, grabbing his knee after I'd gotten a pressure dressing on the injury. "Put your knee on Marca here. Push hard."

My bet was the Lost Elves knew they'd just been kicked out of the fortress. Now they either wanted some revenge as they raced for the desert floor, or they just knew we were in the way and they weren't stopping to be friendly.

The legionnaires weren't great at swapping belts on the RPDs. I had to help them every other time. I went dry on my weapon as we tried to keep them back. I chucked it to the side, swung the slung Commando around, and started firing bursts on massed clusters of the enemy. We were holding Tower Seven, but it was clear we weren't going forward. Alpha was on the right of the Stairway. Bravo on the left.

The Legion captain was going from badly wounded legionnaire to badly wounded legionnaire, picking up weapons or belts of ammo and then hosing the snipers above us who were doing the most damage. If the enemy was firing at him, he didn't seem to care. He was clearly going to kill them all.

Suddenly the elves began to beat their shields above us, screaming and signaling they were ready to charge. And there were a lot of them now building up there.

I heard a small, tiny voice and realized the radio on my back had its volume down. I rolled over on my side, hugging rock to avoid enemy arrow fire.

"Task Force Hawthorn... Any element, Task Force Hawthorn on this channel... Say again..."

I couldn't believe it.

That was when the black darting flash of an MH-6 Little Bird streaked by on the desert floor below our position.

"What the hell!" shouted Joe, who was swapping mags and trying to get shots off on the snipers above.

"They're going to push us!" shouted Corporal Chuzzo from nearby. He was on his knees and swapping out a belt for the RPD. An arrow had torn off a huge chunk of his cheek. Another one was sticking through his forearm. Blood dribbled down over the linked ammunition he was getting ready.

"Bite off more than you can chew… Dogs," he gasped breathlessly and began to fire too-long bursts at the enemy once more.

Task Force Hawthorn was the original designation for every spec ops element going through the QST to save the future that had started this whole thing off.

I grabbed the radio phone mic because that's what these old radios used.

"Little Bird, Little Bird!" I shouted over the battle. "This is the Ranger detachment with Task Force Hawthorn."

There was a long pause. The helo was coming around out there on the desert floor. And it was unbelievably beautiful.

Then…

"Rangers… this is Gunfighter Two," came back over the PRC-77. "If I mark your weapons fire correct, you look to be in real big trouble. Say again, you have mucho bad guys heading down the mountain on you."

The elves fired off a tremendous spell at us and suddenly a fireball, all green and dark, slammed into the tower and exploded everywhere. Rock raced off into the sky and a huge thunderclap followed.

And then the elves came.

Otoro stood before them, both swords out, and chopped them in half as they surged forward. But it was like trying to hold back the sea… and it was nothing compared to what was stacking up above our current position.

Captain Tyrus took the stairs, the sixty held up, advancing as he sprayed the oncoming elves intent on overrunning his wounded men. They could try, but he was not going to let them pass.

"Rangers, pop smoke on your position and give me a vector to lay down some chain…"

We'd taken smoke grenades from the Chinook, and I was glad we had. I shouted at Joe over the gunfire, telling him what was going on. Joe was on one knee and shooting at the elves above. They were like a waterfall now, an endless wave streaming down the near-vertical stairs like an out-of-control flood that would never stop until the world was drowned in blood.

"We got air support incoming, Sar'nt… marking our position now. Heads down!"

I pulled out the compass, got an azimuth, and keyed the mic.

"Gunfighter, we need fire one hundred meters north of our position at a three-four-two. Give us all you got!"

The pilot came back a second later as I heard the beat of the blades out there on the desert floor.

"Gunfighter inbound hot… heads down, Rangers!"

CHAPTER THIRTY

THE MH-6 Little Bird, when armed with the M230 chain gun in area defense mode, can fire six hundred and twenty-five thirty-millimeter rounds per minute. The sound of its gunfire is a brutal series of explosions as the gun unloads antipersonnel rounds against targets on the ground using highly accurate targeting.

The pilot used everything he had on board... and the waterfall of bad guys stopped at the end of it.

I ran forward and tackled Captain Tyrus just as the pilot began to fire. The captain was forward of the smoke I'd popped, and I dragged him down as the Little Bird tore hundreds if not a couple thousand elves to shreds just tens of meters above and ahead of us.

Every army needs leaders like Captain Tyrus. Even if his own generals wanted him dead.

The pilot finished and the Little Bird tore off into the desert, magic missiles chasing it away. But the battle was over. The Rangers were breaching and clearing the defenses above. The Lost Elven mages died clutching their spellbooks.

"Gunfighter Two to Rangers... welcome to the Ruin. Our six will be in touch shortly. Nice to see you."

And then Little Bird was gone.

EPILOGUE

I was walking wounded.

The Ranger medics came and got the wounded legionnaires, seeing to their wounds and getting them ready for transport to the casualty collection point. They offered stretchers for Joe and me.

Sergeant Joe declined. "We'll finish on our feet," he said.

We passed through the dead the Little Bird had made, and those our little force had slaughtered. Some things you just don't look too closely at.

We didn't drop our weapons. We didn't drop our packs. We followed the stretchers with wounded legionnaires, explaining everything that had happened. Getting backslaps, and even hugs, from the Rangers.

Fellow Rangers told us they thought we were dead. And were glad we weren't.

Joe's platoon came running down the stairs.

Some of them were crying. That's okay.

We made the courtyard of the fortress. Captain Knife Hand was away, finishing the cleanup in the dungeons below. But the sergeant major was there. There was an old blacksmith forge nearby, and he had his blue percolator set up on it already. As if he knew.

It was maybe ten in the morning. It would be a beautiful hot day. Cooler here in the pass. Better than the hellish desert below we'd lived in.

I smelled coffee and I suddenly got all choked up... like I was gonna cry. Maybe I was.

"Don't cry, Ranger," whispered Joe as we approached the forge. "Smaj hates that. And it's just coffee. Seriously."

Then he ripped off the Ranger tab on his shoulder and handed it to me.

He shook my hand and walked off to his platoon to do the never-ending business of an NCO. Picking up right where he'd left off before he fell into the surge of water at the citadel and was sucked into the Mouth of Madness and carried away to the horrors that lay within and beyond.

That seemed like a million years ago.

We'd had an adventure out there, Joe and I. I would think of it often, because it was more than just that. Much more.

The sergeant major handed me a canteen full of hot coffee.

"You look like ya been rode hard and put away wet, son."

I took a drink and closed my eyes for a long moment.

"Good to go, Sergeant Major. Good to go."

The End

ALSO BY JASON ANSPACH & NICK COLE

Galaxy's Edge: Legionnaire
Galaxy's Edge: Savage Wars
Galaxy's Edge: Requiem For Medusa
Galaxy's Edge: Order of the Centurion

ALSO BY JASON ANSPACH

Wayward Galaxy
King's League
'til Death

ALSO BY NICK COLE

American Wasteland:
The Complete Wasteland Trilogy
SodaPop Soldier
Strange Company

Made in the USA
Coppell, TX
26 May 2023

17332098R10157